A donkey called Oddsock

John Samson

TSL Publications

First published in Great Britain in 2019
By TSL Publications, Rickmansworth

Copyright © 2019 John Samson

ISBN / 978-1-912416-64-6

Yea, though I walk through the valley of the
shadow of death,
I will fear no evil: for you are with me;
your rod and your staff they comfort me.

Psalm 23:4

Getting away

'We shall go to the ocean, Oddsock. They said that it is very, very big, as big as the sky.'

The donkey nodded his head, then shook it, watching the young boy, looking for guidance, a restlessness twitching in its body. He knew they should move on, get away from this place, but he was bound to the boy. They were twins, born of different mothers, he with one leg black to the knee, the only blemish on a grey coat, while the boy carried a strange pigmentation disorder that left one arm a pale pink to the elbow in contrast to the rich brown of his body, earning him the nickname of Whitearm.

Oddsock twitched his flank to dislodge a fly that was feasting on one of the many small sores that dotted his hide. He nodded his head again to try break the inertia that had settled on the boy.

'As big as the sky,' Whitearm gestured at the blue canopy over-head. There was a glazed look to his eyes, the rapture of the large sky taking his concentration and mind from what lay about him.

The remains of a hut, someone's home, still smouldered nearby. The heat of the recent fire, not quite spent, mingled with that of the morning air, wrapping its warm smoky smells around the everyday shimmer that the sun brought to the land.

'Do you know the way to the ocean, Oddsock?' the boy asked, looking across to the donkey, his eyes glowed within a dark face, smeared white with ash, the idea of the sea possessing him.

Oddsock blinked and swung his ungainly head round to try to gnaw away an itch that ate at his hide. He was agitated, but he could not go, not without the boy.

'That way?' The boy pointed in the direction Oddsock's head had turned, a grin of delight stretched across his face, dislodging some ash which floated lazily to meet the dusty ground.

The donkey swung his head back, drawn by the voice, his eyes catching the bright ones of the boy and he dipped his head impa-tiently. He was not comfortable being here.

'Yes!' Whitearm was triumphant and jumped up. Small puffs of ash and dust exploding from the ground where he stamped his feet. There was energy and movement now and Oddsock gave a slight snort of approval. Something was happening. He watched the young human move around the ruins of the village, stepping over the bodies as if they were not there, the thin film of denial that protected the boy's mind from the horror that lay spilt around him on the ashy ground, fragile and vulnerable, at risk of being rent apart by the slightest jolt.

Whitearm stepped nimbly past the body of his sister – raped and discarded, her barely formed breasts peaking shyly through her torn t-shirt and flies already gathering on the raw red smile that had been slashed across her throat. Her outstretched hand clasped that of Twobites, the young friend who had given Whitearm his nickname. Twobites had miraculously survived being bitten by a mamba on two occasions, but had succumbed to the hard crash of a rifle butt on his skull, administered as he tried desperately to drag the screaming girl from beneath the heavy weight of her attacker.

The ocean. The old men of the village spoke of it many times. Some claimed to have actually seen it and when they sat around the fire in the evening they tried to contain its beauty and vastness in a prison of words, encouraging bright young eyes to dive into the waves of images, eyes both frightened and absorbed. The tides and currents threatening to suck them away in a strong undertow, drag them from the dryness that made the land in which they lived itch.

'The ocean is guarded by trees,' one man had said, bathing in his memories and in the rapt attention he had. 'Tall ones, not like the thorn trees,' he gestured out at the dark beyond the pinprick of light the fire brought to the arid land, a place where the heat and lack of water stunted growth. Trees here were shrubs whose anger at the land for failing to provide necessary nutrients manifest itself in dusty tangled branches, knotted in rage and barbed with vicious thorns.

'And the tall trees produce a beautiful fruit called a coconut.'

The name of the fruit itself was beautiful, a coconut. It was exotic, inextricably a part of the ocean in these young minds that listened. Who among them could imagine a hard, wooden ball full of refreshing juice that made your tongue feel alive? Which of the young minds that wrapped themselves around the fireside stories could really comprehend the fleshy inside of the coconut, 'whiter than your teeth, as soft as pounded yam and as sweet as mother's milk'?

Whitearm had listened, entranced by the stories, a longing grabbing at his breast. One day he would grow and make a journey to this ocean that they spoke of. He had eaten coconut many times in his mind, each time wondering if he had the taste right, altering it again and again as he searched for the perfect mix of yam and juice and milk to create a nectar that best matched the words the men had spoken.

Now, as he rifled through the burnt out remains of his village, looking for anything that he could take with on his journey, anything to appease the fiery devil of hunger that raged in his stomach, he tightened his mind around the words of the men. Even as he stumbled over the body of the one who had first thrown the word 'coconut' into the language of the village, rude red lips marking the bullet hole in his forehead, Whitearm could think of nothing else but the ocean, his young mind seeming to know instinctively that it could not relax its grip on the vision of the sea, to do so would mean madness and there is no room for madness in survival. He had to store up the grief for later when it could be safely released.

Oddsock watched, eyes blinking out a slow, patient rhythm that belied the need to get moving, to get away from this place. The bodies were a constant reminder of those men with their bang sticks that had sent him running into the bushes, slowing only when the tugging at his mane and the weight on his back began to clear the fear from his heart.

The bangs returned when the rushing of the wind in his ears and the slapping of the bush against his legs began to fade, but they were not the loud bangs that hurt his ears, rather distant poppings, as gentle as a grasshopper's chirrup, the sound almost soothing to his mind despite the agitation of his passenger who tugged hard at his neck hair, trying to urge him on and at the same time begging him to return to the village, a plaintive bray, commanding him in human to go back. He understood the sense of the cries, but could not obey the message contained therein. He had never seen or heard bang sticks before, but his whole being screamed that no good could come from such unnatural things. And when the chest of Whitearm's father had exploded in a burst of red, he fled, the confusion and noise disguising his escape with the young boy still on his back, a chance passenger dragged to safety, bouncing on a wave of fear.

The screams that accompanied the noise of the bang sticks died out with the explosions and an eerie silence went up with the plume of smoke that now dirtied the sky. Oddsock's pace slowed with the declining noise until he came to a stop. The rushing wind of escape was becalmed and the hush of the land fell, a heavy oppressive load that the fog of panic had to struggle against as it began to shuffle away from the donkey's mind.

And into the silence, creeping like erosion, his mind became aware of the hands that pulled tightly at clumps of his hair and a face buried deep into his mane, leaking low moans and twitching in despairing spasms. His donkey mind, drawing on its experience of humans, registered the distress and gently nuzzled the naked leg that hung limply down his flank till it slowly drew out the sting of despair and the young human slid from his back and lay, a defeated figure on the dusty floor of the land, strange hiccoughing sobs floating up like bubbles till they slowly faded into a rhythm of an exhausted sleep.

Oddsock, so used to following the will of the humans, stood restlessly by, the lack of movement and instruction from the boy troubling his simple mind. The heat of the day began its silent withdrawal, allowing the cool evening some space to rub its soothing balm over the burnt land, but still the boy did not move. Oddsock risked nibbling at the surrounding bushes, the dust covered leaves, unpleasant as they were, would give sustenance, but he could not wonder too far, and his large head kept turning back towards the prone figure. He wanted a drink, but could not leave his companion and dared not face the village from where the drunken voices of the men with the bang sticks weaved their way to his large ears, surfing on the waves of the day's departing warmth.

When darkness came and wrapped everything up in its softness and Whitearm still did not move, Oddsock settled himself down, his rounded belly just touching the young human's back. The boy stirred in his exhausted sleep and snuggled closer.

It was just before dawn – the time when sleeping and waking start to blend into one another – that Oddsock heard the men leave the village, passing close to where they lay. He lifted his head, his ears erect like small radars. Whitearm stirred and, sensing the danger of the noise, Oddsock lightly touched him with his nose, a reassuring move that allowed the boy to settle again.

The men moved through the bush quietly, a ghost army whose eerie march startled the plants so that they shook a little in fear and whispered hushed warnings to each other. The bang sticks made use of the last of the moonlight to wink coded messages amongst themselves.

'I shot four.'

'I got two, one in the back.'

'Fifty yards and right between the eyes.'

Oddsock shuddered at this grisly conversation just as the snap of a twig nearby sounded an alarm. The glint of a bang stick, a few yards away, gleamed an evil eye in search of prey. The donkey huddled closer to the boy, trying to wrap him in a protective layer without startling him awake. He could not see the bleary eyes that floated above the flickering light of the bang stick and the eyes, dulled by last night's alcohol, did not see him.

The gleam from the bang stick settled, blinking in its suspended state, while a low grunt followed by a muted grumble floated half a body above it. The gleam wobbled for a bit then came the sound of water hitting the dusty ground, a dull flat noise in the quiet of the early dawn, as if the earth were too embarrassed to receive this particular liquid. A pungent odour, fat and acidic, got sucked into the slipstream of the sound, catching in the donkey's nostrils which twitched as they contained the sneeze.

The rolling thud of the noise slowed until it became a series of thumps, like a trail of full stops ending a sentence.

Nasal passages were cleared in a throaty rasp and a ball of spit hit the ground in a final exclamation mark thud!

The gleam jiggled before it moved off in pursuit of the ghostly hiss that slid through the dark in front of it.

Oddsock waited for the quiet to pour into the space left as the hushed noise of the departing army moved off, then rose clumsily to his feet, taking care not to wake the boy who still slept, exhausted by grief. A thirst scratched at the donkey's throat, the pain of it driving him to return to the village in search of water.

Whitearm's body twitched slightly, his young mind adrift in an ocean, a sky on the land, surrounded by coconuts. The paralysing terror had slowly been shaken loose from his body by a constant trembling, allowing the shaking to subside as it was no longer needed. The small circle of bush that the boy had crawled into gave scant protection. Time, at first stretched and taut, had eased and grown to fill the gap between him and the image of his father's look of surprise at the lifeblood that gushed from his violated chest.

He slowly opened his eyes and stared out between the bushes. The commands of his mind turning his limbs to stone, unmoving and tense, and trapping the screams and moans that threatened to overflow through his mouth. Instinct held him to the ground like a starfish slapped onto a rock.

So this was the war the men of the village had spoken of, not with smiling eyes and light hearts as they had when they talked about the ocean, but war was a quiet thing, whispered of, with a serious brow and knowing looks, and not mentioned when they realised that children, hiding in the shadows beyond the reach of the firelight, were still awake and listening. War was not for children's ears. Even the women who were never scared to gossip about others as they went about the day's work, even they would lower their voices and check that the young ones were not near before huddling together to mention the name of this strange god, talking in hushed tones as if to say its name out loud would summons that angry deity.

But the children heard. They were never far from the adults, never far away when the women closed ranks, or the men thought the children were asleep, there were always young ears some-where, listening, absorbing. And they passed the news around in wild-eyed wonder, as if sharing a forbidden fruit stolen from their mother's store. The image of this god – a rampaging force gorging itself on the people and the land to appease its insatiable hunger – grew and swelled in the young minds, drip-fed by whispered words accidentally discarded by the adults.

'If war comes, I will beat it away with my stick'. The bravado in the eyes of the youngster who brandished a gnarled branch, faded quickly as those around stepped back in fear, expecting the wrath of this god the elders spoke of to strike the boy dead with a force as strong as lightning. You could not defeat war with a stick. Everyone knew that. You could not defeat war. Only a bigger, more powerful god could do that, but they knew of no deity that big.

And now war had come. It struck fast, like lightning, without warning and with lethal bangs and flashes of light. It had not come from the sky as Whitearm had expected, but disguised in the form of men, angry men with eyes hardened by hate yet gleaming with a primitive lust that could not be satiated.

The men's faces danced in Whitearm's thoughts, his mind feverish with fear, but slowly the realisation came that he had not seen the god, rather he had seen the slaves of the god who carried its forceful anger in bang sticks.

He did not know what the village had done to upset the war god so much that it sent its slaves. Maybe it was the boy with the stick, a stick that could not bang or flash. The cheek of daring to challenge the war god with that would certainly have caused its ire. You cannot challenge a god with sticks that have no lightning, not a god that can send its slaves to punish you. It was as if the god was saying, 'You have threatened me with a stick, I am so powerful that I do not even need to come and teach you a lesson myself. Look, I have slaves to deal with people with sticks'.

Only a bigger god could stop the war god, not a stick. Whitearm began to tremble again. He knew of no god bigger than war, no god that would even match the power of the lightning sticks that the slaves had. He hoped that the war god could not read his thoughts. If it could, it would anger him that Whitearm dared to think about a bigger god. The boy shook uncontrollably, his fear and grief stirred up again like a whirlwind. He wanted to cry out, let out all those dirty, hot emotions that scratched and burned in his mind. He wanted release from the ball of thorns in his head, but instead he felt Oddsock lie down next to him and the fires within him died as he moved closer to his companion. Oddsock was not a god, but he was a friend and that was better than any god.

The smoke carried the souls of the dead, drifting close to the earth, frightened to move too far from the roots of the lives it held in feathery fingers. An acrid bitterness clung to the air which screamed out, 'What did we do? Why us?' The trees bared their thorns at the smoke, warning it not to contaminate their branches.

Soon after the ghostly army had slithered away, a dull, inky light began to leak over the horizon and splatter itself across the sky. Wispy clouds slashed claw marks across this muted canopy.

Whitearm felt the absence of Oddsock before waking and this absence of comfort eroded his sleep till he forced his weary eyes to open. He lay still, his body craving a quarter measure of the adrenaline hit of the previous day, his mind craving complete obliteration of the emotional hit of the previous day. He fought with the fragments of memory that threatened to crystallise into the full-blown picture of the horror.

If his mind was right, if the ball of thorns in his brain was real, then he could not move, he must lie here and die, let the sun dry him out, let the hyenas eat his flesh and the ants pick his bones dry, and his bones must surely crumble to become one with the dust.

Slowly, matching the creeping march of the morning across the sky, he closed his mind against all that had happened, all the screams, all the shouts, all the bangs and lightnings, every evil glare of the slaves, even the pungent smoke that still assailed his senses. None of this had happened. It could not have happened.

'I do not believe in the war god,' the words, whispered, took form and rattled in the air. 'I believe in the ocean. The ocean is big, bigger than the sky, bigger than the war god.'

He paused, listening for the retribution that his blasphemy might produce, but none came. He had shaken a stick at the war god, but his stick was not an insignificant limb lost by a tree, his was a giant stick. The ocean god would protect him.

He pushed himself up, letting the dust fall from his body and the cool morning air, pregnant with the heat to come, caress his skin. His mind created the sounds that should have come from the village, the bleating of goats, the laughter of children and the dull thud of the women pounding the yams.

The smoke that the breeze carried did not smell right and he wrapped his mind tighter round the image of the ocean to keep him from thinking about the odours that the wind bore. The glaze fell over his eyes and he moved nimbly through the low bush towards the village. He felt the absence of Oddsock acutely now and longed to tell his companion the news, 'We shall go to the ocean, Oddsock'. The donkey would understand. The donkey would know that the ocean would protect them.

The last wisps of smoke meandered lazily up from the charred remains of a young boy, tickling Oddsock's nose. He recognised this farewell from the one who, in life, had been a source of irritation, always blowing yammy breath up his nostrils whenever they met. It would make Oddsock sneeze, so he avoided the lad, but now this final nasal attack was a peace offering, an apology and a plea that they part on good terms. 'I was only a young child,' it said, 'I meant no harm, it was my uninformed mind's way of saying I envied your friendship with Whitearm, I just wanted to be friends, but did not know how to ask.'

Oddsock nodded his head, his nostrils flared slightly and then he sneezed, a farewell salute to the fallen boy.

Whitearm scrounged in amongst the debris. There was not much of use, the slaves of the war god had taken or burnt what little food the village had. Turning over the collapsed roof of a friend's house, he discovered the charred remains of what had been the family chicken and he tore hungrily at the meat, the tough flesh, white and stringy beneath the blackened skin, provided a burnt offering to the devil in his stomach and appeased it enough to reduce the growls to a low mumble of discontent.

They had poisoned the well, dropping bodies into it, the blood of the victims changing the muddy brown water into frothy pink wine, bitter and vile. However, they had not discovered the secret supply, stashed away by the men of the village whose hushed tones had first dared mentioned this god called war.

There were too many gourds to carry, so Whitearm drank his fill, pretending it was cool, sweet coconut juice to fool his mind from tasting the brackish warmth that ran helter skelter down his throat.

Oddsock drank quickly from the small pool of water that the boy poured into a large bark dish, afraid that this precious supply would leak through and be stolen by the ground before he could get his share.

A few of the gourds were tied to the donkey's back with rough twine and he accepted the burden, knowing that this meant they would be on the move soon. The remainder was reburied, a libation to the departed or perhaps, just perhaps there were others who had survived.

The heat was gathering and would soon be drawing out the stench from the bodies. Whitearm stood for a moment, his eyes roaming the land, rebuilding what had been destroyed, yet also knowing it was gone. A single tear washed a trail down his cheek, clearing the dust and ash. But that was all he could afford right now. They would understand, the departed, they knew that water could not be wasted, so they waved thin, sinewy arms of smoke in farewell and watched him walk slowly away, the donkey following without need of tether or call.

A deep hush fell over the village and the land began the slow steady process of absorbing the dead into its dusty belly. Save for the one teardrop that had fallen from Whitearm, there was no one to mourn the villagers. The water in the gourds, reburied just in case, would also make its slow way back into the earth and feed the roots of a strong tree that would stretch out branches like open arms, a tight twist would crown the plant in a wreath of thorns. It would stand as a sign that a god bigger than war, a god not known to the people of the village, had seen what had happened and would remember.

Whitearm wanted to look back. His short life was tied to the village by an umbilical cord that he could never name, but could always feel, as if the land itself tugged at him wherever he went, a child strapped to its mother's back. He wanted to look back, to run back to that mother and wrap his tiny limbs around her. But he could not. The ocean god was calling and he had no choice but to obey. He had to stretch that umbilical and if it broke, so be it. He had to try and be born into a new life. His old life was dead, and he felt that acutely in his soul.

As long as his surroundings were recognisable, his steps were painful. Each tree, bush, rock held memories that clung like the dust that covered the leaves and branches or shimmied with the heat that disturbed the air.

There, that was where Twobites had his first encounter with the mamba. No one expected him to live, but he had struggled with the poison, writhing and wrestling with it for ages while his mother wailed and his father looked on, grim faced. Whitearm had jostled with his other young friends to peek in at the scene, fear and excitement churning in their young minds, knowing that something significant, something out of the ordinary had happened, but the urgency of action that the adults displayed, dulled the gloss on the energy of the moment.

Each memory grew and faded as the trigger for it approached and then quietly crept behind the boy's back. He catalogued the thoughts and packed them away under a blanket of oceans.

He stopped at a large thorn tree. This one was an important one and needed to be properly processed. Oddsock dipped his head, nodding sagely. This place meant something to them both and the boy wanted to imprint it on his mind for he knew he would never return to this place.

It had been a lazy afternoon, fat with heat and licked by a rasping tongue of dust. Life swung gently in a hammock of lethargy, a soupy, syrupy thickness clinging to its movements. A small herd of goats huddled in a corner of the freckled blanket of shade below the tree, a scent of indignation rising from their poverty battered coats at having to give over half the blanket to the human who sat, oblivious of their presence, throwing stones at a distant rock. The clunk and thud of hit or miss marking out the seconds and minutes of his boredom. He stopped to look at his hand, all colour drained from it by vitiligo. Yesterday none of the other children had noticed, not even that morning and in all likelihood tomorrow they would not. But his solitude that afternoon was a direct result of his ghost arm. Yesterday it had been the girl with one leg noticeably shorter than the other who fell victim of the constant ebb and flow of prejudice amongst the kids. Tomorrow, perhaps, they will remember Twobites and shun him, fearing that he was a mamba magnet.

There was no pattern to their childish discriminations. They would flow in random tides over the group, the undertow curling the waves so that they would crash down on whoever happened to be in the way.

They could – should an outside force threaten them – stick together as a group, a solid front against anyone who opposed them. Only they could exile one of their number, send them to the naughty corner for a few hours, or even a day. But nothing brought them closer than an attack from outside, be it by a parent or nature.

On the day that he was recalling one girl, Whitearm could not remember who, had decided without reason that his particular peculiarity gave him an unfair advantage as they played at smashing piles of cow dung with sticks. Her objection spread quickly amongst the players and Whitearm was forced into solitary confinement with only the goats for company.

He knew the donkey well for he had even been taunted once when the tide of prejudice dumped itself on him. 'You and your twin brother should have been taken out and left in the bush when you were babies.'

'I have no twin brother,' he had retorted.

'Yes you do. There.' His persecutor pointed at the donkey. 'You and the donkey were born at the same time, you are twins.'

He had burned with anger and shame as he knew that he could not deny their shared birth dates. Even his mother had once joked about his twin brother, the donkey. Their similarity in terms of mis-coloured limbs had strangely not yet come to the fore, as if through their coordinated arrival they were automatically expected to have similar defects. It bubbled beneath the surface waiting for that perfect moment to be released, that moment when a strong spring tide required giant waves to crash down it.

The young donkey arrived slowly, stopping to taste the leaves along the way, the heat sedating its movements, evaporating energy. The goats were no company, they sat blinking at the glare of the day, a gathered tribe wary of this stranger who was part of their daily lives. Whitearm clicked his tongue to attract the donkey, more from hope than expectation, the possibility of being ignored quite real. He was the outcast of the day, why would this beast feel any differently towards him.

The unexpected noise startled the donkey and he stumbled back a few steps, preparing to dash. Another click of the tongue was needed to reassure the animal. He knew the boy. Not one of those he would stay away from, not one who threw stones or lashed out with a switch plucked at will from a nearby bush and applied to his flank for no reason other than that he was there. He eyed the boy with suspicion, yet still Whitearm clicked.

And then he waved, a pinky-yellow hand that clashed with the rest of his body. The donkey began to slowly nod its head, as if agreeing with its thoughts, as if saying this one is like me, it has one leg different to the rest.

The donkey knew nothing of their shared birthdate but, recognizing a kinship in a shared birthmark, slowly edged closer.

The boy smiled and held out a welcoming arm, waiting to stroke the grey coat when it was within reach, his need for company speaking to the donkey's suspicious trust. The dusty hand, its defect momentarily forgotten, gained in confidence as it patted, sensing the donkey's acceptance but not yet aware of the bond the donkey now felt.

The sting of rejection that the day had delivered melted slowly in the young mind. Here was a connection, a friend. When all others had deserted him, this donkey had chosen to be his friend. He stroked the animal and, looking down, noticed the odd sock. The hand stopped, the mind raced, the heart leapt. They *were* twins. He put his pale arm next to the dark leg, a giggle boiling up inside him.

The goats, sensing that something was happening began to shuffle to their feet, not sure if what was coming was good or bad.

The boy's eyes darted from his arm to the donkey's leg and back. 'Oddsock.' The name was whispered as if something precious had been discovered. Whitearm held up his pale hand. 'Whitearm' he pointed, 'Oddsock. Whitearm.' His non-discoloured finger moved rapidly between the two objects of his fascination. The giggle was freed and erupted into laughter as he grabbed the newly named animal around the neck in an affectionate hug, scattering the nervous goats and startling the donkey.

The boy and beast stood silent now. That day when their umbilical cords had knotted together, that day of happiness, every detail needed to be collected and stored in the mind. It was all they could take with them. Whitearm knew that it was only because the war god did not know about it that he had let the memory survive. The tree where he had sat on that day was untouched by the slithering slaves of war. They had taken the goats, Whitearm had seen the remains, stripped of their meat, lying in the ashes of a prepared fire. Others lay around amongst the bodies of the villagers, dead eyes wide in surprise.

But Whitearm did not think of the goats, they were an incidental detail which cluttered a scene too pure for a dirty goat. So they were lost. The sun shone brighter and the heat, like the goats, was blocked out of the memory, replaced by a comfortable warmth. Perhaps the donkey was painted a little too brightly in this memory, an angelic glow seeming to radiate from it and where was that startled look when first summonsed by the click of the tongue, or that initial twitch away from his hug before settling? These were details that the war god's men had inadvertently taken, stuck to the bottom of their shoes like the sticky berries that grew on some of the bushes around the village.

'Come,' Whitearm said at last, 'we must go. The ocean is waiting for us.'

He moved off slowly at first, the scene of his first connecting with Oddsock sending out invisible hands to clutch at him, hold him back, or at very least, hinder his escape. But he knew he must go. This was now the war god's land. He had won it by having greater force in a battle, there was no ocean god here to stop him.

'He can have it,' Whitearm thought as he tried to quicken his pace. 'It is dry here, there are only thorn bushes to eat and there are no coconuts. Coconuts will give the war god a belly ache because they are sweet and good. A war god only eats thorns and that is why he is angry, because the thorns are bitter and prick at his belly. An angry god cannot have a happy belly, an angry god will feed on all that is bad because it does not know how to be good, because it would not be a god if it became good.'

Each step became easier as he moved further from the village, the bushes had less memories with tentacles trying to hold him back. He paused as he reached the outer limits of all his previous excursions from the village. He had not ventured past this point before, so he waited, giving the surroundings a last chance to pull him back, but there was not sufficient strength in their familiarity to keep him. Oddsock, oblivious to the significance of the border about to be crossed, had wondered past and into the unknown territory. The pull to go forward was greater than that trying to keep him back. And this was the way to the ocean.

The land breathed a heavy sigh as it watched the boy go. The brutality and savagery that scarred it would slowly heal as winds, rains and animals would eat away at this rotten wound until all trace would be gone, swallowed up and digested in a silent last supper that the world would never know of.

The war god's slaves had moved on, leaving behind an untidy mess, bodies strewn like litter, unwanted wrappers discarded after they had gorged themselves on the juicy morsels that appeased a base hunger. Stumps of houses, blackened by flames, sat in muted shock, shrunken in on themselves as if embarrassed that they had not done more to protect those who had built them. They had seen off the heat and when the rains did come, had provided the necessary shelter. They had fended off attacks from above, but when the danger was from the ground, from the same species as those they were meant to protect, they had crumbled, their fragile walls unable to withstand the onslaught of the lead stones that hurtled through their thin skin, small stones so frightened by the bangs and flashes around them that they fell over each other in an effort to escape.

The thatched straw roofs surrendered quickly to the flames that jumped from the hands of the war god's men, burning bright for a few seconds before plunging in a glowing mass, unable to wait for those below to decide whether to be crushed by this terrible load or to escape and try to outrun the lead stones that flew through the air and would cut down anything that got in their way.

The screams had died and their echoes had melted away on the breeze, scattered across a deserted landscape where they became one with the land. The flames no longer fed by the adrenaline and excitement of the slaves, had slowly shrivelled to glowing embers before expelling their last smoky breath and resigning themselves to a life of ash.

And from these silent ashes had come a nervous movement. But it was not a phoenix-like bird arising, renewed and invigorated to a new, more powerful existence full of promise. No, what arose had been a frightened little boy full of innocence, bewildered at the harshness of a god he had only just heard of, a young mind unaware that this brutal act meted out on his family and friends was not part of a cause and effect chain. The village had done nothing to deserve this, the community was an innocent one that lived in harmony with nature and its surrounds. Its only sin against the war god was that it existed and happened to be in the way of the slaves as they hunted the land, hungry to please their master.

Grief

The direction of the ocean, elusive and invisible like a god, could only be believed in. It was not a tangible thing like a rope that the boy could grasp and pull himself along. It had to be felt and fumbled for and then trusted to be right. The nod of Oddsock's head was a sign that the ocean god was there and waiting, guiding him by means of this strange donkey-angel, pulling him across the boundary of known and unknown when he faltered in his faith, unsure of what lay beyond the limits of his existence.

Whitearm's legs made the steps required while his soul trembled with doubt and his mind screamed out in fear. But Oddsock was there before him, moving slowly into territories new, frightening and exciting, moving slowly towards the ocean.

The devil in his gut poked at him in stabbing spasms. The burnt chicken offering had subdued the hunger, but was powerless against the nervous knot that twined emotion round emotion into a tightknit jumble that expanded and bloated his stomach, egged on by the devil. Surely this imp was a foot soldier of the war god too. It fought against the boy and his will to find the ocean. 'Go back,' it shouted from within. 'Go back. This way is unknown, full of danger. You know nothing of what lies beyond, you know nothing of the ocean. Do you think that the ocean could be more kind to you than the war god? The ocean is angry too, just like the war god. It will smite you in the same way the war god dealt with your family, your village. Why do you want to go and die at the hands of a god you don't even know? Why not stay and die in your own land, stay with the people you know. If you go, you will be too far away to join your ancestors when you die, and they will not be able to find you. Stay. Stay here in the land that now belongs to the war god. The ocean will kill you and you will not be able to come back. Do not trust your life to the ocean.

The gap between the boy and the donkey widened and the animal stopped suddenly, as if commanded by some unknown being, and looked back to see what was delaying his friend.

'Coconuts,' the boy said.

'What?' The devil was confused.

'Coconuts. A god that wants to kill people for no reason would not produce something as lovely as a coconut.'

The devil laughed and tried to re-twist and tightened the loose threads of emotion that were unravelling from his tightly constructed ball. 'You think a coconut is a good thing? Coconuts are poisonous. If you eat them you will bleed from your eyes and your ears until all your blood is gone, then you will be a shell that will walk the land, neither dead nor alive. No one will come near you, you will have no friends, no donkey for company, no birds will sing to you. The ocean will not have you and the war god will spit on you. Coconuts,' the devil snorted, 'they are more evil than the war god.'

'No!' Whitearm screamed. 'No, coconuts are good, they have juice that is sweet and makes your tongue feel alive. And it has flesh that is whiter than teeth, softer than yam and sweeter than mother's milk. A coconut is not poison!'

It could not be. To allow this exotic fruit, spoken of with so much affection by the elders, to be referred to in such negative terms would be to deny life. Too many of Whitearm's hopes were bound up in the ocean and the coconut was the ocean's representative. There could be no evil in this and the boy screamed out his tantrum, the high-pitched protest bouncing and ricocheting around the bushes, ruffling the leaves and scaring the birds.

Oddsock started at the noise, his knees bent slightly in preparation to launch himself off anywhere away from the threat this unexpected outburst brought.

The devil laughed, but was not quite as sure of itself now. The concentration of emotions had loosened, he had lost this battle and needed to regroup. He would come back stronger, but for now he was content to just plant the seed of doubt, a nasty, spikey and shifty emotion with poisonous barbs that dug into a mind and slowly spread a festering infection through the whole being until it consumed the soul.

The doubt began its work, but was interrupted by a grey snout and wet nose softly nudging the boy, gently reassuring and quietly softening the pain till the doubt faded.

The landscape did not change but the trees and the bushes, although familiar in species, were not the ones that Whitearm knew. They were strangers to him, the branches shaped differently to those that surrounded the village. This one spread further from the trunk, that one curled up where the one the boy knew curled down. The differences, slight as they were, excited Whitearm. He was into unfamiliar territory, an explorer searching out new lands. And yet the similarities made it safe. He knew this kind of landscape, how it behaved, what animals inhabited the area, what threats it offered and what rewards. If you knew which plant to look for, you could eat the fleshy leaves for sustenance, providing both nutrients and liquid. You also knew which trees the mamba, that foot soldier of the devil, preferred to hide in, pretending to be a branch but carrying a deadly sap that its thorn-like fangs would release at the slightest provocation.

He knew how the heat behaved here, how it sucked energy from the land and bent the horizon, creating a ripple across it, hiding the truth, yet luring one on with unknown promises and a duplicitous nature.

The sky was his sky, the great canopy, intensely blue, quietly calming and reassuringly unchanging. And it was big, as big as the ocean. But you could not touch the sky. It was up there far away. You could not stand on your tiptoes as you did to reach some branches of a tree. Even if you climbed to the top of the tallest tree, even then the sky would still be far away. The sky was not like the ocean. You could touch the ocean, the elders had said. You could walk into the ocean and its cool waters would wash away the heat of the day from you. But the sky, you could never touch the sky.

The boy looked round to check that Oddsock was still following. The donkey ambled along quietly, lifting its head when Whitearm turned, acknowledging that he was still there and gave a quiet snort to say that he was grateful he was still needed.

Whitearm was glad of the donkey's presence. It was a balm against the unseen undercurrent of unease that washed around inside him, there, but well-hidden so that he knew only of it through the hearsay of his mind, but there was no empirical evidence to support the rumours and without the proof, he could not admit it into his conscious thoughts. The donkey was alive and so long as he could clutch onto this fact, he did not need to address any of the issues of the dead. But the hidden tides continued to ebb and flow inside of him.

He hit out at a low branch with the stick he carried, hoping that a burst of energy and release of vengeance on the world would negate the increasing tightness he was feeling in his gut, as if someone or something was wanting to wring out all the emotions that soaked inside him, lead-heavy emotions that could not be squeezed.

A bird, frightened by the sudden attack on the tree, fled from the top branches, the safety of height allaying its fear of the unknown tremors from below. Safety first, get away, circle, assess, then, should it be nothing, return with caution, but never to the same tree, that tree has been tainted with a violence.

The boy did not have the luxury to circle and assess. He could only make his judgements on what he could see from the ground. He was without valuable intelligence gained from the air. The bird knew, but did not, could not, foresee the danger, nor would it take sides. All it saw was a young disconnected from the herd and as struggling to catch up. The main group had passed through at first light with this young not too far behind. Once settled back on a new branch, she chirruped her encouragement to the lost one.

'Keep going, you will soon catch up with the others.'

The boy acknowledged the bird with a smile, the guilt of disturbing this friend momentarily eased the tension in the stretched emotions within him, a welcome relief that flowed warmly through his body, unaware that this letting down of his guard would precipitate a violent attack from those suppressed emotions that gathered as a rebellious horde, tightly wound and ready for their moment to seize power.

Oddsock sensed it before the boy. Something in Whitearm's gait triggered an alarm. The footsteps became laboured, shoulders dropped and his arms fell limp at his side, yet his mind had not registered. This was the final defence, but it could not withstand the constant battering from the grief that had waited patiently, plotting its attack till it burst through the last wall that the young mind had erected.

The force with which it hit knocked the boy to his knees and he clutched first at his stomach, then his head, as if trying to contain his sanity therein, trying to stop the troops of reason from scattering in a disorderly and panicked retreat. But he had no authority over them. They, like Whitearm when the war god struck, had fled in terror in the face of this sudden and violent attack.

His body collapsed in on itself and he withered till he was a dry log cradled in the dust, foetal and grasping at lost memories of the womb to hide inside. A slow unnatural wail built like a wave, growing inside until the weight of it caused a catastrophic collapse in a crashing yowling sound that rippled eerily across the landscape. The bushes rustled uneasily as the sound rattled through their branches, a grief-laden primal screech that seemed to rip at their fleshy bark, wanting to tear off the protection it offered and strip them as naked and raw as the emotion itself.

The boy's body convulsed in spasmodic spurts as if his rational self were being ejected in shattered shards of shrapnel, exorcised in stuttering machine gun succession, a firework factory up in smoke, unable to contain the outward-bound missiles of all that was once precious within.

The vacuum created by the vacating sanity rapidly filled with an ache so intense it battered his body, shredded his mind and squashed his soul so that his whole being writhed in the agony, blindly thrashing around, too panicked to even look for escape as he threatened to drown himself in the overpowering crash and thud of waves of images that ran through his mind, re-creating the moment the war god had unleashed this ungodly punishment on him.

His father was shot over and over again in his battered mind, chest bursting open in protest at the invasion of the alien stones flung with brutal force from the bang sticks. His mother just fell over as his eyes desperately turned back to witness the scene while Oddsock carried him away from the mayhem. She lay where she had fallen, face down in the dust, arms at strange angles. The screams of his sister had reached his ears as he fled, he had known hers among the others as if their blood bond had given it a special pitch that only he could identify. His mind had taken a picture of his young sibling's body when he had returned to the village, but had stored it in a mental camera, unseen until the time was right for the picture to be developed. And the time was now. The camera gave up its stored image in burning high definition that hurt the eyes and scorched the brain, yet would not allow the viewer's eyes to move from it.

The pain poured into him as the barriers erected in defence crumbled against the onslaught of this tide. He felt as if he could take no more, the torture of these thoughts slowly tearing into him, building to a symphonic crescendo of noise and discord as memories clashed violently against the inside of his head and against each other. The turmoil of it all lashed viciously around his mind. It felt as if this agony would never end, that he would have to live with this crippling pain forever. He could see no release from it. The irreversible had happened and nothing, not even the ocean could rescue him as he floundered in the intensity of this emotional attack.

Then slowly, like a trickle of water from a dying spring, he began to become conscious of something outside of his grief. Beginning as light splashes on the periphery of the vast black cloud that threatened to completely engulf and suffocate him, it grew in strength, chipping away at the darkness, an antidote to the poison the war god had injected into him, slowly fed into his system, evaporating the hurt within him, as silent and unseen as the sun's heat that slowly dries out a puddle.

From deep within this emotional pool, he stretched out his white-gloved arm, searched for and found the source of this balm, his hand gently stroking the long grey nose that nuzzled him, poking around to find the human, the young friend lost in that strange jerking body.

'Oddsock,' he whispered, the sound muffled by the deep mist in his mind, a mist that was beginning to swirl and depart. The name, mentioned so quietly, was spoken with true reverence, as if it were some holy name that belonged to a god and which man could only utter in most hushed of tones so as not to offend. He lay still, his hand unmoved on the donkey's nose, afraid that should he be disconnected from his companion he would at once be hurled back into the tempest from which he had just escaped.

The air that he frantically grabbed at while lost in the storm, now began to find a natural path to his hungry lungs and with it, a sense of peace slowly settled on him like stirred up dust returning unnoticed and unfelt, coating him before he was aware of it. His body felt the poison retire, reluctantly kowtowing as it left to the power that had vanquished it.

The boy drank heavily of this new emotion that was re-inflating his soul, restoring balance and tranquillity and was soon able to open his eyes and push himself up.

Oddsock nodded his head in satisfaction that his companion was returning to normal and moved a few paces off to give the boy some space and to sniff at a small shrub which, he decided, was too bitter to eat.

Whitearm was unsure what had just happened to him. The initial shock of the attack had numbed his senses enough that he had been able to walk through the devastated village without really taking in the scale of what had occurred. The fear that incapacitated him as he lay hidden in the bushes and had acted as an anaesthetic preventing the pain for a while, wore off quickly and without warning. This had subjected him to a level of distress that he could never have known before, could never even have conceived that such agony could exist.

But he was emerging from the other side of it, shedding that ugly brittle exoskeleton and dragging himself into a more mature existence, an awareness that his tender years were not designed for. It settled on him, an ill-fitting garment, dirty and torn, something he had to wear, but would take a while to grow into.

He sat still, the heat of the sun stinging his neck with a thousand tiny insect bites and tried to adjust to this new state. Conflict as he had known it had meant words, raised voices and the occasional push of another who would not bend to his way of thinking. But those emotions were fragile things that would quickly crumble in the face of time, the fragments forgotten as friendships reconstituted themselves. The idea of revenge was something his mind could not form. The village with all its hierarchies of elders, young men and children, had as yet been untainted by this emotion, there was no word for it in their language and consequently no ability to conceive of it as a notion. So he formed no thoughts of tracking down the slaves of the war god to pay them back for the loss that had cut through him as savagely as the bullets through his father's chest.

His mind, becalmed and bewildered, struggled to readjust to the moment, echoes of the recent storm of thoughts still rumbled around his brain, muted pain flaring up in lightning flash attacks, receding slowly into the distance. He held his head, helping to steady it and reached deep inside his thoughts for a brown hairy ball full of the most refreshing juice in the world.

'Co-co-nut,' he said the word slowly out loud, stretching it like a plaster over the wound his mind had suffered.

'Coco-nut,' now with more speed and confidence, the pull of the mysterious ocean and this exotic fruit dragged him to his feet.

'Coconut, coconut, coconut.'

His small body, battered by the emotional attack, was not as quick to respond to the healing taking place in his mind. His legs shook, his arms felt heavy and drooped at his sides and even his head seemed to be too big a load for his neck, but his mind was leading the way. If it could recover, then his body must follow.

'Come Oddsock, we must move on. The ocean is waiting for us with coconuts, we must not keep it waiting.'

He began to walk again, his pace slower than before, but his footsteps no less determined.

The donkey grabbed a last mouthful from a plant it had found that better suited his palate and, head down, trundled slowly after the boy, pleased to be on the move again. They had not yet put enough distance between themselves and the horror of the village.

A lazy haze settled over the land, heat and dust mingled to create a soupy thickness to the air as if conjured up by some malicious imp that found amusement in making progress through the land a task, an effort to push through this perpetual curtain that impeded progress and, one could perhaps argue, prevented those who travelled through it, from striving for a goal, a punishment for daring to want a life better than the one the fates had thrust upon them.

The boy was, however, unaware of the force that tried to deny him his dream. He could not turn back, there was nothing holding him to the village anymore. He had snapped the last of the strings that held him to the village, offloading his grief had lightened his burden and all he had left was a hope that the ocean god would welcome him in cool, loving arms, a hope that the love and

friendship he had shared in the village that had been washed away
so suddenly by the flood of violence that the war god's slaves
brought, that that love had somehow washed down the rivers that
lead to the great sea and that it would be waiting there for him in
abundance, a prodigal returning to the arms of those who love
him, and who awaited his arrival with excited impatience.

The malicious imp was no match for the determination that now
crystallised in Whitearm's mind. It could make the going difficult,
throw hot sludgy dust-filled air in his path to try and distract him
from his mission, but these things were, at the moment, minor
irritations in the steadfast mind of the young lad who plodded
slowly, but with unfailing faith, through the land.

The donkey had faith too, but it knew nothing of oceans and
coconuts. The stories the elders had told around the evening fires
were mumbled human noises that struggled to cross the dark
stretches that lay between the wavering light of the fires and the
quiet solitude that he had found at the back of one of the huts.
Oceans, coconuts, gods meant nothing to him. All he knew was
that he should follow the young boy. This was his only connection
to anything living. The wilds around the village were frightening
areas filled with unnamed animal scents that, to a lone donkey
signalled danger. But the humans had always protected him, kept
those hinted at threats at bay. So if the boy moved on, he had to
follow if he were to stay alive.

He caught a guinea fowl, his quick hands following instructions
passed to him through watching his father and mother at work.
The neck clicked as it snapped, the feathers were tough to pull, but
that is what his mother had done so he kept going despite the ache
in his fingers that were unused to this labour. Somewhere in his
mind an ember of shame burned as this was not work for a boy, a
man in training. Catching was his work, plucking and cooking was
not, but the ball of thorns in his stomach demanded that he be fed
so he had to be mother and father, woman and man. He alone was
the village, he alone had to take on the roles of all. The ordered life
of the village fell on his shoulders and, while his mind ached to
return to his normal role of child, free of any major responsibility,
he knew that if he was to survive, he could not, must not, allow
that young carefree person he had been just a few days previously,

to have the free rein on his life as it had before the war god's men came.

He wanted to mourn that loss within. His body was not yet ready to take on the responsibilities that his parents had. The ache in his fingers as they clutched at the feathers, the strength he lacked, reminded him of his inadequacies. A rogue tear escaped from his eye as he continued to prepare his food, betraying his inner thoughts and he wiped it away with an angry hand, annoyed at the betrayal of self. This was a new enemy to him. The war god's men had come and gone, but now he faced this enemy within, this helpless pitiful child fussing over its lost freedom. He had to harden himself against this weakness. He sniffed and, ignoring the pain, grabbed a handful of feathers and yanked again and again. His hand moved in a flurry, rushing to complete the task before he could no longer bear the agony.

'I will do it, Oddsock. I am a man, I will not be defeated by a task that woman can do.'

The donkey lifted its head at the sound of its name, but quickly returned to grazing on the dusty plants when it realised that it had not been called. It could sense the frustration build within the boy, but this was not a distress that needed intervention. It was a childish tantrum of the boy's own making, not an external factor causing heartache. The boy needed to go through this one alone, he needed to learn from the experience and grow. Besides, going too close with those flying little fists could well result in an inadvertent punch on the nose.

Whitearm won the race. Just. His hands had reached overflowing levels of pain as the last feather was uprooted from its fleshy berth. He sat back and smiled. He had achieved and he let his hands lie limp on his lap as a reward for their work.

'I must make my hands stronger, there will be much work like this before we get to the ocean, and I will need to be strong to open the coconuts when we get there,' he told Oddsock as he waited for the pain to ebb slowly from his fingers. The men in the village had not explained how you got the juice out of the coconut. They spoke of the hard wooden shell that kept the fleshy sweet yam-like fruit and the cool refreshing milk safe from attack by birds and other animals, but never said how a young boy could get at it.

Whitearm puzzled over this as he waited for his hands to regain their feeling. Had the men just forgotten this important piece of information, or perhaps they never thought any of the children from the village would ever see a coconut, so it was a waste of time explaining. It could not be that they wanted to keep the extraction method a secret in case the village came across a coconut, then only they could get at the flesh and juice and then only they could eat and drink it. That was not the way of the village. If good fortune came it was shared by all. And if one suffered loss, the village suffered loss. They would not have kept the secret to themselves.

He flexed his fingers, the sharp pain had burned down to a dull one now. He would soon be able to start making a fire to cook his catch.

He could eat the whole bird, the village was no more, so he had no one to share the good fortune with. He would leave some behind, an offering to the spirit of the village. He had to share the good somehow. But how could he share the bad, the loss of his family and those he loved, those who had been his life until now? All taken from him. The ultimate loss, so swift and so complete. There were not enough villages in the world that could truly bear the loss he had to share. His recent outpouring of grief was all his small body could manage. He knew that was far too inadequate to properly mourn the destruction of his village, but he could do no more.

That is why the war god is so powerful, he can inflict a pain so great that one person cannot come close to properly acknowledging it and cannot come close to digesting it all. If he could share his pain with everyone in the world, they would all have such a small bit to bear that they would hardly notice it. Maybe if every person in the world had to carry such grief every time the war god struck, they would not like it and they would find a way to stop the war god, he thought.

He did not know how many people there were in the world, all he had known was the small number in his village. There had been visitors from outside, but never very many and they never stayed long. The men in the village who had spoken of the ocean had also talked of places where there were so many people you could hardly walk because they all got in your way. If you could imagine that everyone in the village was a whole village more and every cow and every goat and every chicken were all whole villages, and everyone in those imagined villages were whole villages of people and everyone in those extended villages were also a whole village, then maybe you could know what these places called cities were like. But none of those young minds could expand to accommodate the mass of people the men spoke of, no matter how big their eyes got.

These thoughts were getting too big for him and the pain in his hands had subsided. He gathered up wood and scrub to make a fire and set about rubbing the sticks together as his father had taught him. The pain seeped back into his hands but did not reach the earlier levels and the smoke soon jumped up into a flame, catching the dry leaves and twigs and it was not long before the fire was burning healthily.

The sun had withdrawn itself from the world and the dark crept over the land bringing with it a slight relaxing of the heat, but Whitearm knew it would not retreat much further.

The bird cooked quickly, dripping bits of fat into the fire in hissing splashes, but the guinea fowl is a lean, tough bird and does not provide a lot of juice in which to cook. The result is a chewy chicken, slightly dry but packed with gamey flavour. To Whitearm, however, flavours and juices mattered little. There was a devil in his stomach that needed to be appeased and he ate quickly with no thought for taste.

Oddsock turned down the wing that was offered. He had eaten his fill and drank sparingly of the water the boy offered, as if knowing that the precious cargo he carried on his back was to be consumed with care. The boy too drank very little, just enough to soften the dusty rasp in his throat. The mosquitos began to whine and he tossed some dried elephant dung that he had found while savaging for wood on to the fire. The rich earthy aroma pleased his nostrils but irritated those of the insects and they retreated.

With his belly full, his thirst muted and the soft smells of home gently caressing him, he felt a satisfied lethargy take hold and for the first time since the war god's slaves came, he relaxed, staring into the fire and freed his mind of the thoughts that had so crowded it of late. He did not even let the ocean enter his mind, rather letting it float on a spongy raft of feelings that were formless like mist, yet soothing, allowing him to think without shape till it all faded and he fell into a deep sleep.

An encounter

The morning stretched languidly, gently caressing the land awake, brushing away the darkness and pouring its warmth into the air. The bird woke as the first fingers of sunlight tickled the trees and set about her morning business, flying between trees, greeting friends and catching breakfast.

As she found a breeze and glided over the dusty land, she spotted the human young curled up in the shade of a small tree, its animal friend sitting quietly nearby, watching over him. The bird swooped down and landed near the donkey, nodding its head in greeting before scrounging in the dust for some tasty insects and then studied the human closely, head cocked to one side. She still maintained a respectful distance, one could never be too cautious.

From her vantage point in the air, the bird had seen the rest of the human herd camped not too far away. It moved slower than the stray, its sheer mass slowing its progress. Also, it seemed to linger in places as if reluctant to want to move on, rather being pushed by some invisible force that it had to obey, than propelling itself of its own volition. The human young would catch up with the herd by nightfall if he continued in the right direction.

Whitearm woke to the sound of bird wings fluttering to safety as he stirred and sat up slowly. The night had been restful and his dreams were now locked inside a part of his mind that only they knew of. The events of the last few days were slowly finding a home in his head, somewhere they felt comfortable to stay quietly, their presence felt, but not intruding on their surroundings.

There would be days when those memories would prick in his brain, play with the equilibrium of mind as images would suddenly flash up on the mental screen in his head. Sometimes a word, a sight, often a smell, would trigger these things to be trundled out and displayed. But, by and large, they were already being trained to sit quietly and behave.

His mother was not there to ensure that he washed, nor to provide a little food to start the day with, but some of last night's guinea fowl remained unpicked from its bones and he completed the task that he had started at dinner. With his loss came a degree of freedom. He had no one to tell him what to do, when to do it or how to do it should he decide to make the effort.

He had to obey the devil in his stomach and the imps that stuck small dry thorns into his throat. They had supreme command of his life at the moment, but just as powerful was the unseen umbilical between himself and his twin, the donkey. This, without seeming to touch his mind, steered his emotions and actions with unseen strings. So too did the concept of the ocean and its coconuts pull at him in a way he could not explain. Without the latter he would not have moved. He would have remained in the wreck of the village watching those he had loved decay and crumble back into the dusty earth, a slow attrition of his surroundings that would assail his nostrils with powerful odours and fill his mind with an unmoveable stench that would taint both his senses and his sensibilities. The ocean was strong, it spoke to him, called him away from where he no longer could exist.

The bird chirped a greeting from the safety of a tree, a cautious hello for she did not yet know if the human young could be trusted. The boy smiled and returned the greeting, waving his pale hand. The interaction giving him some impetus to move and he pushed himself slowly to his feet, mindful that sudden movements would frighten his new friend.

The night had disoriented him and he was unsure which direction to go. The ocean was not going to make it easy, but that did not ruffle his mind. In his short life he knew that easy things were never as good as those you worked for. The food his mother prepared, while always dealing with his hunger, never tasted as good as the guinea fowl, patiently stalked, painfully plucked and then roasted on a fire he had started. The hut his father had built, and which housed him was a good shelter, but held none of the adventure and excitement of a pile of sticks he and Twobites crudely fashioned into a rough hideout.

He looked around, noting the trees and bushes, trying to recall the direction he had been going in before he tired and stopped for the night. The sun would be different in the morning than the afternoon and he could fix a direction from that, but the dark of the night had served to confuse him and his confidence in Oddsock's nodded direction had dissipated, sucked into the dark vacuum of night. He needed to be reassured.

'Oddsock, which way?' he asked.

The donkey tossed its head to acknowledge that it was ready to move and Whitearm nodded.

'That way? I thought so.' He did not want to let on that he had lost his way and he had seen how the elders would act when they had forgotten something. They would pretend that they were just testing the children, making it look like they were helping them to learn, but really needing to be reminded themselves. It was a game they played.

'Whitearm, you are a big boy, can you remember the name Mzeko has given to his new child?' The man had smiled, his face said, 'this is a test to see if you remember', his eyes said, 'I have forgotten, please could you remind me, but do not treat me like a forgetful old man.'

'Yes, the child's name is Shishi.'

Oddsock did not make him feel forgetful, the donkey just indicated the way and began to plod slowly in that direction, presuming that the boy would want to continue in the same way that they had been going the day before.

The bird, seeing the movement, chirped its approval and moved ahead of them, flitting from tree to tree, occasionally climbing to check on the rest of the herd, sometimes swooping to catch an unfortunate dragonfly or tsetse, darting through the air with a speed too great for the unfortunate insect to escape.

Whitearm felt good. He had packed away the emotions that had caused his collapse and his sleep had restored his childish good spirits. The lack of adult intervention to his morning served to cheer him further. He missed the company and noise of family life, but a subtle undercurrent, driven by the missing authority over him, injected a freshness into his life. An excitement of possibilities that he could grasp at, unfettered by the dictates of his elders, bubbled inside him. If he had said to his mother or father, 'I want to go to see the ocean,' or 'I am going to see the ocean,' he would have been laughed at, scolded perhaps and, if he had, as was his habit at times, persisted with a whiney demand, he would have been punished.

But now he was free. He could go to the ocean and no one could tell him he could not. His only companion would be Oddsock, and the donkey shared his goal as evidenced by the nodding of his head whenever Whitearm asked for directions. They were twins. They thought alike. There would be no protest from Oddsock.

As he began to walk, he hummed to himself, almost unconscious of the noise emanating from his throat and certainly unaware of the connection of the tune to the song that his mother had sung to him as a small child:

> *Here is the sun, my child*
> *May it warm you*
> *Here is the moon, my child*
> *May it guide you*
> *Here is the wind, my child*
> *May it sing to you*
> *Here is the rain, my child*
> *May it sustain you*
> *Here is my love, my child*
> *May it shape you*

The words floated below the radar of his mind, their presence disguised by the hummed tune which in turn passed through his head like mist, its presence a thin veneer over the mood which he carried.

The sun began its day slowly once it had appeared over the horizon, stoking the embers of warmth that had made it through the night, building slowly, degree by degree, as it headed to its mid-afternoon target when walking would not be an option and life in the land would come to a standstill.

The war god's slaves were not as quick to get going. Their master had moved them on quickly from the scene of their destruction, perhaps not wishing them to dwell on what they had done. Rotting corpses in the bright light of morning were not good for morale. They were a stark reminder of the atrocities that had been committed and there was no adrenaline rush of battle to disguise the fact that they had caused this. Without that eruption of chemicals within his men, the war god was concerned that the inhumanity of their actions would be revealed to them. He could use the words of their leader to temporarily blind them to their loss of humanness, they would have some impact, but words would ultimately lose their grip on the feeble minds of his slaves. The eyes of those killed would stare accusingly at the men and slowly they would lose the taste for destruction, shamed into submission by the victims.

So he moved them on quickly, stealing away from the village in the early hours of the morning when the adrenaline had subsided and the lack of light denied the dead their chance to attack the consciences of those who had brought destruction to the village. They crept out into the darkness leaving all images of the killing the day before in amongst the ruins.

They yawned and scratched at themselves now as the war god gave them a reward of a slow morning. The mood of the camp warm and relaxed, the men joking with each other as they enjoyed the leisurely pace allowed to them as they prepared for the day's march. There was food, as much as they could carry from the village, and water, packed onto the backs of unwilling donkeys, angry red stripes glared from their flanks where they had been struck to force them to obey their new masters. Few of the slaves met the accusing looks of those wounds and those who did, hardened their minds, justifying their actions with the war god's words, 'they are only animals'.

The war god was pleased with his men. They had killed without question, the destruction of innocent lives feeding his insatiable lust for blood. And it would have its rewards. It would draw other groups of slaves out to fight against this group. In the big cities men, the slave drivers, his henchmen, would sprout forth and justify their actions using words that an ignorant populace would not question.

'Harbouring spies.' The war god loved that phrase. It made those on one side feel righteous while enraging those on the other, allowing them to feel justified when committing their own atrocities.

This helped the tit-for-tat mentality ensuring longevity to wars and ultimately to the war god himself. If he had been aware of the survivor of the slaughter, he would not have been pleased with the mental processes taking place in the boy's mind. There were no thoughts of revenge, the war god's lifeblood. This would not help his cause. But the war god was too busy rewarding his slaves to concern himself with such a stray.

The preparations to move began to gather pace, like a stiff limbed giant shaking off the dust of rest and slowly easing the aches that had built up overnight, grinding them away through laboured movement that grew gradually to fluid steps.

Oddsock paused. The warmth of the morning, which had been a light cotton sheet, was turning into a thick woollen blanket, lying heavy on the land and making movement underneath it turgid and slow. The boy's pace had slackened and his will to progress was waning. His head, which had been erect, and eyes that had been busy now drooped, studying the dusty ground that moved slowly beneath him. He no longer hummed.

There was a scent in the air that the donkey was not sure of. It smelled something like the village had before the men came, a homely smoke from fires used to provide sustenance and companionship, not the harsh acrid smoke of chaos and destruction. But it was not as pure as the village smoke had been. There was an undertone to it that Oddsock could not quite determine and it made him wary.

The boy with the white-gloved hand did not seem aware of it, walking without thinking. Oddsock did not want to continue towards these offbeat smells, not until he had had time to consider their implications, but his friend showed no signs of stopping the mechanical movement in that direction. He slowed his pace till Whitearm was walking next to him, then gently guided his twin towards the shade of a tree by angling his body across the boy's path, causing the somnambulant youngster to alter his route by degrees. Once under the tree the donkey stopped across Whitearm's path and waited for his friend to bump into him.

The glaze over the eyes shattered and Whitearm focussed on his surroundings.

'We should rest a while, Oddsock,' he said, his tone a gentle chiding of the donkey for being too eager to move on. 'We must conserve our energy, we have a long way to go to the ocean.' He stroked Oddsock's mane, his colour-starved hand expressing the body's gratitude while the mind remained too haughty to admit that it was the donkey who had the idea that they needed to rest.

They sat in the shade, drawing on the coolness this freckled blanket cast on the ground, the change in temperature, although only a few degrees, began to re-animate the boy, but he did not speak.

Oddsock settled himself near to his friend, leaving enough space for their respective body heats to melt in the cooler shade without causing the other discomfort. His nostrils sought out the smell again and he did not like it. The scent below the scent that he had picked up on earlier was of fear and suffering, something excreted from the glands of donkeys he knew in the village. Mingled in with these was the smell of donkey blood. Not blood pumped out of veins in large quantities, but that which seeps slowly from hides struck with switches, a smell he had encountered before, but never alongside the fear he now sensed.

He shuddered. Whitearm was walking towards those odours and seemed intent on going on in that direction. If that was what his young friend wanted, then so be it. He knew he could not survive on his own. He knew that he had to follow, albeit reluctantly.

The sun turned the sky white, bleaching it with a powerful splash of light across the heavens that hurt the eyes. The usual blue shrunk behind this harshness, scalded into retreat. The land kow-towed to the heat that the bright sky bombarded it with in pulsing strikes. The birds took refuge in trees, too lethargic to fight against the onslaught. Animals sought shelter under the trees, under-ground and where they could find it, underwater.

A breeze tried to drum up support from friends to form a wind, but the lack of interest from the others left it sheepish and it soon returned to the earth to lie and wait for a better time to play.

What chance did humans stand against this attack? Even those around with all manner of weapon that could decimate most life forms – guns, knives, fire, axes – were powerless against the strength of the sun.

The war god could have no power over his slaves as they wilted in the face of the heat. He could try and command them, urge them, threaten them to move, but the heat was such that they would rather face the wrath of an angry war god than fry in the brightness.

He was a canny leader, knowing when to advance and when to maintain his position, knowing that to attack the sun would be foolish, but knowing too that the bright heat could only burn for a short while. The sun's arsenal would deplete and be restocked in a predictable pattern and so he let his slaves rest, lounging lazily in whatever shade they could find, smoking cigarettes, playing cards, swearing, joking and sleeping. Sweat oozed out of them and soaked the group in a fruity funk of humanness that shimmered in the air but went unnoticed by the men whose nostrils were bored of the smell.

And so time passed in a vacuum of activity as the sun plodded slowly across the sky, wearied by its own radiance and heat, its slow steps trudging along a well-worn path like a slave pushing a grinding stone round and round in a seemingly endless journey.

The grasshoppers were the first to become aware that the worst of the day was over and rubbed their legs together to sound the first notes for a call to action. The grass, where it had managed to grow, yellow and dry, began to come to life again as insects buzzed and bounced.

The renewed movement in the insect world caught the eyes of the small birds and they started, lazily at first, to swoop down for a snack or two.

In turn, the larger predatory birds noticed that their food was on the move and began to float round in effortless circles at a slightly higher altitude where the air was cooler.

Mongooses, lizards, snakes and other small animals became more alert, wary of the threat of attack from above and their restlessness transmitted itself to the larger antelope who began to move out of the shade to areas where grazing was slightly better, their ears, eyes and nostrils on constant lookout for incoming lion or leopard or cheetah.

Whitearm was an early starter in this chain of waking. He stood and rearranged the dust on his clothes. Thoughts of the ocean still drove his young body on while his mind was not experienced enough to judge how far it could push his physical being.

The air was cooler but still had a lazy lethargy about it. It no longer fried to a crisp the will to move. The sky was regaining some of its blue and the odd cloud rode high across it.

The war camp was slower to respond to the reawakening of nature. It stretched and yawned, moving in languid motions, trying to evict the stiffness from its many limbs. Guns were hoisted over shoulders with leaden movements, a reluctance to get going endemic within the slaves' ranks.

But the war god knew it was time to move them on in search of fresh blood. Inaction was a great enemy and, using his slave masters, he drove the army to action and it began to glide quietly through the bush, always on the alert against attacks.

Whitearm and Oddsock were well past the slaves' night camp by the time the army had started to move on from its afternoon siesta. The donkey not wanting to investigate the pungent odours that lingered like a heat haze over the camp, had steered the boy gently around it, giving it as wide a berth as he could. Whitearm, happy to be moving and relying on Oddsock to show him the way to the ocean, did not notice the diversion, his legs surprisingly sturdy given the frail appearance their thinness gave off. He was again lost in a world of his mind's making, not overly aware of his surroundings, choosing to replay happy scenes from the village in the days before the war god came. This protected him from thoughts that could cripple him, hinder his progress towards his goal. He had almost convinced himself that the carnage had not occurred and that he was heading to the ocean as a young man, let out of the clutches of the village to take on this important task.

'Go to the ocean, Whitearm. Gather as many coconuts as you can carry and bring them back to us,' the imagined command came clearly from the elders gathered in his mind.

It was a life or death mission he had been sent on. If he could return with the coconuts, he would save the village from thirst and starvation, the white fleshy yam-like fruit filling their bellies and the juice slaking their ravished throats. His father would be proud, strutting around the village offering his bounty to everyone. 'A gift from my brave son,' he would tell them. 'My son who walked all the way to the ocean and carried back enough coconuts so that the whole village would never go hungry or thirsty again.'

And his mother would sit shyly with the older women as they made a big stew from the five guinea fowl he had just happened to kill on the way back from the ocean. They would use the juice of the coconut to cook a feast, the likes of which the village had never seen before. 'Your son is a brave young man,' they would say to his mother and she would smile and look over at him, pride shining in her eyes. 'Yes, he is,' she would reply in her quiet voice, not wanting the cry of joy in her heart to escape through her voice as it felt too good in her breast to release.

Even his sister, who usually regarded him as a nuisance and hindrance, would tell her young friends, 'Yes, my brother is a brave young man and strong. He carried all those coconuts back from the ocean by himself.'

His friends would never make fun of his arm again, they would grow up and tell their children the story of Whitearm who fought all sorts of wild animals to bring back the coconuts and that the juice from them spilt on his arm and turned it white. Children would find ways to make their arms white so that they could pretend to be this village hero in the games they played.

'They will remember you too, Oddsock,' he verbalised his thoughts to his companion. 'That is Oddsock, the bravest donkey in the world, they will say and they will know you are brave because you are my twin. The other donkeys will all want to be your friend and the people of the village will feed you the best food they can find.' He patted the donkey's back with the reverence due to the hero he had just created.

The fantasy was important to him. It aided his progress, taking his mind from the dreary landscape that he walked through, a distraction from the heat and the thirst that irritated his throat. The glory this dream promised drove him on to his goal. It also shut out the horror of what the war god had done, kept his family and friends alive, defying the barked orders of the bang sticks that said they should be dead.

His dream was his fuel, allowing him to walk with confidence towards the evening, protected in this cocoon, oblivious of the shrinking gap between himself and the slow-moving slaves of the war god who trudged ahead of him.

The war god was growing concerned. The long hot march through this godless land was not good for his slaves. They were starting to grumble, inwardly of course. Not one of them was brave enough to make known their inner dissatisfaction. The recent hit of blood and adrenaline had served only as a quick high that, instead of appeasing their addiction, had rather fired it to greater heights and they craved action. But the land was desolate, devoid of human life for them to terrorise.

The slow draining of the rush that had excited them was also leaving space for a trickle of doubt to creep into their minds. A sense of lost humanity and humanness flittered across their sub consciences and this, if not quickly stemmed, could create problems for the war god. He needed a distraction so commanded his slave driver to call a halt to the march and gave him permission to break out some of the rations of alcohol and drugs. This always served to divert the slaves' minds from coming face to face with their baseness of being.

The men quickly forgot their unuttered grumbles as their march ended and the banana beer was passed around. Strong herbs for chewing were also distributed. They liked the mind-numbing effect the leaves had, it cleared the brain of the thoughts that did not sit well inside the head and, although they would deny it, kept them loyal to their master.

The sun, seeing the end of its daily journey in sight, hastened its steps and plunged into the horizon sending up a spray of orange across the sky before the black curtain of night took over.

Fires were lit in the camp more for light than warmth and the men sat around them, their voices growing stronger as the war god's potions took hold.

Whitearm did not want to rest, he had a mission to complete. The village could not survive long without the life-giving coconuts from the ocean. He pushed on despite the reluctance of Oddsock to move in the dark. The moon spread a thin veneer of light over the land, but the donkey was uneasy. You could not tell what dangers lay just beyond the reaches of the moonlight. This was not a safe land, animals and man had proved that. The lions that had dragged off one of the village's precious cows, the hippo that the elders spoke of with respect, the scorpion, the snake, even the buzzing tsetse or mosquito could cause problems.

The boy continued to move, so Oddsock had to follow, trudging slowly behind his twin. It was time to rest but his companion seemed oblivious to this, as if he had forgotten that the dark was not a time for walking. When it was dark you sat around the fire and talked and laughed, all worries and woes of the day fading like the afternoon light that had given itself over to the blackness of night. It was a time when the village would gather, share news and forget any differences that may have flared up during the day. The elders would tell their stories while the young men would sit watching the young girls and the children's eyes would open wide as if their ears were not big enough to accommodate all the wonders the old men spoke of.

Even though the village no longer existed, surely the boy should respect the tradition and stop. The only thing the donkey could think was that his companion was heading towards the smell of fires and the muted sound of voices that squeezed though the dark, coming to them as a part of the night, carried on the moonlight, but not as smooth. There were jagged sounds within the voices, noises that lacked the gentle rounded curves of the village evening talk. And there was the acrid smell of the bang sticks that covered the softer aromas of cooking and fires that were associated with the village.

Perhaps it was some kind of homing instinct the boy was following that kept him moving toward these men who had obliterated the village. Oddsock brayed softly, a questioning of the boy. 'Do you really want to continue in this direction? You are my friend, you are a human, you know best, but I feel I must just check,' the muted sound said.

The boy's thoughts returned to reality and he stopped suddenly, looking around as if lost and trying to place where he was. The noise of the camp, so much closer, hit his senses causing obvious discomfort.

'Quiet Oddsock!' the command was urgent and the donkey fell silent, its decision to speak up vindicated by the reaction. He swung his head to indicate that they should change course, move off in a different direction to avoid the men with the bang sticks.

Perhaps I could throw some blood into the mix, the war god mused. The alcohol and drugs were deadening the slave's minds to their barbarity, but some strife within their ranks would keep their edge. The violence against the village had been a selfish act on the war god's behalf. He fed on the panic, brutality, blood and death, gorging his fill on it, the feast made sweeter by the innocence of the victim and the lack of reason for the attack. It was senseless violence in its purest form and he drank heavily of this nectar.

But his slaves were men, not gods. They had consciences that could be pricked, an in-born sense of right and wrong that needed to be well-managed and overridden occasionally in order to achieve his goals and feed his lust for blood.

Just a trivial dispute thrown in between a couple of his slaves and they would soon be at each other's throats, forced to obey a stupid instinct within their psyche that he could rely on to get them to follow his will. He was in a mischievous mood and tweaked events as only he could.

There was a push, a push back, a shove, a shove back, then a punch was thrown and returned. Voices were raised as two slaves began to grapple and the others quickly took sides. The war god grinned evilly.

Whitearm did not hear the boy approach and the boy did not expect to see anyone out there in the dark. They stopped, both as surprised as the other. The boy reacted first, raising his gun and pointing it menacingly.

'Stop! Who are you?' he commanded, his language coated in an unfamiliar accent, but the words climbed through the disguise and hit Whitearm hard enough for him to obey.

A slave of the war god, his mind yelled at him while his eyes did not move from the bang stick in the boy's hands. A slave, but he is a boy, not a man. The incongruity stuck him.

'Who are you? Put your hands up.' The boy slave twitched the bang stick.

Unsure what was required of him, Whitearm held out his hands, palms up.

'My name is Whitearm. I am called this because I have a white arm.' He turned his afflicted limb to show the boy slave. He could not recall seeing a slave this young when they had attacked the village, and the blurry fuzz his mind had wrapped the memory in, offered no elucidation.

The boy slave stared at the arm, momentarily forgetting his gun which took the opportunity to stand at ease, pointing at the bushes rather than at Whitearm.

'How did your arm go like that?' Curiosity was overriding his menacing stance. The sounds of the fight in the camp was a fine misty drizzle in the dark quiet around them, so faint that it did not penetrate through to the slave boy's mind.

'I don't know, I was born with it this way,' Whitearm studied the limb now, the question had never occurred to him that something had happened to cause it, it just was and always had been.

The slave continued to stare. 'It is not witchcraft?' he asked, fingers tightening on the gun, bracing himself to flee, a panicked look flashing across his face.

'Witchcraft?' The thought had never entered Whitearm's mind. He studied his arm again thoughtfully. 'Witchcraft?' he repeated. Could it be that his difference was caused by a curse of sorts? He had never regarded it as being so. Even when it had been his turn to be outcast for the day, the others using his discolouration as an excuse for banishing him, he had not once put it down to a curse, it just was.

'If it was witchcraft would I be here to show you my arm? Would my parents not have abandoned me to the wild animals, the hyenas and lions?' He had heard the stories and found relief in the realisation that his survival proved that he was not cursed. He stared at his hand with renewed interest.

'Where are your parents?' The slave was beginning to join up some dots that led to this strange boy's presence here alone in the middle of nowhere.

Whitearm looked up and then at the bang stick. He too was making connections.

'They are dead. Men came to our village and threw stones from their bang sticks and my mother and father are both dead. My sister too.'

The two boys both looked at the gun, one with suspicion, the other with guilt.

'When?' The word struggled to escape from the gun bearer's lips.

'Two days ago.'

Silence fell between them now, a thick and tense absence of sound that turned the dark into a syrupy sludge of suspicion and fear that seemed to suck the air out of the bush.

'They made me do it,' the slave lifted the gun and pointed it at Whitearm, wary of potential pent up revenge being unleashed.

'Who?'

'The men. I am sorry.' The apology did not bring relief nor the lowering of the gun.

Whitearm studied his emotions. He should be angry with this boy with the bang stick. He should grab a stone and throw it at him, or find a thick branch of a tree and hit him. But there was something in the slave's moonlit face that did not sit right with that. The eyes of the boy said, 'I am a slave. I cannot help but obey my master. If I were free I would not do this, but I am not free, I have no choice.'

'How do they make you do it?' Whitearm could not comprehend how the god could make a slave of a boy as young as himself. He had always been free, his only masters were his mother and father who had ruled his life with love, never forcing him to inflict pain on another, only punishing if he caused another pain through harsh words or a punch or a slap.

The boy with the bang stick was unsure how to react. Where he had expected rebuke and violence he got curiosity, almost sympathy. He began to point the stick to one side, paused, re-aimed, then relaxed again.

'They have my brother. They say they will kill him if I don't fight for them. They are not nice men, listen, you can hear them fighting. They have got drunk and they take drugs and then they fight. I am glad I am on sentry duty, I hate being in the camp when they are like this.'

The sounds of the anger stirred up by the war god's cunning, pierced the innocent bubble the boys had created around themselves and they both listened, the slave boy with a sad and resigned look, Whitearm with some fear, his only relief coming from the distance the noise had to travel and the darkness that it had to travel through.

The boy with the bang stick broke off the contemplation first with a sigh and then a shrug. This was his lot in life.

'I should take you to them, that's what I am supposed to do,' he paused, considering the consequences of disobeying his instructions, then shrugged again. 'But if they don't know we have spoken,' he continued in response to the widening of Whitearm's eyes and the fever of fear that gripped the orphaned boy, 'then they cannot do anything, can they?'

Whitearm shook his head, not sure what he was agreeing to.

Having made up his mind, the slave lowered the bang stick again. 'What are you going to do now? Where will you go?'

'To the ocean,' the answer was out of his mouth before his brain could warn him against giving out too much information.

'The ocean?' the boy smiled, 'I have heard that it is very big.'

'As big as the sky,' Whitearm smiled and gestured the size of the ocean with spread arms, the boy's smile and knowledge of the ocean giving him confidence to reveal more. 'And there are coconuts there with juice that makes your tongue feel alive and flesh as white as your teeth, as soft as cooked yam and sweeter than mother's milk,' he rattled off the qualities of the fruit using words burnt into his mind by the evening firelight.

The other boy's eyes widened at the description. 'I have never heard of these coconuts, they sound wonderful.'

'Come with me then,' Whitearm was proud of the idea that bypassed his mind and went straight to his voice, but his pride crumbled quickly as its meaning seemed to be a slap in the face of the boy.

'I cannot,' his voice subdued by sadness, 'they will kill my brother if I run away from them.' The noise of the fight was growing, an angry buzz like enraged bees, it came to them quickly now, as if it were offended by the mere suggestion Whitearm had made. How dare he, a youngster, a victim, one who should be dead, how dare he try and steal away one of the slaves?

'Boy! Where are you?'

The voice was rough, edged with anger and it startled the youngsters. The slave motioned silence and indicated that Whitearm should hide quickly. He scrambled into the bushes, his heart slapping against his ribcage.

'I am here, sir,' the slave answered once Whitearm was sufficiently concealed.

The figure of a man broke the darkness that had hung around the boys. He too carried a bang stick, pointing it at the boy as he approached.

'Why have you wondered so far?' The man's eyes did not settle on the boy but darted around, checking that the darkness contained no surprises.

'I needed to relieve myself, sir. That is why I wanted to be far from the camp.'

The man nodded but belief did not come to his eyes. He sniffed.

'Your shit smells like a donkey's.' He stared at the boy, un amused by his own humour.

'Yes sir,' the boy bowed his head, accepting the insult as a more favourable punishment than what he possibly could have received.

'Were you talking to someone?' The eyes still roamed around the darkness.

'No sir.'

'Don't lie to me,' the punch caught the boy in the chest and sent him reeling.

Whitearm grabbed at the gasp that rose in his throat and stuffed it back into his mind, his eyes watching the scene, unable to look away despite the instructions being sent to them.

'Who. Were. You. Talking. To?' The staccato question was accompanied by the butt of the rifle jabbing maliciously at the air just above the boy's head.

Whitearm wanted to stop the violence, to shout out that he was the one who the boy had been speaking to. He fought against the sticky black cotton soil of fear that his confession was bogged down in.

'My brother, I was talking to my brother,' the slave boy called out quickly from behind the protective wall of his hands. His voice carried a trace of insolence.

The rifle wavered for just a second. 'Your brother?'

'Yes sir.'

'He is not here you fool,' the rifle was lifted slightly ready to strike.

'No sir, he is not, but I like to pretend to talk to him, it reminds me that he is still alive.' The little body was still tensed, but his eyes peered from behind his arms that were held up as a useless defence, trying to discern the impact of the words.

The rifle considered the answer, unsure of the action it should take, eventually turning to its master for advice.

'You fool,' the man repeated and lowered his gun, then, as the boy relaxed his arms, stuck his boot heavily into the boy's side, the breath leaving the youngster in a sickening gasp, but he did not cry out, instead grabbed his side, clutching for air.

'Get up!' The man was angry but the voice said to Whitearm that the annoyance lay in a bed of guilt. The lashing out had been an act of frustration. The inner human had lost its temper with the outer beast and the innocent boy had suffered. The shock of the action of kicking a defenceless child prompted a short cease fire between the rational and irrational and he helped the boy, who was still struggling to breathe, to his feet.

'Get back to the camp,' the man paused as the sound of the fighting reached his ears, 'and stay clear of those fools,' he twitched his head in the direction of the noise.

The boy moved off, clutching his side where the boot had hit him. The man cast a glance around, the beast had not believed the boy while the inner human had its doubts. His eyes settled on the bush where Whitearm hid, trying to determine if he could see something amiss or if it was just the dark distorting his vision, moulding the blackness into shapes that were not there. Whitearm held his breath, tensing himself, getting ready to run.

A stutter of bangs came loudly from the camp and the man turned. 'Idiots,' he spat out the word and started to run towards the noise.

The bang sticks spoke briefly in a rapid burst before falling silent and giving over to the shouts of the men, the voice of the man with the boot could soon be heard over the others, instilling order through authority and the darkness began to absorb the noise and dilute it till it became a low mumble in the outer reaches of audible.

Whitearm waited till his sprinting heart had slowed itself to jogging pace before pulling himself cautiously to his feet.

'Oddsock,' he whispered, 'Oddsock.'

The donkey emerged quietly from the bushes, taking the summons to be the all clear.

'Oddsock,' the boy threw his arms around the donkey's neck, the trembling in his legs made standing an effort, so he held on until strength completed its trickle feed back into his limbs.

'Come, we must go. We must get away from those men. I would like to help that boy but what can I do? I am just a boy myself. I do not even have a bang stick. Why do those men do that? He is just a child like me, why do they make him fight?'

He shook his head to let Oddsock know that he did not have an answer. The incident had shaken him, the brutality of the man who still showed a little compassion, confused his young mind and all he wanted was to be far away from it all.

'Come, we will walk for a bit in the night, then rest, but be quiet.'

The war god was not pleased. The idiot slaves had gone too far and he had lost two of them over a stupid dispute about cigarettes. If the slave master had not returned, the loss would have been greater. He cursed the foolishness of man. They were supposed to fight with fists when attacking their fellow slaves, not pick up their guns. This was a waste of ammunition.

He would get his revenge on this group of slaves, ensuring that the donkey carrying the liquor would stumble, causing it to spill and be quickly swallowed by a thirsty land. The slaves in their anger would shoot the donkey. The war god caused their drugs to be stolen by monkeys who ate the powerful herbs, only to be shot by the slaves angry at the insult these primates had caused. The army then marched on, sullen and annoyed with their fate, but when they reached the next village their pent-up frustrations were unleashed in extra violent acts of rape and pillage as they gorged their lustful desires and loaded up with homebrewed beer and more herbs. The war god allowed them this reward, but rationed the loot to small doses.

He did take one further act of revenge. While he had been enjoying the fighting and bloody noses handed out before the shooting began, he had taken his eye off one of the child soldiers for a bit. When the youngster returned to the fold, the war god knew he had not obeyed orders, he had let a potential slave go free and that could not be tolerated. At the war god's direction, a village goat, fleeing in the mayhem of the attack, knocked the traitor from his feet and through the door of a hut, moments before the roof, in a desperate attempt to escape the flames that consumed it, rushed towards the ground, smothering the cries of the boy before they could escape his mouth.

Hunger

The bird could not understand why the human young did not want to join the rest of the herd. It had been so close, but after the night of noise, where there was jostling for power amongst the group, the young seemed to deliberately head off in a different direction to the rest of his species. The noise of the fight, especially the loud bangs, had made for a difficult night, the bird withdrawing as deep into the branches of a tree as she could. She had observed disputes in families of other animals, even been involved in a few squawking spats with her own kin, but the humans were even more intense than the elephants.

When two elephants fight, so the saying goes, the grass suffers. But those fights seldom left carcasses. A defeated bull would slink off and nurse its wounds, perhaps be banished from the herd completely, but it would still walk off. The bird in its early morning reconnaissance had seen the dead, two humans and a donkey. When humans fight, those around them suffer.

The bird, despite not quite knowing why the human young had decided not to join the others, felt glad that it had chosen a different path. Something was right about this shunning of violence, so she swooped and glided through the air above the child, her maternal instincts driving her to keep an eye on him.

Whitearm quickly learned to pace himself as he walked, spending the hottest part of the day in whatever shade he could find, usually falling into a deep sleep under a tree, the dust of the earth seeping into his skin, tingeing his usually brown appearance with a red-orange hue. He became less interested in the fight against this outer coating, not bothering to dust himself off when he stood to continue his journey. He would wash himself in the ocean, was the excuse he made to the mother he carried in his mind. Unlike his real mother, the memory of one was far more indulgent of his whims and behaviours. His flesh and blood mother would not

have accepted that as an excuse, making him go and draw water
from the well to remove the dirt, but the mother in his head would
nod and smile and say, 'Carry on my child. You are grown up now
and you know best.'

And she did have a point as water was precious, needed more as
fuel for the body than as a beauty product. He drank sparingly
from his small supply, but even then it seemed to dwindle quickly.
A fortunate change of direction – a result of nothing more than
Oddsock standing at a different angle when called on for guidance
– led to a dying watering hole that was quickly sucking the remnants of water into itself. Oddsock drank his fill and the boy did
likewise after filling up all the gourds he had.

The discovery of the water, instead of bringing relief to his mind
that had started to dwell on his disappearing supply, prompted him
to wonder how many watering holes lay between where he was
and the ocean. Would he get to the next one before he ran out?
How far was the ocean? The excitement of his adventure began to
lose its lustre as the needs of the body fired themselves up and the
heat continued to hinder his progress. The ocean struggled for
attention against thirst and hunger.

When he did manage to put those basic needs aside, his mind
searching for a distraction to block out the hammering messages
from throat and stomach, he took to dwelling on his encounter
with the boy soldier, trying to comprehend the position the young
slave found himself in.

'They have my brother. They say they will kill him if I don't fight
for them.'

The boy was a prisoner in a jail without walls, like the donkeys
and cows of the village. They were free to wander away, but the
alternative to staying in the confines of the village was not a
pleasant one, facing the wild world without protection. The difference was that he could see that the boy slave was not happy being
a soldier. If he liked the job he would not have lied, not have
subjected himself to the punishment he received in order to protect
a frightened urchin from a fate similar to his own.

Despite the dark and the fear that coated the memory of that
encounter, the boy slave's eyes, clear in the moonlight, carried a
look of defiance, as if by enduring the punishment he was victori-
ous, as if by refusing to give up Whitearm to the man, he was

taking revenge on his master. Whitearm could not quite understand this. Why be beaten so that someone you do not know can
stay free?

He had not had a brother, only a sister, but the effect would be
the same surely? If the war god took his sister and said to him, 'You
will become my slave and if you do not do all I command then I
will kill your sister,' he would have obeyed, he would have done
everything asked of him so that his sister could be kept safe. Or
would he?

It was the evening after his encounter with the boy slave that
Whitearm finally had a chance to think about it. His mind had
been frazzled with fear and concentrated on one thing only, to get
as far away from the war god's men as he could. That thought
dominated as he pushed on through the heat of the day, the sun
ravaging his throat with thirst as he continued to move, all the time
making sure that the place where the noise of the slaves had come
from was at his back. Oddsock struggled behind him, sensing the
need to be gone from the area, but disliking having to walk in the
heat.

As the evening fell softly like a bird gliding to the ground,
Whitearm stopped and looked round. He could no longer sense the
raised fighting voices and loud shouts of the bang sticks that had
followed him throughout the day with a near tangible presence, a
beast in pursuit. He sagged to the floor, exhaustion pulsing through
his heated body and mind. His throat was afire with thirst and that
devil had returned to torment his stomach. It was with great effort
that he only took a few sips of his precious water. The trees around
here did not offer the right leaves for him to find moisture, but the
few swallowed mouthfuls eased his baked mind and he began to
feel safe from the war god's slaves.

His thoughts about the boy he had met, grew out of a necessity
to ignore the attack on his gut by the hunger devil and he drew
himself deeper into his questions. He tried to imagine how he
would have reacted had he been the slave with the bang stick and
if that boy had been the frightened animal trapped and at his
mercy. Whitearm had known the pain of a beating and would
never actively seek one. His had come when his boyish enthusiasm
for life conflicted with the norms of the village and it would drive
him to do things with little thought of consequence. But the slave

boy knew what was coming and actively sought it. That had been written in his eyes. He had done so in order to deflect attention from Whitearm, but there was something else in that look, something that spoke to Whitearm. His young mind struggled to comprehend the way the boy's eyes had faced his punishment. There was purpose in what he was doing.

Whitearm scratched through his mind to place where he had seen that emotion so clearly on a face. His only experience was the village and he slowly narrowed down the looks he had seen in his short life till a face jumped up, looking at him with a smile splashed across it and that same look etched in the eyes. It was when Twobites had confessed to his mother that it was him who had broken the eggs the chickens had laid. All the boys knew that it had been Twobites' younger brother who, in running excitedly during a game of catch, had not looked where he was going. The sticky innards and some shell fragments still clung to the youngster's bare feet, nearly blackened with dust turned into dark mud by the added moisture.

His mother ignored the obvious evidence as she berated Twobites for not being careful and metered out the required spanking. Twobites had taken the punishment with a proud glint in his eyes, the pride not at the deception, but because he was protecting his brother.

Whitearm remembered his own reaction to the incident. As with the slave boy, he could not understand why Twobites had been prepared to take the blows due to his brother, his young mind still learning that the needs of others, especially those close to you, play as much with your emotions as your own selfish needs and that doing things for others could be as rewarding, if not more so, than tending to your own.

As he sat puzzling over these thoughts, breaking the somewhat complex ideas into digestible chunks, his mind, against his wishes, threw up the screams of his sister as she was attacked by the slaves. His one wish at that moment had been that he could be the one being abused and that it was his sister speeding away on Oddsock's back. Perhaps it was a selfish thought in that the mind was fooling him into believing that the actual pain his sister was being subjected to was not as severe as the pain evoked by having to listen to her distress and not being able to do anything to help.

Slowly the understanding drizzled into his conscious and began to soak his thoughts. One knows oneself better than one knows any other and it is that not knowing that causes the pain. How is that other person coping with their ordeal? If you knew for sure that they had the mental mechanisms required to get through it and to come out the other side with minimal damage, then perhaps the pain of helplessness would not extend to wishing to change places, but the ego would always tell you that you are better equipped than your loved one to cope with the atrocities being inflicted.

The slave boy had been playing the brave one, accepting the punishment he received because he felt that he could endure that better than Whitearm would cope with being made a slave. Gratitude flooded through Whitearm as he realised the fullness of what had occurred. He hoped that the slave boy would one day find his brother and that the two of them could run off together, leave the grasp of the war god and perhaps find their way to the ocean. The thought that the war god may not let his young saviour have that pleasure touched his mind lightly before being brushed away. It felt as if allowing the idea residence in his brain would somehow give it a life that would transmute itself from his head into reality. Whitearm could not allow this to happen, as much for himself as for the slave boy.

Each morning chipped slowly away at the rock of Whitearm's resolve to get to the ocean. Rising from sleep became a greater and greater task, the weariness of the previous day's movement gaining in strength through tiny, almost unidentifiable annexations of the boy's body, spreading aches and pains at a slow glacier-like pace.

Hunger too began to eat away at his frame, pulling his skin closer to his bones as the small layer of fat that had resided there was sacrificed as fuel to keep the body moving.

His luck at catching the guinea fowl that first evening of his journey did not hold and he tried to pluck sustenance from the dusty trees, but the leaves were bitter and fought with his stomach, leaving him doubled over and retching.

He soon learned that when he did manage to find food, the odd small animal he could catch, that he should not gobble it down in a frenzied race to appease the devil in his gut. That seemed to anger his tormentor further. So he would eat slowly, chewing the food well, taking small mouthfuls and hoping that the demon would accept this offering with good grace. Saving some for the following day would have the devil in a grumpy mood, still torturing his stomach, but that was more pleasant than the violent protestations from being overfed. A meal of leftovers became the best offering to the devil, calming him to a level where he would poke lazily at Whitearm's innards with considerably less vehemence than when there was no food.

Water, although scarce, could still be found. Usually brackish and muddy, but it eased the thirst that was a constant companion to the hunger. His throat was always dry, filled with the dust that lived in the air.

Oddsock suffered too, but was able to eat the foliage they passed by and found the water more palatable. However, his ribcage still floated just below the surface of his hide, two grey washboards, pockmarked with little sores. But the donkey did not complain. He followed, or led the boy, depending on his friend's strength and will to move, keeping alert for signs of the war god's men. His nostrils monitoring the changing smells in the air, but the army had moved on to a different territory for Oddsock picked up no recent scent of them.

A murkiness slowly descended over the terrain they travelled through as more effort was required from Whitearm just to propel himself forward. His eyes lost focus on what was around him, fatigue and hunger robbing him of his capacity to process all aspects of his surroundings. He moved forward in a daze, his mind shrinking into itself, taking refuge from the tide of hurt and exhaustion that assailed his body. His outer defences slowly crumbling in an attempt to protect his inner self; his goal, that of getting to the ocean, was wrapped up inside his head, his most precious possession.

The mornings passed slowly, the need to keep moving dragging Whitearm from his dusty floor bed, gravity sucking at him more strongly each morning as if the ground wished to pull him into itself, the dust from which he was made was tempting him back to be one with it again. Yet each time the call of the ground screamed loud in his mind, he would release a wave from the ocean he had locked up in there. 'A crashing wall of water as tall as the tallest man,' the elder had said when trying to describe the phenomenon to young minds that had only seen water in trickles.

The waves would douse the impassioned flames of the dust and wash the mind clean, clearing the way for the boy to lift his body again and start to move.

Oddsock, as stubborn as the saying, would always be ready, waiting to move as soon as his twin had found the strength for the day.

Once up and moving, the tide from Whitearm's inner ocean would retreat as a sense of responsibility toward Oddsock began to kick in. He no longer required the large sea to keep him moving as that was a dream, something for the waking moments. Oddsock was real and present and, in the boy's eyes, needed to be cared for and there was no one else to do this.

Before setting off he would take a moment to pet his friend, talking softly to him, telling him everything would be alright. 'The ocean is nearby, I can feel it. We will be there today, or maybe tomorrow and then we will drink coconut juice until it comes out of our ears and eat the sweet flesh of it until our stomachs are so full we will not be able to walk,' he would say.

Oddsock would listen to the quiet words, feeling the certainty in the boy's language. He would nuzzle his friend in thank you for the attention he was getting and in return would unknowingly give purpose and meaning to the boy. Despite his obsession with the ocean, the bond between Whitearm and the donkey was an unrecognised incentive to continue to live.

The routine of finding shade when the sun reached its peak became second nature, especially as the absence of food sapped Whitearm of his energy. He would lie motionless for two or three hours, conserving all energy for the afternoon walk. Flies and other insects would appear and disappear on his skin like black spots of light flicking on and off. On one occasion a snake moved over his prone body, pausing to study the boy, its forked tongue darting in and out of its mouth. Its eyes, cold and unfeeling, dared Whitearm to try something, but the boy did not flinch, the exhaustion of the morning walk numbing his body to inertia. The snake, a non-venomous one, lay quite still under the stare from the boy before gliding off in search of a friend to tell the tale of its encounter.

'A huge human it was and I climbed over it. It was so scared that it did not move. Ha! It probably thought I was poisonous.' And it would laugh as though the danger it had been in was nothing. All the other snakes would know that you don't come face to face with a human and escape without some attempt being made on your life. To stare one down was the act of a very brave or very stupid snake.

Like the mornings, getting going again once the day's heat moved from sharp, stinging and silent to a hazy, lazy buzz, was an effort of will. Most days it would be Oddsock who started proceedings, getting a little restless and unnerved by the lack of movement from his twin. He would stand and, after snacking on whatever leaves were close by, would edge over to where the boy lay and begin to gently nudge him with his nose, a puzzled look on his face, as if to ask, 'Are we not moving on this afternoon?'

Whitearm would get slowly to his feet, using Oddsock to steady himself when the dizziness of starvation threatened to rob him of balance. There was a blur of incomprehension about the boy as if his life bewildered him, the hardships he endured before the war god's slaves came, a distant paradise, a time spent playing with friends, trying to steal the odd morsel of food from nature to supplement the one small meal a day his mother managed to prepare. He remembered too, with some happiness, waiting out-side of Twobites' house as his friend fought against the mamba poison, the elders preparing potions and poultices, the recipes of which had tumbled like dominos through generations, as inevita-ble as gravity and the laws of physics. Even if Twobites had not made his slow recovery, slower after the second bite, his death would have been within the laws of nature.

But the deaths from the frightened stones running from the bang sticks, they were not part of the ordered nature of life, they were an aberration that even the elders knew nothing of. They knew its name, war, but they did not talk of what war did, nor how contrary to nature it was. In his dazed state, Whitearm could not work out if the elders were ignorant of what war could do to one, or if they knew, but did not want to tell.

He tried to imagine himself as an elder, sitting by the fire, stories piled high in his mind. But would he talk of what happened the day the war god's men came? Would it have helped if the elders had told the village what to expect? How could they have defended themselves against the power of the bang sticks?

The questions began to consume his mind, compressing the ache of hunger into a tight wad in his stomach, ever present, yet never the centre of attention. The passing of time however, had other plans and the hunger knew it could not allow those other thoughts to control the boy's actions. The hunger had to keep a balance. If the boy could suppress all awareness of it, then he, as host to the hunger, could die without really knowing why he had died. However, if the hunger made too much of its existence, it would spur its host on to greater efforts to find food and in that way, the hunger would put its own existence in jeopardy. So it developed a system of hibernating when food with sufficient nourishment was found, never quite dying off completely but hiding in the stomach, awaiting the moment when it was needed to spark its host into action. Then it would flare up and fight against the sense-numbing thoughts in order to gain supremacy in the psyche.

Evenings were the best time for Whitearm. The air cooled to levels where he could breathe without scorching his lungs and he could rest with a clear conscience knowing that he was not wasting precious hours being inactive while the ocean beckoned. Surely the ocean must know that moving through this landscape after dark was perilous. Animals lurked beyond the wall of dark that surrounded him. And men. War men. Whitearm knew from his encounter with the slave boy that they could be anywhere, hidden by the blackness the night brought. Even the moon at its brightest could still not cast enough light on the land for him to move with confidence that he would not stumble across the war god's men.

The ocean must also know that a boy – for despite being thrust into a world of adult responsibility, Whitearm was still a boy – could not move without the need for rest. The ocean was good, the ocean would understand, the ocean must understand.

So he would rest in the evenings, letting not only his body, but his mind relax. He would talk to Oddsock who sat quietly beside him, a loyal companion, listening to him mumble, sometimes incoherently, sometimes with painful clarity, depending on how sharply the thorns of his memories would dig into him. The donkey would react accordingly, not responding to the words which he could not understand, but moved by their inflection, knowing when the thoughts cut the boy deepest and would dip his large head close, as if seeking attention but acting as a distraction, allowing Whitearm to pet him, always seeking the boy's oddly coloured arm, making a joke of rejecting the other normally coloured one by tossing his head away, much to Whitearm's delight.

The gentle teasing would ease the sting the memories brought and there would be evenings where the boy would hug the large neck in gratitude for the companionship the donkey gave.

Oddsock felt the hunger in the boy, the hollowness of the gut that would rumble in his ear when the boy held him close. He watched, eyes blinking a sad symphony, as the boy would chase guinea fowl that would scatter amongst the scrub, littering the land with squawks and panic, pursued with growing desperation. On the rare occasions when the hunt was successful, Oddsock would bray a victory cry, his head nodding passionately in celebration of the boy's obvious joy.

Those evenings were the best. The remembrances of war could not penetrate the barrier of joy that surrounded the boy and the donkey as the human would eat, slowly as he had learned, feeling the weakness of hunger gradually crumbling inside him. Oddsock was not needed on those evening but was not excluded. The white hand would constantly seek out and stroke the animal's flank, almost as if it were doing so under no instruction, yet if the donkey had settled a little too far to reach, the boy would suddenly become aware of things being amiss and would shift closer to his twin before settling again into a state of absorption with his cooking and his food.

The nights could vary. Tiredness from the day of walking would close his eyes soon after the darkness settled over him, the heat that had shouted at him all day would work to close down his mind, but the hunger that ate away at his stomach would dance with his dreams. And it was a fickle dance partner, some days perfectly in step with the dreams, executing foxtrots and tango with the flowing grace of waves lapping at a beach. But there were nights when the timing was off and the hunger would tread clumsily on the toes of the dreams, heels crashing down like the butt of a bang stick with bone crunching anger, pain shooting through the boy's sub-conscious, yet the walking and heat conspired to keep him in his sleeping state, prolonging his agony while his inner mind would writhe and twist and try to escape the sharp claws that dug into him. His body would twitch and low moans would escape his lips till the donkey, feeling his distress, would nuzzle him gently, nudging the hunger off the dancefloor, leaving the boy to a black and dreamless sleep from which he would wake slowly, picking his way along the path to consciousness with wary steps, as if afraid that his nightmares would be waiting for him when he arrived back into wakefulness.

The bad dreams left him dazed, moving slowly, fearful of the next step, yet too frightened to stay near the space where his mind had been attacked. He trudged, his feet sulky and petulant, not wanting to obey, yet afraid to fall behind the mind that kept moving forward.

On the nights when some food was found, the dreams danced alone, gliding across the floor of his subconscious, a rapt satisfaction painted on their faces, but with a body drooped and dripping sadness at its solitude and inability to share the good fortune with another human. Whitearm was unaware of the cause of the melancholy that these moments brought. He would celebrate the acquisition of food with Oddsock, hugging the donkey's large neck, laughing excitedly into the musky, dusty hide.

For his part, Oddsock would bray and nod his head, sensing the excitement and good news, but he could never voice this joy in a way that the young human could understand. This did not affect the animal the way it did Whitearm. Oddsock was content to be with the young boy, not missing the company of other donkeys.

The hyenas were hungry the night they came, soft paws padding across the dusty floor, heads bent low to the ground as if following a scent. But their noses caught little of the odours on offer, their progress powered by instinct yet hindered by malnourishment. This was the lean season, a time when the land withdrew its meagre ration of food and animals spread themselves thinly across its plains in search of life giving water.

The famine had cut into their number. The pack, once large, powerful and arrogant, was now decimated, a handful of survivors. Some had succumbed to the hunger, slowly shrivelling up and giving up, too weak to jostle for a place at a carcass should they be fortunate enough to find one. But the largest loss occurred one fateful night when, driven by desperation, they made a daring raid on a human encampment. Usually such raids would be fruitful. The humans kept chickens and they could be in and out with half a dozen birds before the shouting and stone throwing began. But that time the humans, possibly because of the general lack of food in the land, had been more vigilant. The shouts came quickly, the stones hurled even quicker and with lightning force that those hit by them would be knocked sideways almost before the loud cry of effort the humans gave could frighten the pack. Most of those that the stones hit lay where they fell, only one or two managed to limp away, but inevitably fell soon afterwards.

The encounter had made the survivors wary of the humans and they now moved in wide arcs around any scent of human they encountered.

The leader, a wiry beast covered in a patchwork of fur and raw, red skin, was the first to realise they were close to a human. He stopped, glaring round at the one behind him who, so wrapped up in its hunger, had bumped into him. A malevolent smile to which no humour could ever attach itself was a permanent fixture on his face. He sniffed at the air and the others followed, realisation leading to restlessness. They eyed their leader, looking for a decision. He took his time, weighing up the power of the scent against the strength of his hunger.

There was not a mixture of human smells on offer, just one and a donkey. Could the four of them win in such an attack? He tested the air again to check he had read it right, then looked round at the pack. There were four, himself, a female who frightened easily, a male who in better days had been their leader, but injury during the attack on the humans had left him lame in one leg and with the disability came the abdication from his role. The last was still a youngster, a fighter like the leader, but inexperienced and a survivor more from luck than skill.

The youngster was up for confronting the human, its eyes hardened in the fading light and a rancid globule of saliva escaped out the side of its mouth. Its body tensed, facing in the direction the scent was coming from, awaiting the command.

The female was restless. You don't attack humans. That was the rule in normal circumstances. We are scavengers not hunters. The recent 'hunt' and the resultant loss of her mate, still raw in her mind, had dented an already fragile confidence. So too had the depletion of their number. Before she would wiggle her way into the middle of the pack, the surrounding wall of bobbing hides protecting her from fear. Now she felt naked and exposed. She would follow wherever the new leader took them, her only choice being whether to like it or not.

The ex-leader was nervous too. In his day he had been as fearless as his specie's genes would allow, but he could now no longer rely on strong forepaws to help him through any dangerous situations, the knee joint smashed by one of those super-speed stones, still ached and he was acutely aware of his reduced agility. He too would follow, his loyalty a mixture of an in-bred instinct to be brave and a nagging fear of abandonment and the obvious death that would quickly result.

The three predators watched their commander, sensing his hesitation, their minds moving along the same track of thought. They were not completely averse to attacking and killing, necessity had helped them across that bridge. Scavenging and feasting on others' left-overs meant that you relied on others. When they were not there, you had to turn inwards and that meant doing the killing yourself.

Stealing from the humans was one thing. What was proposed here was possibly taking the human. The scent told them it was a young, disconnected from its herd and therefore vulnerable. But where was the rest of the herd? The leader sniffed the air slowly, trying to detect any trace of the rest, but there was nothing. Frothy saliva began to accumulate in the corner of his grin and then slowly he began to move forward.

It had been another day without food but Whitearm still built a fire, his tired mind working on automatic, forcing his limbs to gather the wood and twigs, then rubbing the sticks together till the friction-induced spark would ignite the dry grass. The smaller bits of wood would take on the flame, their dryness grabbing hungrily at the warmth, unaware that it would consume them. The bigger branches and logs would be slow on the uptake, lumbering in the wake of the fire, catching up through persistence rather than speed till they all crackled, cackled and spat in warm unison.

Whitearm sat a few feet away, staring into the fire, the flames playing cruel games with his mind which wished to switch off for the night and hopefully shut out all the things that it was still too young to be processing. The gentle swaying of the flames distracted him, the rhythmic motion building a hypnotic field around his thoughts, trapping them inside his head where they shimmied and shuddered in an attempt to break loose, but could not, their presence painfully felt but not comprehended.

Beyond the reach of the light, eyes began to appear, keeping downwind to avoid detection. Wet black noses grasped at the scents that travelled on a breeze so slight it barely moved. The hyenas began to size up their prey. They could not see the source of the donkey smells, but the young human was clearly visible in the firelight.

Four drops of saliva hit the dusty ground simultaneously. Courage was building within the small pack. Even the nervous female began to believe that they could soon be feasting on young human flesh although there did not seem to be much meat on those bones. The leader moved quietly in front of them, padding back and forth, his eyes, ears and nose taking on as much intelligence of the situation as they could.

The retired leader stood tensed, ready for action, his lame leg held up high to prevent accidentally knocking it or, in the heat of the hunt, forgetting about the injury and placing his weight on it. Echoes of the pain from the last time he had accidentally tried to use the paw still rang in his brain.

The youngster joined the leader in pacing, showing his willing for the fight, impatience beginning to build. Why were they not attacking? What was the leader waiting for? Its evil grin turning into a sneer of contempt at the seeming lack of courage. They had seen their target, a small human. Surely it could not see off four hungry hyenas if they all attacked together. He turned to eye the female and the wounded one. He would get the best share of the meat on offer, he could easily see them off and, if he fought for it, he could push the leader out the way, he was sure. He grinned evilly and in the criss-cross to-and-fro movement that he and the leader danced, he began to push ahead of the others, edging closer to the human, vile sticky saliva running freely down his jowls.

The leader wanted to growl, to warn the youngster off being too hasty, but to do so would be to lose their advantage of surprise. He had no choice but to follow. The female and ex-leader brought up the rear, knowing that the best bits would probably be taken before they could get near. The scene was tightly wound, a ball of energy waiting for release, tense and expectant.

The youngster broke first, moving into a sprint straight for its target which lay in a slight stupor awaiting sleep. Nearer and nearer till suddenly its body flew sideways as the rear hoofs of the donkey smashed against its skull. He landed a few feet off and did not move.

The female pulled up suddenly in fright, causing the ex-leader to knock into her rear, his damaged leg clashing painfully into the bony flank of his companion, a distressed wail issued from his throat as it rushed to escape the agony.

The leader, on hearing the cry, glanced round, the momentum taking him slightly off course and luckily missed the flying hoofs of the donkey as they flew out for a second time. However, the second's delay allowed the human to grab a burning log from the fire and, by the time he was focused on his prey again, a flame whooshed past his nose, singeing his whiskers and drying his saliva, the heat sending a searing shot of pain through his face. He yelped and changed direction mid-air, paws scrambling wildly to gain traction. The hoofs caught him a sidelong glance, bruising his ribs and banishing the air from his lungs.

The female had turned and was moving off quickly, her meagre appetite for the hunt rapidly disappearing. The ex-leader hobbled quickly after her, his leg throbbing, his ego screaming at him to stay and fight, but his survival instinct chided the ego for its stupidity.

The leader became a follower, slinking away after his companions, the grin still on his face looked sad as it cast a glance across at the lifeless youngster, regret at the further reduction in their numbers weighing against the relief that his main rival for leadership was no longer a threat.

The chase Whitearm gave was lacklustre, a few swings of the burning log and a couple of yells before his weakened body called a halt to these proceedings. He returned to the fire and laid the burning branch down close enough to grab again should the need arise.

'That was close,' he told Oddsock as he patted his friend's neck in gratitude. The donkey stood nearby, ears alert for a re-match, but eyes docile, enjoying the attention.

The meat of the young hyena did not taste pleasant. It was tough and gristly, but served to fill the moaning hollowness in his gut. He did not sleep that night, conscious of the possible return of his attackers, but the food in his belly gave him strength to remain alert till dawn when he ate what he could and began the new day's trek.

'This is what the war god does to the land,' Whitearm told Oddsock as they moved slowly through the heat, 'hyenas do not attack humans. It is not in their nature. But the war god has made them angry and hungry. It has taken away their food, so they will attack anything now. The laws of nature have been broken. Before the war god came, I would not eat hyena meat, but now I am so hungry because the war god has taken away the food and I will eat anything even if it is not natural to do so.'

He looked over at the remnants of the carcass he had strapped to Oddsock's back. He knew that the meat left would not last long in the heat, but he had no appetite for it now. His stomach had been stuffed as full as he could make it and this reactivated his taste buds which now felt that they could be picky. Whitearm shook his head, with hunger dropping down the list of needs for the moment, he could afford to think for a bit, but the thoughts tasted as unpleasant as the meat had. He did not like the unnatural order that the war god had brought to his life.

The ocean. He dug deep into his mind to re-listen to the old men tell their stories of it and began, for the first time, to wonder if it really existed.

Bruised and sore, the hyenas moved away from the boy's scent, not looking each other in the eye, each ashamed of what had happened during their brush with the human young. Their faces drooped again, but luck was with them after their defeat, an old buffalo had left its herd as they went in search of water. It knew that its time was near and after the rest had moved on, it lay down and let its life slowly fade away in the sun. The hyenas were the first to get to the corpse.

Sanctuary

Whitearm opened his eyes, his senses telling him that someone, or something, was very close. Oddsock was strangely quiet and this alarmed him even before he felt the unknown presence. The pale face that greeted his open eyes stared down at him, studying him and sent shockwaves through his body. He pushed himself backwards, away from the dreadful apparition, his ears hearing the distant scream that his mouth, not having time to tell his brain what it was up to, was emitting.

The pale figure jumped back, the sudden movement and noise of the boy evoking the involuntary reaction.

'Holy Mother of God!' the voice came from the deep pink lips that floated in a sea of yellowy-pink face, the words just strange sounds to the boy's ears that had never heard English before.

Whitearm backed himself up against a tree, his eyes wide as his eyelids tried to run away from his eyeballs, the panic in his mind preventing him from working out a route around the obstacle blocking his retreat.

'It's okay, I won't hurt you,' the voice came softly, gently, in his language, but covered in a layer of uncertainty, as if saying, 'I am using these words, but I do not know for sure if they are the right ones.'

'It's okay,' the voice came again, soft and feminine while the pale figure held out its hands, palms forwards to show that she held no weapons.

Whitearm looked at the white woman, then beyond her to where Oddsock stood watching him, a slightly bemused look on his face. The lack of fear or alarm in the donkey fell on his mind like a net of fine mist and cooled his heated thoughts of peril. He returned his attention to the womanly voice, taking in the human shape of this ghost and the human tones in with which it spoke and, except for the fact that she wore a wild bush on her head, he began to accept that she was perhaps human. The elders had spoken of a tribe with skin the colour of the moon, but which did not shine. They had also spoken of strange head garments that, so the rumour went, were stuck so well to their heads that you could not pull them off.

There were mixed stories about the white people. All agreed that they were unpleasant on the eye. Some said that they could not be trusted, they cheated men of their possessions, they claimed land – which belongs to all men – as their own and would not allow others to even let their cows cross 'their' land or to take water from the rivers or dams that they said was their own. There had been mention of this the first time the elders spoke of the war god.

But there were also stories of pale men and women who would come and live with the people of a village. These white people claimed they were there to help, but despite their good intentions, they were stupid, not knowing how to grow things or even how to look after a cow.

Whitearm scurried through his thoughts, some lying under a coat of dust that had gathered during his journey, all of them having to be plucked from the mouths of men now dead and whose memory lay solely in his small mind.

Was this pale creature one of the good or bad white people? He had no words from the elders to draw on that would give him a clue. There was nothing in those stories that said a pale person who had three eyes cannot be trusted, or one who has an upside-down nose is from the nice but stupid lot. His eyes searched the woman's visage for a clue, but nothing came. His back was still pressed hard against the tree as if he were trying to be absorbed into its trunk so that he could become one with it and in that way hide from the eyes of the strange person and be relieved of having to make this difficult decision.

The woman waited patiently for him to decide. The corners of her mouth were pulled down, but this seemed to highlight a warmth in her eyes that told him she was smiling. It was a gentle smile that became more radiant as she eased herself onto the ground, sitting with her legs demurely folded to the side of her body. Her face said, 'I will wait for you to decide if I am good or bad. You are free to go if you wish. I will not harm you.'

Whitearm felt the tree trunk relax its grip on his back but still he would not move. The woman searched the ground around her then picked up a small stone which she held up between her thumb and finger to show him. Her movements were slow, deliberately designed to be non-threatening. She placed the stone in the palm of a hand and showed it to him again before bringing her other hand over it and rubbing them together. She then held them up, showing him two empty palms.

Whitearm stared. Where had the stone gone? The woman smiled, the corners of her mouth pulling down further and the light in her eyes growing brighter. Her hands moved again, her fingers furling and unfurling like the wings of a bird as it groomed itself, then suddenly she pulled the stone from her ear, holding it up again between thumb and forefinger and looking at it in feigned amazement as if to ask, 'How did that get there?', her laughter gentle and soothing.

The tree now peeled itself completely from his back as he leaned forward, watching the trick, wondering what powers the woman had that she could do that. She could not be one of the war god's people, they threw stones out of their bang sticks with mighty force, stones that killed. This woman could make a stone pass through her hands up her arm and neck and come out of her ear and still laugh and smile.

'It's a...' she seemed to wait for the unfamiliar word to arrive and when it did it was wrapped in uncertainty, '...a trick?' the questioning tone wanted to know if he understood.

'Look,' she said and held the stone up again. This time she moved slowly, revealing the sleights of hand in a way that was obvious, yet still seemed to maintain the integrity of the trick.

Whitearm grinned as the mystery was unveiled. She was not a god or a witch who could cast spells, she was an entertainer, like one of the elders in the village who could make an egg come out of his mouth. The women, and especially his wife, would get very cross with him, which always made the trick funnier for the children.

'Would you like some water?' the woman suddenly asked, again her use of his language uncertain.

He nodded before he could consider any consequences of saying yes.

'Come,' she said rising to her feet and dusting her skirt off. She made no move towards him, no threatening gestures, turning her back and taking a few steps before glancing back to see if he followed.

'Come,' she said again and held out her hand for him to take if he wished, 'I won't hurt you.'

The hand held out triggered memories, fresh and recent, yet half a lifetime old for Whitearm's young mind. His mother, a few steps ahead and in danger of forgetting he existed if the gap grew bigger, would, as if following an instinct, stop, turn, smile and offer her hand, waiting for him to catch up. Plump little legs would pound along the dusty path and he would secure his berth beside her and all would be well with the world again.

The hunger, tiredness and his mind, battered and bruised with grief and fear, had bombarded him with all that the strange world beyond his village had thrown at him. But this now crumbled in the face of this memory of his mother and it was as if all was well again. And as those moments resurfaced when he escaped the rough seas of feared abandonment and docked beside his mother, he craved the feelings of contentment and the sense of being safe. Deeply hidden recollections of being cocooned in a watery womb radiated their warmth into his mind without fully revealing themselves. He pushed himself to his feet, his head reeling slightly from the movement of blood and he moved, almost blindly and quite mechanically to grasp the offered hand. A dizziness suddenly engulfed him and he stumbled, the outstretched hand and the safety it offered, agonisingly close, yet as far away as the ocean. Then all went black.

Something cool lay across his forehead. His eyes stayed closed as he let the soothing balm, that could well have been imagined, seep slowly into his skull, his mind sucking it through the bone, letting his thoughts, that had been tossed like sparks from a fire, settle slowly into the quiet calm pile of ash that signified the end of the night and a new day, a new start.

He would tell his mother about the dream. Tell her that he had seen a white woman and that she had performed a trick, making a stone disappear. But it was just a trick, he would tell her because she would start to look at him with that face that said, 'you are being foolish, my child.'

'Just a trick, ma,' he would say, 'she didn't really make it disappear, but hid it between her fingers. It was a good trick, ma, you should have seen it.'

He would tell her this when he opened his eyes, but it was good to lie in the dark, feeling the coolness against his thoughts. He let a smile trickle over his lips as he imagined his mother's reaction to his dream and heard a movement nearby.

'Ah, so you are still alive.'

The voice was real, the woman had not been a dream, his mother would never hear his story. And yet his brain felt cool enough to accept this without panic, the words spoken just before the blackness, returned to him, 'Would you like some water?' His tongue was rough and dry in his mouth and the offer spoke to his closed eyes. You cannot drink with your eyes closed.'

The blackness that had descended on him so suddenly was preparing to leave after a visit of who knew how long, but he needed to help it on its way so with an effort, he opened his eyes.

The room was less dark than the blackness. Where there had been nothing but feelings and thoughts, there was now a figure, a silhouette a shade darker inside the lines of the shape than outside, but he knew that the dark within the dark was the pale woman. The elders were right, this skin the colour of the moon did not shine like that great ball that illuminated his night sky.

'May I have some water?' he heard the words, spoken in a voice that wanted to be his own, but crackled like a bird left cooking too long over the fire. Somewhere under the charred skin of his utterances was a polite pleading in a language that did not have a word for 'please'.

'Certainly,' the coolness lifted from his forehead and a soft hand touched him. He heard water nearby and something cold and damp was placed back on his face, then the silhouette withdrew and he was left to the quietness of the room. He wanted to touch whatever had been placed on his forehead, but the pale woman had placed it there for a reason, so he felt that he should leave it undisturbed.

He reached out tentatively to touch the nearby wall, the smoothness under his fingertips surprising him. Walls were made of mud and branches twined together, rough and knobbly, they should not feel like this. He ran his hand across the surface, back and forth, marvelling at the sensation, until he heard the woman return.

'Water,' she said and, leaned forward to help him sit up, then let him sip the cool liquid from a strange container. 'Slowly,' she eased the flow while he enjoyed the sensation of his tongue and mouth being freed from the shackles of dryness. The water tasted so sweet and he wanted more, he wanted to drink it till it started to pour out of his ears, but the pale woman forced him to go slowly and soon his stomach, unused to such free-flowing water, began to say that this was enough for now. He nodded his head to convey to the woman that, for the moment, he had had his fill.

'Do you feel better?' Although he could not see it, the voice contained that turned down mouth smile and her words were becoming more confident in his language.

Again, he nodded, his body had already absorbed the liquid, pulling it quickly to those parts that needed it most.

'Are you hungry?' her voice did not stop smiling and she lifted the coolness from his forehead.

'Yes, I have not eaten for many days,' his own voice had returned, the crisp fried sound it had made earlier was gone, drowned and soaking in the sweetness of the water. He felt his saliva, almost forgotten, return to his mouth as the realisation that if the pale woman had water this good, she must surely have food that tasted excellent.

'I thought so,' she said, 'are you strong enough to walk a little way?'

Of course I am strong, I have walked halfway to the ocean already. He wanted to make the boast, but doubt crept into his mind. Should he let her know where he was going? He decided just to nod, but as he stood, he felt the blackness close to him and reached out to the wall for support. He felt his arm being caught and slowly the blackness receded, but his legs were not listening to his mind too well, they shook and he did not know if he could trust them to work.

'Slowly,' the woman said again and led him gently from the room.

The light outside was warm, but not too hot. He needed to blink away the dark of the room and the blackness that still floated as wispy feathers in his eyes. Thoughts tumbled over each other as his head tried to keep its balance and within his tumbled mind, one word broke loose and fell onto the safety net of his tongue.

'Oddsock.'

'Hmm?' The woman whom he could see closely now, looked at him quizzically, the downturned corners of her mouth lifting slightly and the smiling glow in her eyes faded in the same proportion.

'Oddsock, my donkey. Where is he?'

The glow returned to full force and the mouth turned down in its inverted smile.

'Oddsock. A perfect name.' She seemed to be talking to herself, then to him she said, 'He is fine, he is grazing round the back.' Her free arm indicated the other side of the building that they had just come out of. He wanted to turn and look in that direction, but his head threatened to swirl again so he just nodded slowly.

'We will eat and then I will take you round to him. You need your strength first.' She led him slowly to a small table with two chairs and guided him on to one. He sat awkwardly, not used to sitting like this. Chairs were for the elders, not for children. The children sat on the floor at their feet. It was only as a special treat that they could sit with the adults and then they would have to be as still as a lizard in the sun or they would lose their privilege. But the woman did not seem concerned if he moved or not as he could not help twisting in his chair to see what she was doing now, but she disappeared into the building again through a different door.

He studied the building. It was not like the huts of the village, this one looked strong, like an elephant. The war god with his bang sticks and his fire could not burn it down as they had done to his own home. This was made from stones, but none that he had ever seen before. The stones he knew were different shapes and sizes, mostly rounded or having jagged edges. This building had stones in straight lines, shapes unnatural to nature and he wondered what god could create something like that. Surely not the war god, that was a god who did not build, but rather broke down and burned.

After a while of staring, the imposing façade of the straight-lined building slowly began to lose its grip on his attention and his gaze changed to the surroundings, moving as quickly as the sloshing of balance in his head would allow him. To the right of the building was a small garden, the plants in it neatly lined up like the angles in the building, but they were new shoots. Food would be some time coming from there.

Further to the right a strange arrangement took Whitearm's gaze. Small trees had been planted in rows, but they were unlike any he knew. They had a trunk that would reach up to his hip, he guessed as he studied them, and one single branch across the trunk, sticking out equally on either side and it had no leaves or thorns. The unnatural square-ness of these branches sat well with the lines of the building, but not with Whitearm. Again he wondered what sort of god could get trees – those magnificent plants whose only master should have been nature – to grow in such a way. A tree grew how it wanted to, its branches twisted and turned as if the tree were dancing as it stretched out its limbs. But these strange small trees were not happy. They did not dance. They stood, arms outstretched, and Whitearm recalled the words of the slave boy many nights ago, 'hands up' he had said. The trees were 'hands up' as though they had been commanded by someone with a bang stick. He looked for, but could not see, the bearer of the bang stick.

'Here is your food,' the voice was friendly and brought his gaze back round, a little too quickly. He grabbed at the table to steady himself again. The pale woman looked across to where he had been concentrating his gaze and the smile left her eyes as she stared at them. She too does not like the trees being 'hands up', Whitearm whispered to himself and watched as the woman's lips quickly said 'soundless' words and she touched her head, her stomach then each breast in quick succession before returning her eyes to him and forcing the corners of her mouth downwards so that the light could come back on in her eyes, but it did not shine with the same intensity as before.

'Come, eat,' she gestured to the food in front of him. The portion was small and he felt disappointed, but drove those thoughts from his mind, hoping they would not show in his face. This woman was good enough to share her food and water, he must not be ungrateful.

'Slowly,' she said as he began to eat, 'your stomach and food are strangers. You need to introduce them so that they can become friends once more.' She smiled her upside-down smile again, then gestured for him to continue.

The food tasted good, but the pale woman was right, his stomach no longer knew food and wanted to kick it out. He sat still after the first few mouthfuls, remembering how he had trained himself on those days when he had managed to find food. Slowly, allowing his stomach to remember. The animosity it had toward this intruder eventually began to fade and he soon finished off the plate. Despite the smallness of the portion, he felt quite satisfied. The good feelings between his stomach and the food spread to include those in his head and he found he did not feel as dizzy.

'Better?' she had watched each mouthful, the smile never fading from her eyes.

He nodded gently, still not quite trusting that the dizziness had left his head.

Her eyes suddenly lifted to look behind him and he turned.

'Ah, your friend is here.'

The donkey came quickly to him, head nodding an excited greeting, the joy of the beast clear on the long face which was soon embraced in mismatched arms, the young boy's head resting on the grey neck, words of friendship, quietly mumbled, tumbled into the long ears, the donkey blinking a happy Morse code of acceptance of the words.

The dizziness took a few days to vanish completely, spinning in ever tighter circles in his head till it consumed itself totally and Whitearm found that he could move without fear of the tempest that had risen and fallen in his brain.

The pale woman fed him, gradually increasing the portions as his stomach expanded and settled. He did not notice the contraction in the amount of food that she put on her own plate. All the time the corners of her mouth would stretch down to keep the light of her smile shining in her eyes.

Every morning she would go into one of the buildings, emerging later with a serene look on her face. Whitearm watched and wondered what happened there, but could not get up the courage to investigate, the fear that somehow this would break the spell and he would be cast out kept him at bay. He chose rather to explore the area. Nearby he found another village that the war god's men had visited, stumps of what had been huts stood in a clearing, the dusty black paint left by the fire that had swept through the village touching everything, even the ground around them.

Unlike his village, there were no bodies left lying around, no unseeing eyes bearing witness to the brutality that had occurred. In their place 'hands-up' trees had already started growing, so many of them. Whitearm could not understand the purpose of such trees. They had no leaves for the animals to eat, or fruit for the birds to pick at. They were dead trees without reason. He wondered if the war god's slaves had planted these trees as a mark that they had been there. He pictured his own destroyed village, imagining what it would look like with these strange plants strewn around the compound, a pang of regret at leaving his home passed through him. Had he stayed, he could have pulled out these weeds of war as they grew.

They spoke very little at first, most talk revolved around food and the sweet tasting water that the woman seemed to have some secret and endless supply of. She had told him that her name was Sister Constance, an unusual name, especially when she translated 'sister' into his language. No one called themselves 'sister' as part of their name. You could call a girl sister even if they were not related to you, but you would not then add their name to that. However, the pale people seemed to want the person's given name to sit next to 'sister', so he complied and called her in the manner she wished to be named, his tongue always struggling as it navigated itself around the unfamiliar sounds needed to say her name.

Oddsock stayed close to him as he explored his new surroundings. He moved slowly as the strength seeped back into his body. Like the renewed vigour his limbs found, so this new place settled in his mind and a feeling of 'home' began to grow in him.

He started to wonder how a sister could also be a mother as Sister Constance took on the maternal role recently vacated by his natural parent, throwing up conflicting emotions in the young boy. The umbilical, long disposed of, still held a powerful sway over him, demanding a lifelong loyalty that he willingly gave. But the hand that now fed, the eyes that smiled and the gentle inclination of a head that radiated love and caring on a level that felt more spiritual than earthly, cast a spell over him, nearly as strong as the invisible cord that tied him to his birth mother.

He was given small tasks to perform, light work to match his enfeebled state and designed to aid his recovery, putting some substance on his muscles and growing in their demands as his body became more able. There were chickens to feed, a small garden to tend to and the compound needed to be swept clean. He set about these chores with a light heart, happy to be of some use to the woman who had rescued him.

His work took him all round the small settlement, but he avoided the building where Sister Constance would go in the mornings and evenings. This was her sanctuary, her private place and, despite a burning curiosity about it, there was a sense that this was something private and should be inviolate which kept him from even peeping round the door.

The ocean, that longed-for goal that had so occupied his thoughts and kept him alive as he continually strove for it, was slowly slipping from his mind. Like the tide going out, the memory of the sea receded, leaving only dry sand and a thin ragged line of detritus as evidence that it had once visited this far up the beach. It would appear in his mind in light, soft focus flashes as the tasks of his new life took precedence in his thoughts. The idea of escaping to this mystical body of water had been born out of a necessity to find a reason to survive, but now his survival seemed less threatened and he no longer needed this to spur him on.

There was an almost unnatural lack of curiosity from either Whitearm or Sister Constance as to why they were where they were, as if they both already knew that the other was a survivor of the war god's wrath, but neither wanted to, nor could, talk about it. An unspoken agreement arose between them that they would not tell their stories, not yet. The pain so private and personal that to even think of the events in each other's presence would trigger an excuse to be elsewhere. Sister Constance would disappear into her private house, tears sitting close to her lower eyelids, while Whitearm would find himself wandering through the ghostly remnants of the nearby village, the haunting scenes reminding him of the horrors he had witnessed, but the quietness of the place bringing a calmness to his mind. He began to talk to the hands-up trees, despite their lack of use, their stubbornness of being began to charm him. If something without use could exist and continue to exist, neither growing nor shrinking, how much more could something that had a purpose or a use continue to be. *He* could continue to be, whether he had a use – which he felt he did now – or even if he were forced, through whatever events may take place in the future, to return to his unguided wanderings in search of the ocean, he would continue to be.

Their lives seemed to connect and disconnect as they drew near, then parted as the departed came between them. It had to be Sister Constance who broke this cycle, Whitearm did not have the language to do so.

'They came on us so quickly,' she said one afternoon as Whitearm brought her the eggs he had managed to find. She was sitting on a small chair outside the building they shared, her eyes looking across at the hands-up trees a little way off. Whitearm nodded and sat on the ground at her feet, sensing that the time had come for stories to be told. He had been good at identifying which of the elders would be the one to do the talking in the evening, there was a look in their eyes, a certain posture to the body and an aura that hung around them as if the story were some kind of elixir that brightened a man's being as it began to reach boiling point within him, awaiting release.

It was different with Sister Constance, but she had a different story to tell. The elders had generally spun yarns about wonderful and amazing things, things that left you wide-eyed with your mouth hanging open, hoping that the words of the story would float into it and take root and grow on your tongue so that you, when you became an elder, could tell a story as incredulous as the one you were listening to. But when they spoke of things that the children were not meant to hear, their demeanour changed. Eye did not meet eye, bodies hunched as if trying to trap the story inside their huddle, not letting it stray too far. Mouths stayed closed, refusing to let what was being said find fertile ground. Sister Constance had a story that was not meant for children's ears, her demeanour told him that. A slight awe spread in him that he, young as he was, would be trusted with an adult story. He sat quietly, making sure that his mouth was closed so that he would not be burdened with such a dreadful tale.

'We knew about the war, but we kept praying that it would not come to us. They hit the village first,' Sister Constance paused, her eyes moved towards the nearby hands-up trees, then decided against looking at them and continued. 'The others were all up in the village, they were preparing for the...' she paused, thought for a moment, then said the strange English words, '...Easter service.' Whitearm nodded, not really understanding, but feeling that, as he was being allowed to hear an adult story, he should at least appear to understand it like an adult. Sister Constance went on, not stopping to check if he was following. 'I was still here when I heard the screams and shots. I wanted to run and help. I really did, but...' again she stopped, this time her eyes made it to the hands-up trees, '...Lord, forgive me.' She did the forehead, belly, left breast, right breast movement with her hands which Whitearm had come to accept as a sort of nervous tic that she had.

It took her a while to start up again and Whitearm sat quietly waiting. The elders did not usually pause for this long in a story, even when they were talking about things that were not for children's ears. But Sister Constance was a pale person, and unlike the elders, was a woman, so she was obviously not used to proper story-telling. He would have to be patient and hope that it would all make sense, that is if she ever finished telling the story.

'I am not making sense to you, am I?' the corners of her mouth turned down in that funny smile as she suddenly looked at him and realisation flashed across her face.

He wanted to shake his head to say no, he did not understand, but also did not want to upset her, so sat still, staring at her, hoping that she would not want an answer.

'No, I am not making sense. Let me start again,' she was back into her storytelling and Whitearm felt himself fade in her consciousness.

'There were five of us white people. Father Slater, Sister Rose, Sister Rebecca, Sister Shannon and myself.' Her eyes were back on the hands-up trees again, then, as if ashamed to look at them, returned her gaze to Whitearm, then moved on to the distant horizon. 'We had been here about a year.'

After its initial stumbled start, the story was up on its feet again and moving. She kept the words simple and explained, where her grasp of the language allowed, what she could. Foreign words would flicker in and out of the narrative, sometimes causing a jitter

in the otherwise smooth flow, at other times they blended in with
the locals, the flow of the story disguising their alien nature.

Her tale was not too dissimilar to his own and Whitearm absorbed the details, laying them next to his own experience. The
war god's men had arrived unannounced. They had shot indiscriminately. They had set fire to the village homes. They had taken the
cows, donkeys and chickens. Sister Constance had, by some miracle (and a nervous tic, forehead-belly-left breast-right breast) been
spared. All this matched his own story.

There were differences though and these intrigued and, at times,
puzzled the boy. The war god's men had left the mission untouched, undiscovered even (what was a 'mission'?) All their supplies in the building were kept safe from the raid (what are
'supplies'?) As the only survivor, she had buried all the dead and
erected crosses on the graves (what are 'crosses'?).

When she had finished the story they sat quietly together, she
trying to re-digest the unpalatable memories that had been resur-
rected, this time sweetened slightly by the fact that she could share
them with another human being, while he sat contemplating the
strange words that spattered the story and remembering his feelings when he had walked through his own devastated village the
morning after the attack. He could now do that one thing that he
had yearned for most that horrid morning. He reached out his
discoloured hand and took Sister Constance's in it, feeling the
reassurance that only human contact can bring. Silent tears fell
from the nun's eyes and she pulled him close to her and hugged
him. The sun, unable to stand the emotion of the moment, turned
red-faced, then hid behind the horizon. As the air cooled and the
moment had run its course, Sister Constance released Whitearm,
held him at arm's length and, with the corners of her mouth turned
down, said quietly, 'Now it is your turn.'

He kept back the ocean. It was his secret that he shared only with
Oddsock. Sister Constance did not need to know of it, not yet. His
chance escape from the slaves, the role of Oddsock, the decision to
leave the village ('there was nothing left there, I had to go') and
even his encounter with the slave boy, those stories could be told.
But the ocean? That was a sacred one, a secret that he could not
trust to anyone but Oddsock. Not yet.

Sister Constance had held on to her tears when he spoke of the slave boy, shaking her head in sadness and nodding when he tried to explain his theories as to why the boy had acted to save him. They were there, the tears, lurking in the background like beasts and figures standing beyond the reach of the firelight at night. Whitearm knew what it was like to be just outside the circle of light, able to see without being seen. The tears that sat on Sister Constance's eyes were able to weep without being wept.

They ate little that night, the stories and memories holding the knocking of the stomach at bay, requiring more of the processing capacity of the brain to allow it any spare to think of food.

The following morning the day seemed brighter to Whitearm as he set about his chores with a renewed vigour. The cloud and dust of his ordeal, not only in the village, but the subsequent journey, had cleared, a life-giving shower of emotions emptied the clouds and settled the dust.

Reaching out his hand and being accepted into Sister Constance's arms marked a mother and child reunion and he felt that he could go back to being the young innocent he had been before the tragedy occurred. There was more to be done round the compound than there had been back in the village, but that, he accepted, was simple arithmetic. The number of tasks did not decrease in proportion to the number of people. Water still had to be fetched from the well whether there was one, or one hundred, of you. The chickens had to be fed and tended, eggs collected and he could not do that while his sister went off to get firewood for the day as he no longer had a sister to go collect firewood.

His new mother, the one who called herself sister, would cook and clean and do all the 'mother' chores, and still find time to disappear into her building every morning and evening. Every seven days she would spend longer there and then the day would be less busy with only essential tasks being carried out. The day before, extra water was fetched and extra firewood gathered, leaving the time free while Sister Constance was in her building. Whitearm would take Oddsock and walk to the burnt-out village where the donkey would graze on the dry grass and leaves around the place while he would do what he could to keep the place tidy. Now that he understood the hands-up trees – crosses as Sister

Constance called them – were markers where she had buried the villagers, he felt a need to ensure that the dead rested in a neat and clean place. Memories of bodies strewn at odd angles around his own village, left to the animals, the elements and time to rot away, prodded at his mind. He could do nothing about it now, but in tending the graves of those nearby, he believed that these dead would communicate with the dead of his village and that they would explain that he had been unable to do anything for them, but was trying to make amends now.

The work in the burnt-out village soothed him and he began to count the days, eagerly awaiting the next seventh one. The spirits of those who lay under the hands-up trees inhabited the village like aftershocks. They welcomed him, sensing the innocence that life should be about. He, despite his own earthquake that he carried in his memories, still viewed the world with wonder and excitement, still strived for a goodness that he believed in. The ocean, although temporarily absent from his mind as the stability of being with Sister Constance eased the need to find it, still clung to his aura in gentle lapping waves and blue tides. The spirits of these new elders smiled because they saw possibilities in the future, a future where the war god would have his comeuppance. Could this youngster who had twice escaped the clutches of that evil tyrant be some sort of saviour who would ultimately defeat the war god and bring peace back to their land? They hoped.

The spirits of the young among those who had been slain watched Whitearm in wide eyed wonder. 'He's the one,' they would chatter to each other, 'he lived,' the defective colouration of his arm surely being the key to his survival. Maybe the war god's men had been too scared to shoot him, worried that the pale hand was some sort of mark of a powerful spell that protected him and would curse the one who tried to kill him. The young spirits would cast off their bewilderment at their too early arrival in the next world whenever Whitearm came and would dance around him, chanting his name.

The adoration the dead village gave him seeped silently and invisibly from the charred ground and out of the tips of the crosses, a vapour that wrapped itself like a second skin around the boy's body, securing it in a kind embrace that felt of home.

Sister Constance never visited the village, always taking a longer route round if she needed to go that way and she would do her strange hand movement which Whitearm slowly began to realise was her trying to draw the hands-up tree in the air. This tree was important, but he could not work out the significance. The ones in the ground were markers, that he knew, but why make the sign across her breast?

The mystery deepened as one day when he was alone in the compound and curiosity, which had been shy around him, plucked up the courage to nudge the boy with its elbow and incline its head toward Sister Constance's special building, the look in its eyes saying, 'don't you want to know what goes on in there? Go on, I won't tell.'

It watched, pleased with itself, as its young protégé, after checking round to see that the coast was clear, moved towards the building, stopping only to check that his constant companion, the donkey, was following and would be nearby should any problems arise.

Minds are strange things. They can build cathedrals where there are small churches, throw dark rugs over well-lit rooms, illuminate a dark and dank space with soft light and neutral aromas, put a pretty face on a voice. Until the eyes are able to gather the necessary intelligence, the mind is at liberty to do what it likes, shackled or freed only by past experiences that colour the present idea of what will be revealed in the future.

Whitearm had so little experience of the pale people that to attempt to create an image in his mind of what lay beyond the door was futile. His time with Sister Constance had given him little insight into her life, scant clues that she was very different from him or those from his village. She cooked, she cleaned, she looked after the chickens, she ate food, she built fires, she sat and told stories in the evening. None of these things clashed with his ideas of what a person should do.

The difference lay primarily in her obsession with the hands-up trees and with the time she spent in her building. The building itself was also different. It had solid walls made of stones cut in straight lines. Unlike the knobbly surface the walls of a normal hut had, this one was quite smooth, as if the winds had blown away the bumps.

The door moved easily when he pushed it, then he stood a moment on the threshold. Behind him, curiosity grinned and gave him a shove in the back, sending him stumbling, as if falling through thick mud, into the room. Fear played the role of the mud, almost pushing him back, but curiosity stood like a closed door behind him.

The room was not well lit, only four small fires burned near the front of the room, bunched together and shivering like small animals caught under the paw of a dark beast. He looked back to the door which had creaked closed, forbidding the outside light from entering. Oddsock had not followed him, but he could sense the presence of his donkey friend just beyond the wooden barrier and he relaxed, turning back to study the room.

There were benches set up in neat rows on either side of a path that led straight up to the front where the light of the small fires struggled for survival. A strange scent was sprinkled over the air – not unpleasant, slightly spicy, a memory of a stronger perfume – like water slowly receding after a crashing wave.

He eased himself onto one of the benches, awe overriding any concern of chastisement for sitting where it was customary only the elders were allowed. He felt the blood moving round his body, not racing, not crawling, but a healthy pulse, a steady beat of life close to the surface of his skin.

The air seemed heavy, like pregnant rain clouds, purple and swollen over a land greedy for the piled-up moisture. A sense of peace pervaded the room, seeping out of the pores of the building and dancing in the auras of the small fires.

And yet...

Whitearm's eyes fixed on the dimly lit hands-up tree that hung on the wall above a small table at the end of the pathway the benches had left. It was not just a tree, there was a man hanging on it, his arms stretched out wide as if inviting Whitearm into them.

And yet...

Whitearm tried to brush away the echoes of the sunshine that still danced in his eyes and casting a drizzly mist over his vision. His body moved to the front bench without informing his mind, instinctively realising that in order to confirm the brain's suspicions it needed to be closer. His eyes, entranced, did not leave the figure.

Surely this man was not pinned to the hands-up tree by large stakes? The red teardrops of paint falling from his palms and the one threatening to drip from his feet, betrayed the anger with which they must have been driven in.

Whitearm sought the eyes of this man but before he could focus on them, he noticed the hair and he shrank back, folding his small body on the bench, yet unable to drag his eyes away. The man had a thorn bush for hair, the sharp points growing painfully into his skull, red blood seeping slowly from the wounds, like snails rushing from a pile of salt.

The sense of peace drained quickly from his body, his muscles tensed, a scream stillborn in his throat.

He felt a hand on his shoulder, cool and, despite its sudden appearance, reassuring.

'I see that you have met our Lord,' the voice was cheerful and calm.

Another God

The nun stood a long time in the door of the small church staring after the departed child, a silent prayer forced its way out of lips that were reluctant to move. The cause of the boy's sudden departure still puzzled her and she threw the whispered prayer up to her god to 'keep him safe.'

She had not denied him access to the church, nor had she insisted that he go in, hoping that he would come to God of his own volition. Her heart, at first rejoicing when she realised he had entered the small church building, was now confused and, though she struggled against it, was already heavy with the doubts. Had she got things wrong? Had she chased the youngster away rather than attracting him in?

She looked back into the gloom of the sanctuary, the flames of the four candles that she diligently lit each morning in memory of her departed brethren, danced excitedly in the breeze, they too were agitated by the events. Her eyes then lifted above the soft haze of light that hung over the memories and she caught the eyes of her Lord. The anguish the carver had etched into the wood cut to her soul with a sharp knife of pure ice. For an instant she felt that the pain in those crucified eyes were caused by her own actions and she sank onto a pew, her knees no longer prepared to bare the weight in her heart.

The eyes did not leave her, but the pain slowly ebbed away, as if soaked up by the figure on the cross. He was her saviour, he would not let her down. Slowly the despair in the eyes changed from accusatory to a look that shared her pain. She felt the heaviness in her breast evaporate, hot air being pumped into her balloon heart and it rose with quiet calm within her. The Lord had this in hand, he would sort it out. She eased herself onto her knees which had either forgotten their recent petulance, or they too felt God's power, giving them strength to hold her up. She prayed quickly, a bullet point prayer, firstly for the one whom the bullets had not found, then, as the light from the candles flickered a reminder, for those that the bullets had found and had done what bullets do. She crossed herself, stood, dipped her knee in a curtsey to the figure on the wall, re-crossed herself then headed out.

'Our Lord.' The word translated rather crudely into chief.

Whitearm sat in the deserted village, his back to the hands-up trees. Sister Constance had said, 'I see you have met our Lord.' He did not know that he even had a 'Lord', let alone shared one with a pale person. He was not sure about this 'chief'. How could a man attached to a hands-up tree be a chief?

'I have escaped from the war god's men twice. Once with your help and once with the help of a boy whose brother is held by them to make sure he fights for them,' he told Oddsock. What need do I have of a man who can only be a victim of the war god? He cannot help himself if his hands have been attached to a hands-up tree with stakes. How can he help anyone? You need your hands and feet free to help others.'

The peace of the village was not as it should be. He felt the hands-up trees dancing behind his back, mocking him. He had been fooled. At first he had thought they were trees. Then he realised that they were just markers. But now he knew that they were set there as a reminder that the dead belonged to the war god.

Even their chief had fallen victim to that angry deity. But they still laughed at his naivety.

He had to get away. It was now clear to him that the war god was everywhere in the world. He had to get to the ocean. The war god was not at the ocean, the war god could not eat the coconuts that grew by the ocean, of that he was sure. He should go. But what of Sister Constance? She had been good to him, feeding him, giving him water, sweet tasting water, when he so needed it. What if he left her? Where would he find food and water again?

His stomach and throat ganged up on his mind. Would it be better to stay with a full stomach and wet throat but always be a slave to the war god, or should he journey again and be at the mercy of the land and the hunger and thirst it brought, but at least be free from the clutches of the war god?

He turned his head quickly, expecting to catch the hands-up trees pulling faces at him behind his back, hoping to shame them into stopping, like Twobites' father had done when Whitearm and his friend had stood behind the man as he worked, their faces twisted, tongues lolled and mouths struggled against the laughter bubbling inside. But, like Twobites' father when he swung his head suddenly, there was no mockery going on, the hands-up trees stood as they had always done just as he and Twobites had stood innocently watching, and yet there was an air of guilt about them.

How things had changed in his life. Not that long ago he had been the naughty child making fun of the adult, now he had grown, he was the serious one turning to tell the youngsters to behave, his ability to be a child, so recently recovered when Sister Constance had found him, was being snatched away again. He needed to make difficult decisions and his mind was objecting to this.

He patted Oddsock's neck, a gesture that always comforted him and gave him the strength he needed to continue, as if his twin had a magical force that could revive him. The donkey snorted its quiet approval of the gesture and nudged the boy gently with his long face. Whitearm began to feel the blood flowing inside him again, a steady beat, like it had when he first sat in that building, calm and natural. There had been something about that pulse as he sat there that did not conform with the predicament of the hands-up tree man, something unnaturally good, as if the hands-up tree man could still exert that peaceful feeling despite what the war god had done to him.

He saw some of that quality in Sister Constance too, as if the memory of what the war god had done to her father and her sisters was not carried inside her. It was not as strong as it was in the hands-up tree man, but it was there. She mourned, but did not let this disturb her peace.

His own feelings about what the war god had done were like the hard outer casings of a coconut, while the memories of his mother, his father, his sister, Twobites and everyone in the village were the soft innards. That was why he had run out of the building, the hard shell struggled against a forceful awareness that he was wrong to feel that way. An embarrassment especially as the eyes of the man to whom the war god had been particularly vengeful, had stared into his very being. Everything about him seemed known to those eyes, his childhood, his naughty youth, the time he had dared Twobites to pick up the mamba, the time they had managed to slip the farting herbs into the food his mother was preparing – the man on the tree seemed to chuckle at that one – but he knew. The eyes made him feel deeply sorry for the bad things he had done, and the one that cut him most deeply was the hard coconut shell he carried, his anger at what the war god had done to his village felt heaviest in the presence of the man on the tree. It shamed him so that he could not bear to be in the room with the man. Or Sister Constance. He did not feel good enough to be with them.

The hands-up trees behind him were dancing again, he could sense that, but this time he let them mock him. They would have to answer to Sister Constance and the man with the thorn tree hair, 'Our Lord'. The movement that he perceived behind his back stopped abruptly and he swung round, the laughter of his adversaries silenced by his thoughts. But it was not his mind that had silenced the mockery of the small markers, it was Sister Constance who stood silently watching him, the hands-up trees standing like well-behaved children around their mother.

Jesus. The man on the tree had a name, one like no other he had ever heard. And he was God's son. Which god, he was not sure, but it sounded to Whitearm that it was the god of the pale people and they only had one. He studied his limb that had conspired to name him. The discoloured area seeming to splash into the rich brown at his elbow, throwing up small waves that blurred the line between where he was white like Sister Constance and where he was brown like his mother and father had been. Was the god of the pale people also the god of his right arm?

Sister Constance was smiling at him again. She sat on the roots of a large baobab that grew near the small collection of hands-up trees. 'Do you understand?' she asked kindly.

He was not sure that he did really. Before the war god came there had been the ocean god and before that, before the elders let that name 'ocean' slide into the language of the village like a fresh egg slipping into a well-oiled pan, before that there had just been the sky. The gods were multiplying and he barely knew how to add yet.

And this new one had children. The war god had slaves, but no children. The ocean had coconuts, but no children. The sky had clouds, but no children. How could a god have children, especially one that doesn't look like a god? There were lots of fathers as well. One of the people under the hands-up tree markers by the buildings was, Whitearm had thought, Sister Constance's father. Father Slater she called him. Then there was the father of Jesus, a god, but Sister Constance also referred to him as 'father'. 'God our Father,' she said. Whitearm knew that this god was not his father, his father lay in the village with his chest burst open by the stones slung by the bang sticks. So when Sister Constance talked of 'God our Father' she must have meant that this god was the parent to her and this Jesus man. That would make him her brother. And was 'God our Father' the same Father Slater who lay under the small hands-up tree outside? But if he was a god, how could he be dead? Had the war god killed 'God our Father', the god of his right arm?

'No, Sister Constance, I do not understand.' His confusion bubbled over into a quiet confession, half-whispered for fear of causing her offence.

But the pale woman continued to smile. 'It is confusing when you have never heard it before. Let me try explain again. Maybe it is the language, you see I do not know all your words, so sometimes it is difficult to know exactly what to say so that you can understand.'

Whitearm nodded slowly. He had never thought about language before. In the village they had their words and a way of speaking which, he felt, had been there forever and had been surprised when he first heard the elders talk of another language. 'They speak,' the elders said, 'but their words are just sounds to our ears, but when their ears hear them, their brains make the sounds become words.'

Sister Constance had not yet used individual words that he did not understand, but if he was to comprehend what her god was about, he would have to make his brain work at turning the combination of the words into something he could understand.

'You must tell me when you do not understand what I am saying.' It was important to Sister Constance that he got to know about her god and so he nodded again and told his mind in the most serious tone someone as young as he could manage, that it must do everything in its power to turn the sounds of Sister Constance into things that made sense.

'God made the world and everything in it, all the trees, the animals, the people, the sky,' she paused to see that he understood.

He concentrated on the words, they were all ones that he knew and they all made sense as individual words – 'god' he knew, 'made' he knew, 'everything' he knew, 'the sky', he knew – but when these words gathered together in his brain, it was like a village meeting before the elders called it to order with so many words colliding into each other that none of them had enough space to allow its meaning to settle. There was so much that the pale person's god had made. If he looked around him and if Sister Constance was correct, her god had made just about everything he could see. Even – and this one was the biggest chunk of meat in the stew of words, a chunk that had to be chewed well – even the sky. The pale god had made the sky god? He asked the question, feeling a little more confident to do so.

Sister Constance looked like she wanted to laugh, but she didn't. She kept her faced serious and answered, 'The sky is not a god. It was made by God.'

'God our Father?'

'Yes, God our Father.'

'The whole sky?' the boy gestured.

'Yes, the whole sky.'

This was a big thing to digest and he studied the dusty ground, the bland monotonous brown of the sand freeing his mind from distraction while he thought.

It was hard to believe, but had the elders ever said that the sky was a god? It was very big and they always looked to it with great reverence for the rains and sun and the night, so he had just presumed that it had to be a god.

'The sky is God's house. He built it so he could live there,' Sister Constance tried to make the understanding of it easier.

'And the ocean?' The question tricked him. He was looking at the sky, trying to comprehend the significance of what Sister Constance had said and the question saw its opportunity, sneaking out of his mouth while the boy was preoccupied. His eyes jumped from the heavens to the earth around him, desperately searching for the rogue enquiry, hoping to capture it and lock it back inside his mind before it caused damage. Even Oddsock, on hearing the word had started, his oversized head nodding its disappointment at the prison break and a low bray rattled out between his teeth.

'The ocean? Yes, he made that too.'

'God our Father?'

'Yes, God our Father.'

'He made the ocean?'

'Yes,' Sister Constance nodded. 'He made everything,' she gestured.

He stared at her in disbelief. How could that be? He struggled to digest it. Not the 'everything' part. That was a periphery to be stored in part of the brain for later rumination, but the ocean, like the sky, was made by God our Father. This would mean that the ocean was also not a god. It may be as big as the sky, but if Sister Constance was right, it was not a god. He was not sure if this was good or bad and he examined his thoughts.

'Is the ocean God our Father's bath then?'

This time Sister Constance did laugh. 'Yes, I suppose you could say that.'

Oddsock began to chew on leaves nearby. Mention of 'the ocean' had not caused them to move on, to leave this place where he was happy.

'Do you think that God our Father would let me climb into his bath if I got to the ocean one day?' There had been no mention by the elders that the ocean was a deity's wash room and this could have serious consequences for his plans, should he ever move on from here.

'Oh yes, people often go play in the ocean, God does not mind.'
The odd nature of this doctrine cast an air of doubt over the words.
None of Sister Constance's training had prepared her for this
question and she knew that she would not find a verse in the bible
that read, 'and I, the Lord your God, will make available unto all
nations my great big bathtub for all to enjoy,' unless it was hidden
away in one of the minor prophet's books or perhaps the Apocry-
pha that she did not know so well.

The truth of the matter was that God did not mind people
swimming in His ocean. He did not smite those who did, unless
you counted those who drowned, or those who fell prey to sharks
or other wildlife that could cause such catastrophes, but on the
whole, swimming in the sea was a pretty safe past-time, if you
looked at the statistics.

'In fact, I think he likes it if people climb into his bath,' she threw
the doubt off her words.

Whitearm felt quite satisfied now. There were still many questions about God our Father, the god of his right arm, that he
wanted answers to, but the panic about the ocean had gone from
rough seas with large waves crashing onto a beach, to a placid
mass of blue water gently lapping against golden sands. He was not
sure if he would ever get to the ocean, but now knew that if he did,
he would be welcomed and would be safe there.

During her evening prayers, Sister Constance cried quietly as she
went through the routine words that the lips knew so well that they
could recite them while storms raged in the mind behind them.
The gentle susurration of the prayers, expelled as a breath, filled
the room like mist, the words, confident in their meaning, yet in
her heart were doubts. How she wished that it had been her body
lying beneath one of those crosses and not Father Slater's. He knew
how to get the message of Christianity across to people to whom it
would appear strange and alien. He was truly born to minister to
these people, yet God had taken him and the people he came to
save, leaving behind little Sister Constance, a woman young in
years and even younger in her faith, to take responsibility for this
lost soul who had, according to his story, wondered across a land
ravaged by war and teeming with dangerous wild life, to arrive on
her doorstep, bones wrapped in skin. Why had God left her to take

charge of this orphan on the doorstep? Why not save Father Slater who could handle the situation far better than she ever could?

She fretted as much for the boy's spiritual well-being as for his physical health. Apart from encouraging the strange doctrine of God's bathtub – surely not the best way to bring a child to Christ – her food supplies were dwindling. What to do when she ran out had been a question she had put off answering. When she had been alone, there was still plenty and she had hoped and prayed that someone would come rescue her before she had to make a decision on that issue. Leaving the settlement frightened her more than staying and possibly starving. But now there were two to feed and the boy needed it more than her. She had shrunk her portions to help nurse the boy back to health, but she could feel her own body turning in on itself as the hunger boiled in her gut.

They would have to leave eventually. The chickens were not reproducing, the supply of meat on them dwindling as she watched and the eggs were becoming more scarce. But where would they go? She had no idea how to survive in this harsh land.

The prayers she knew by rote tapered off as the urgency and enormity of the problem slowly squeezed her lips closed, the tears that had so far refused to accompany her dry sobs, now gathered on her eyelids, feeling forced into action, but still reluctant to participate. She turned to look at the crucifix, hoping that those eyes that had endured far worse than she could ever imagine, would give her strength, some reassurance, but her sight was too blurred to focus.

'Lord, help me.' Her lips freed themselves of the spell and the prayer came out loud, not with shuffling steps on a carpet as her earlier petitions had been, but high heels on a wooden floor. 'Help me to know what to do. Guide me so that I can save this boy. He is one of your sheep, an innocent in a guilty land. Show me what I must do.'

In her heart a prayer hid itself under the waterfall of blood in her aorta, 'Lord help *me*, save *me*. I am one of your sheep, save me.' The redness of the blood that thundered down on the prayer, disguised the embarrassment it felt for being so selfish. But God sees what goes on in our blood streams.

Her prayers became more feverish, bordering on demanding, then retreating as she realised the error of her ways, only to come back again reinforced with desperation that seemed to travel through her body like her blood. Her eyes closed and she heard the prayers echoing in the room as if it were someone else shouting at God, someone else demanding that God help.

Slowly into that hailstorm of emotions came a realisation that her hand was being tugged. Someone was trying to pick the lock of her interlocked fingers. The prayers stopped abruptly, the ones behind them stumbling into their backs and causing all to collapse in a jumbled heap.

The boy did not speak, just pulled at her hand, urgently, the tug shouting, 'Come quick!' Panic rose in her breast, clambering over the prostrate bodies of her prayers.

'What is it, Whitearm?'

He did not respond, just pulled and she followed, almost tripping over the emotional obstacles that lay strewn across her mind.

Outside, the sun glared at the teardrops that still rested on her bottom eyelids, threatening that they return to their dormant state or face evaporation. Large lumps of the darkness from the church lumbered clumsily across her sight, like large beasts, buffalo perhaps, that had been resting but now needed to move on.

The steady pull at her arm led her as she adjusted to the outside world and she had no choice but to trust her guide. They moved across the open space in front of the church, a dusty square cleared by Father Slater and the first missionaries who had built the church in more peaceful times. It looked bedraggled and unkempt, the out of place thought striking Sister Constance as the young boy kept up the pressure on her to follow.

Where is he taking me? What has happened that makes him pull my arm with such urgency? She prepared herself for the worst, her heart sinking as she realised they were heading towards the donkey, Oddsock, who stood placidly on the other side of the 'church square', his blinking eyes watching their progress.

'Is it Oddsock? Is he ill?' she forced the question out, her desperation, trying to sound calm, grabbed at the exiting words, lost its balance and tumbled in a ball of panic behind them. She risked a look at the boy hoping to cover over the words with a calm look and was surprised that his attention was not on the donkey, the concern in his young face was directed at her rather than at Oddsock.

She tried to pull up, stop the boy from dragging her, but the tipping of the balance of food distribution in his favour had weakened her and he was showing remarkable strength and continued across the square with her in tow.

They reached the donkey who nodded a welcome and the boy quickly wrapped her arms around the animal's neck. It took a slight step back, surprised by the sudden gesture, then the boy placed a reassuring hand on its flank and he stood patiently while Sister Constance, quite confused by what was going on, stared at Whitearm, her face asking the question that her mouth hadn't yet worked out how to frame.

Slowly, like a baobab stretching its root-like branches to the sky, she felt a sense of peace drizzling into her, sand in an egg-timer. She looked at the donkey, then at Whitearm, then back at the beast, her arms tightening slightly.

Later, she would shy away from the memory of the event. The tranquillity that began to gush through her veins as she hugged the donkey was quite unexpected and bordered on a religious experience.

And yet...

It should not have been. Her faith – practised and believed – was in God the Father, in Jesus Christ His only Son and in the Holy Ghost, a spirit, a comforter. Why, when she had those three to turn to, did she find the comfort she craved in a simple sharing of affection with a donkey?

She added this guilt to the mental list she kept for when she could next get to confession, if she ever got to confession again. The hope of rescue that had been part of her prayers every morning since the attack, was fading. She struggled to understand God's seeming reluctance to come to her assistance and would often search her life for a reason why she had to endure this punishment. She had tried to be good, most of her sins revolving less around the physical things of this life, but more from her thoughts. But nothing on her 'to confess' list warranted the punishment she was enduring. 'Perhaps God is testing me,' she would tell herself then reset her smile and head out to face the world again.

When next they spoke of God our Father, Whitearm asked about His son, the man on the hands-up tree. He had slipped into the church again and studied the figure, the initial shock of seeing it still tingled slightly in his mind, but if, as Sister Constance had said, this man was the son of the god who made everything, then the man on the hands-up tree must be important too. A chief's first-born son always deserved respect.

Why was he stuck on the cross like that and why did he wear a thorn bush on his head? The questions seemed reasonable to him, but Sister Constance struggled with the answers. The problems of language were twofold in that not only did she need to find the equivalent words that Whitearm could understand, but also she had to translate from her adult grasp of the significance of the crucifixion into something a child would be able to process.

'Sin', 'forgiveness', 'resurrection' were words that did not have easy equivalents in Whitearm's language, but also had an adult heaviness that shrouded them in a dense fog, blurring their meaning, yet leaving them untouched, their core definitions still elusive.

'Bad people put him on the cross. They also put the thorn bush on his head.'

'Why? Why would they do that to the son of a god?'

Sister Constance decided to brush over the 'a god', the boy was not ready for monotheism just yet. Father Slater had been good like that, never forcing his single God on the villagers, rather he tried to slowly roll their various lower-case gods into one great capital letter God.

'They did not believe him when he said he was God's son. They thought he was lying.'

Whitearm knew the punishments he had received for lying and also knew those odd ones, unfairly received, when people's idea of the truth did not match that which he spoke. He could see how someone would be punished where people did not believe the truth.

'And he wasn't lying?'

'No, of course not,' the blurted response revealed worn shock absorbers. 'No. He was the Son of God, he would never lie,' Sister Constance turned onto a smoother road to avoid the bumpy ride.

This made sense to Whitearm after a moment's contemplation. What need does a son of a god have to lie, unless it was a bad god like the war one? You don't have to lie to do good, but you need to lie to do bad.

'What happened to Him on the cross? Was it sore?'

'Sore' was a word used for minor aches and pains, a small cut, a bruised toe. 'Sore' is a sardine. What her Lord had suffered was a blue whale of pain and agony on a level unimaginable to most humans, his desperate cry of 'My God My God, why hast thou forsaken me,' screamed of physical pain and mental anguish. To have all that is good and Godly withdrawn from you must surely feel like burning in the depths of hell, an unbearable pain to body and soul. What Christ felt on the cross went way beyond sore.

'Yes, it was very sore. So sore that he died while hanging on the cross,' she could not bring herself to explain the torture that crucifixion brought.

Whitearm's head snapped up. 'Died?' What sort of a god would let his son die at the hands of people, especially a god that made everything? If this god of the pale person, the god of his right hand, was powerful enough to make everything, surely he could have stopped normal people from killing his son.

Sister Constance nodded seriously. 'Yes, he died, but three days later he came back from the dead, he was alive again.' She didn't feel quite comfortable with how the words came out, but it was the best that she could manage. She expected more questions but the boy was studying the dust again, his young mind processing this revelation.

It made sense. If a god made everything, then he would have the power to bring back to life his son if he were killed. Maybe he had to let his son be killed so that the people who did it would think that he was dead, then he could go and live somewhere else and no one would come looking for him.

They were quiet for a while, the boy absorbing and processing the story of Jesus, the nun pondering a question that had been washing around in her mind for some time, trying to find an answer, yet being too adult to stoop to asking a child. How could a young mind mine the depths that were, she felt sure, required to get to the real essence of her question. Father Slater would have known the answer.

'Why did you take me to Oddsock when I was upset?' The question was not as proud as the adult, the question was itself young and not afraid to flitter around immature minds in order to find an answer. The question was, one could say, a little bit promiscuous.

'Because when I am upset, I always hug Oddsock and it always helps. You were upset.'

Sometimes young minds can make one feel stupid. The tone, the quizzical look on the face all suggested that the answer was obvious and expressed surprise that an adult, who should know better, had been unaware of this basic fact.

Perhaps the real question was not 'why' but 'how'. How did Oddsock have the ability to soak away the emotional upheaval and distress that she had been suffering? The 'how' was a tough one that Sister Constance was sure the young boy who sat next to her would not know, nor would he have sufficient depth to really address the issue. The 'how' remained unasked.

Had Sister Constance known something of Oddsock's history, then the 'how' would have been obvious to her, but neither she, nor Whitearm knew, or could know. Oddsock himself was also oblivious of his heritage.

A donkey's lineage is not something that owners take much heed of, even professional breeders would only look back a handful of generations if records allowed.

Some, if they knew, would argue that the direct line of descent that connected Oddsock to the colt that Jesus rode on that first Palm Sunday as he entered Jerusalem, accounted for the donkey's powers to be able to bring calm to those came into contact with him. Others would say that if such a link did actually exist, it still would not account for these 'powers' but there was a simpler explanation that contact with a calm animal evokes a calmness in a person purely through the usual channels that touching another living being brings. Some get tranquillity from a stream, hugging a tree or sitting listening to the waves lap against the shore of a peaceful ocean. If such things can calm a mind, surely hugging a placid donkey can also evoke such a feeling?

And of course, there will be those who would be quick to point out that if Oddsock were a direct descendant of that biblical beast, why did he have a blemished leg when the one our Lord rode on was without a mark. Those people have probably never hugged a donkey before.

But neither Sister Constance nor Whitearm knew of Oddsock's heritage so they could not add their opinions to this debate and the question of 'how' mingled with the other thoughts in the nun's mind until it lost its individuality within the crowd that loitered there. She returned to her prayers, her concerns no less urgent, but somehow blunted as if the soft roundness of the feelings evoked when hugging Oddsock had dulled the once sharpened points of concern that pricked at her mind.

The dust floated like a fine mist around the dead village, touching the crosses in a gesture of care, a wartime nurse comforting patients in a ward. The air moved languidly, carrying the dust with it, but unable to push aside the morning heat that already sat stubbornly on the land. The spirits slept. Their space, little disturbed, was quiet. In one corner two hens emerged from the bushes, surveyed the area, then began to peck at the ground, their muted clucking a whispered conversation.

Oddsock glanced up at the new arrivals, then returned to his meal of leaves, the tranquillity of the place soothing him after the activities of the previous day. He had no real objections to the taller human, but was yet to fully trust her. It had only been the reassuring white-gloved hand that had prevented him backing out of the hug. He was happy here otherwise. The constant moving before they arrived, while not too strenuous, was disturbing, especially as the journey had seemed to suck away the boy's physical being, leaving him a weak and skinny waif.

Here, Whitearm slept less, walked quicker, looked fatter and smiled more. His reliance on his donkey friend for support was not as great and the hugs had become fewer and further between, a fact that Oddsock regretted, but managed to link in his mind to the better wellbeing of the boy and he took a level of comfort from that.

But it was not just the improved health and the stability the place brought that the donkey liked. There was something else, a feeling that spoke to his instincts, a feeling that told him things here were good, here they were safe.

And yet...

Underneath that heightened instinct, there was something that he could not identify. It was not a bad thing, but it still unsettled him as he could not quite understand it, the unknown aura that surrounded this niggle causing the unease. He found that he was avoiding the building that the larger human would go into every day and in which his young twin was taking an interest. The core of his feelings somehow linked to that structure, as if a memory that purported to be his, but of which he had no knowledge, was leaking out of the building, its tentacle-like fingers probing and searching, trying to gain entrance to his mind, a stranger on the doorstep claiming to be a long lost relative. His dreams were haunted by crowds of people throwing strange branches in his path, branches of a type of tree that he had no knowledge of. He had admitted the stranger, who now sat weightlessly on his back, still unsure if he was being conned or not.

The dust stirred as Whitearm arrived, darting gleefully around the boy as he moved across the former village. It missed the bustle that the people had brought to the place. The bare feet that playfully threw it up in the air so it could dance in and out between legs that were going about daily business, had suddenly stopped their play, bodies thumping to the ground for a final hurrah before falling silent and playing no more. The dust greeted the young one with joy.

The boy hugged Oddsock's neck affectionately, his action born, not of a need for comfort this time, but out of a slight guilt of neglect, an apology.

'There has been a lot to think about, Oddsock,' he explained. 'Sister Constance has a god who made everything.' He gestured. 'He made the sky, the trees, the animals and,' he paused, still not quite convinced, then whispered, 'even the ocean.'

The boy broke a branch off a nearby bush that Oddsock was eating from and fed it to his friend, smiling to himself.

'And then,' he went on after Oddsock had finished chewing, 'this god had a son who was killed but came back to life again.'

He fed the donkey another branch, his smile reappearing as Oddsock ate, then disappeared as he returned to his contemplation.

'Sister Constance says she wants me to accept her god as my God.'

He punctuated his thoughts by feeding another branch to Oddsock.

'I have never had a god of my own. I have trusted in the god of the sky to bring sunshine and rain. The god of animals brought me meat, milk and eggs,' he looked up at twin, 'and friends,' he added. 'The god of plants gives yams and corn and other food. It also gives herbs for healing and the branches and leaves to make houses. I have never met the ocean god, but the elders say that he has coconuts. I have never seen coconuts but they sound so good. I still hope that one day I can taste one.'

He stopped to savour the coconut juice and flesh that his mind conjured up, then went on. 'But I am worried. If Sister Constance is right, if there is only one god, can he really look after everything? How can a god make sure that the sun shines and also make sure that the hens lay eggs and also grow the trees so we can build houses? How can a god do all this and still remember to make the coconuts for the ocean? All this is too much for one god to remember. I have seen that the sky works, the animals do what they need to do and so do the plants, but I have not seen the ocean nor a coconut. What if the god of everything does not have time to prepare the coconuts? What if he cannot stop the ocean from drying up? The elders said it is like a puddle after the rain, but a puddle the size of the sky. But when it does rain and when there are puddles, the ground drinks all the water and soon there is none left. If the god of everything cannot stop the ground drinking up a small puddle, what can he do to stop the ground drinking up a puddle the size of the sky?'

He let the size of his question sink into the donkey's mind, not expecting an answer, it was too big a question for a donkey to answer.

Oddsock shuffled closer, the boy had stopped talking and he nuzzled him, hoping that his friend's problems were solved so that he would pat him.

Whitearm obliged, his discoloured hand stroked the flank of the beast, vigorously at first a smile of enjoyment on his lips as his mind drifted away from the question, but slowly, as if the energy were being siphoned from his hand, the arm moved with less vigour and the smile seeped off the boy's lips while a realisation leaked into his eyes, pushing the lids apart and baring the whites.

'I don't have to decide right now if Sister Constance's god is right for me. If I get to the ocean and if there are coconuts and if their juice is as sweet as the elders say it is and if the flesh is as white as my teeth and soft like cooked yam, then I will take Sister Constance's god to be mine.

Oddsock nodded, hoping the gesture would get the boy to pet him more.

The light in the eyes dulled slightly. 'But I don't know if I will ever leave this place to go find the ocean. Sister Constance is so good to me, she is like my mother. And there is food here. Her god, God our Father, looks after her and I do not know where the ocean is. He looked about him as if expecting a path to open up showing him the way to the sea.

Oddsock followed his glances, wondering if they were going to go back to the building of intrigue, but the boy stayed where he was, further thoughts weighing down on him, making his legs too heavy to move.

Whitearm studied the surrounding area, memories of his village, his family and friends floating up in his mind, the small hands-up trees once again reminding him of his loss and how he had just left the bodies in his village as they had fallen. If he chose God our Father as his god, should he return to his village to bury the dead and put hands-up tree markers out to notify his new god where the dead were?

He had no idea how to return to his village. Like the ocean, the directions had become hidden to him, evaporating in a blur of hardship. Oddsock would know. Oddsock knew where the ocean was, he would also know the way back to the village, but Whitearm could not ask. He had to see the ocean first, to know if God our Father existed before he could return to the village to bury the dead and mark the graves with hands-up trees.

After a long time of contemplation and still no resolution to his problems, Whitearm stood up and moved slowly back to the church to go about the day's tasks.

On the move

The earth spins on its axis, a graceful ballerina pirouetting round the sun, sometimes closer, sometimes further away from the feather light fingers of heat and light that radiate from that central character in this celestial ballet.

Nothing stands still in the universe. There is constant movement, revolving, orbiting, drifting, swooping, running, walking, migrating, travelling, strolling, gliding, fleeing. It is as if the god of everything is a restless one, one that is easily bored, one that thrives on change. Perhaps that all-encompassing deity has uttered the mantra, 'I'll sleep when I'm dead', too full of the joys of life to waste a moment. But the god of everything, the god of Sister Constance, the god of Whitearm's right arm and the god of the ocean (still to be confirmed), does not die. The god that says he is the alpha and the omega, the beginning and the end, this god has no omega, this god will never sleep. And so, neither will the world that He created.

Be it a large city or a deserted landscape, be it by the hand of some great higher being or a fluke of nature, all things move and change. Buildings rise and fall, plants grow and die, returning to the earth to feed a new generation. Humans live and move. Even in dying they *shuffle* off this mortal coil. The body itself is a constant dying and renewal, a movement of old dead cells out while new ones are created to take their place or expand the body.

Movement can be positive, running to meet a loved one you have not seen for a long time, throwing one's arms around another in welcome or offering an arm to support an elder as they rise from their seat. It can be neutral, scratching a nose, shifting one's weight from one leg to the other, or stirring a cup of tea. And, of course, movement can be negative, a wave of the hand to dismiss the pleas of one in need, raising a rifle to shoot an animal for a small part of their body, or the frightened, near mindless fleeing from a marauding army.

We all move. Our bodies can move without changing their location greatly, they can also move great distances. The earth and all that is in it cannot stand still.

Oddsock picked up the scent first, a heady funk of sweat, guns and bloodlust, borne lightly on the air, diluted by the journey, yet still strong enough to disturb the donkey's nostrils. At first he turned his head towards the smell, his nose twitching, not quite believing the signals it was receiving and wondering whether to pass the intelligence on to the brain. But the brain already knew and was already messaging the eyes to seek out the boy and the mouth sounded the alarm.

The low bray was loud enough to get Whitearm's attention, but had not the strength to travel back towards the source of the scent.

'What is it Oddsock?' the boy was quick to understand the message, his young eyes moving in the direction that his twin was looking.

The day was preparing its gloomy blanket of dusk as the light gave a final bow before retiring behind the curtain of night, always hoping for an encore that would never come, yet still looking to the next day's performance.

Whitearm and Sister Constance sat outside the church at a rudimentary table, their small evening meal all but consumed. Oddsock stood a few paces off but as the scent advanced and built up like a storm cloud inflating itself, gathering momentum to spit out its cargo of rain, he moved closer to the humans, his nervousness clearly evident.

'What is it?' Whitearm asked again, his body tensing. Although he could not detect the scent that Oddsock could, his mind was already mumbling 'war god!'

The donkey turned his head again towards the smell of danger, checking that he was right while also warning the boy. He gave a low bray again.

Beside him, Sister Constance shifted her weight nervously, the tension spreading quickly amongst the trio. They strained their ears for any aural evidence to support Oddsock's nasal claims.

'Wait here.'

Whitearm was off before the nun could hold him back. She started to call, quickly bringing her hand to her mouth to stop the cry which had already died in her throat. If there was trouble out there, it was no good alerting whoever it was to their presence. She stood rooted to the spot by fear for a moment, then shook off the emotion. She needed to act quickly and began to move around the compound dragging a branch across the dusty ground to disguise their footprints. The fire, recently used to cook the evening meal, was covered with as much sand as she could find. She chased the chickens, who mercifully did not make too much noise, into the church building, leaving the door open, then gathered up as much of the small supply of the remaining food and water that she could, threw it into a saddle bag that had not been used for a good while and secured this over Oddsock's back, the donkey surprisingly calm in accepting the load. All the while she fired off prayers to her god. By the time Whitearm returned, she as ready to move.

'There are men, lots of them. They are coming and they have bang-sticks,' the boy reported. He did not want to talk of a war god, not to someone who thought that their god was one who made everything. His eyes took in the changes to the compound as he delivered his message and he understood their need to move.

Covering their tracks as best they could, they hurried off at a right angle to the approaching army, Sister Constance leading the way. Her logic was that the approaching men would hopefully continue in a straight line and not catch them. Her other motivation was that heading off at this angle was to go in the direction she had come when she first arrived at the village. Somewhere in that direction lay another mission station. Maybe, if that one had not been attacked, they could find safety there.

They did not speak as they moved quickly away from the village, the bush closing in behind them, leaving only the ghosts of memories. The fallen villagers and missionaries summonsed up in the mind of the departing nun, stood silently watching them go, an emotionless guard of honour, all feeling squashed by the mercilessness of the land and the viciousness of their deaths. They did not know if it would be better for their departing companions to be slain quickly by the advancing army, or face the uncertainty that the wild land brought. They had seen what it had done to the boy, the condition he was in when he arrived, and did not wish that on him again. They also knew what had happened to themselves.

Some of those spirits watching the nun, the boy and the donkey depart, prayed to their god, the god of everything, the God our Father, beseeching His protection for these refugees. Others, who had never accepted the god the pale people brought to their village, chose to weigh up their chances.

'She is an adult, he is just a child. She will take care of him and hopefully, with her guidance, they will make it to safety.'

'Yes, but she is not of this land. She does not know the animals, the plants, how to find water. That was all taken care of for her. But out there she will not know. The boy knows this land. He crossed a great distance on his own. He can survive better than she can. It will be difficult, but he is more likely to survive than she.'

'But she has her white god to help her.' The doubters still had superstitions, unanswered questions about the existence of the god of everything and, if He was there, what powers did He have.

'Yes, but look where their god got them,' the deniers nodded their ghostly heads in the direction of those spirits who stood huddled together, heads bowed in prayer, their hands making the sign of the hands-up tree.

It was only the spirits of the donkeys who watched the trio departing who nodded their heads sagely. They had faith in their counterpart whose departing flank swayed gently as he moved. They did not know how or why, but they felt that this kin of theirs, the one with the odd-sock leg, that he was blessed in a way they would never understand. Their senses giving them confidence in that, although they never understood the details. But they saw the man who had hung from the hands-up tree in that special building. They watched as he, a faded spirit himself, climbed onto the back of the donkey as it left.

The war god's slaves moved into the village quickly, their guns ready for combat, suspicion stretched across their faces, the word 'ambush' rattling in their minds. But there was no one there to meet them, friend or foe. A breeze played spinning tops with the dust across the compound and those of the slaves who were more attuned to these things felt the presence of spirits which skittered around the dead village.

The steady advance of the men painted the ground with a wild pattern of footprints disguising Sister Constance's rudimentary attempt to cover their tracks. Had the war god's slaves been looking for signs, they would have suspected a recent departure and probably given chase, but they were tired from their march and grateful to be able to stop. Even the one who found the chickens in the church did not question why there was no dust on the pews nor why there was not bird mess on the floor.

The pews made good firewood, as did the carving of the man with his arms wide open, although some felt ill at ease as the eyes of the man stared at them from the depths of the fire.

'It was like a curse was being put on me,' one confided in another later on, 'but not a curse.' He searched for the word to explain the feeling. 'It was like the man was looking into me, as if he knew everything about me. He did not curse me, but made me feel a shame like I have never felt before. And that is worse than being cursed. Being made to see everything that you are doing wrong, so clearly. It made me want to throw away my gun.'

The other looked up sharply, as if slapped. You could not contemplate throwing your gun away, that was treason against the war god, punishable by death.

'Not that I would,' the first man continued quickly, realising the significance of what he had said.

The second gave a derisive snort, a slightly over exaggerated attempt at disguising the unease he felt when faced with the eyes of the burning effigy.

A white man's fetish. The rumour spread quickly round the men, unease settling on them as they discussed who had been responsible for throwing the carving onto the fire, no one wanting to take responsibility and no one quite sure, all scratching through the muddled memories of the bustle and movement of setting up camp.

A most likely candidate was decided on and ostracised, the belief being that to associate too closely with this perpetrator would place one in the firing line of any fetish fall out.

The real culprit, relieved at not having been caught out, hid within the crowd of accusers, a freed Barabbas calling for the crucifixion of an innocent Christ.

The war god enjoyed the scene, egging the mob on against the innocent one, a young man who had been forced into the army as a child and who survived the ordeal by taking refuge in the drugs on offer and who now took a perverse pleasure in the warm unconsciousness the beating and kicking brought him. As he slid into that stupor, the pain of the blows ebbing out of him, the blackness slowly taking control, he prayed to any god that would listen, that he would never wake from this sleep.

When he stopped moving, the mob stopped hitting and kicking, suddenly shamed by their actions and none more so than the one who had carelessly tossed the crucifix into the flames. The eyes of the carving, still burning in his mind, were joined by the image of the accused's body flopping unconsciously in time to the blows it received. These scenes would not haunt him for long as he would perish the next day when the army accidently disturbed a herd of elephant. Five soldiers were trampled to death, one was shot by a stray bullet fired from a panicked gun, but this one, this guilty man, felt the sharp stab of a tusk in his back and endured an agonising death, his blood seeping slowly from him as he lay paralysed, the sun burning down on him in judgement, his fellow slaves not bothering to return to see if he had survived.

Some may say that this was an act of vengeance, an angry God our Father, seeking revenge for the man's blasphemous actions. Others would put it down to bad luck, being in the wrong place at the wrong time. There is no God our Father, they would say, this was a pure coincidence. The war god himself would not know one way or the other. He knew of the God our Father, knew what he was capable of, but also knew that chance could be a bitch.

But the elephant attack was an event for the future. Something the men could not predict as they drifted away from their exertions against their brother to find food, drinks and drugs to numb the pain in their lives and a place to sleep, the senior slaves getting the lion share of the provision and the shelter of the church roof under which to sleep.

In the morning, before dawn, they packed quickly and quietly, sneaking out of the dead village like outcasts, dragging an aura of shame behind them. No one glancing at the inert body they had created, which lay where it had fallen the evening before.

The soft morning sun crept silently across the clearing in front of the church, climbing nimbly over the ashy rubble of last night's fires, giving the dark remnants a silver-grey pall. It moved toward the seemingly lifeless body nervously, as if stalking a prey it suspected may fight back. Had someone been there to watch, they would not have expressed surprise if the advancing light had touched the body, checking for signs of life, then jumped back a foot or so to observe and if needs be, flee to safety.

But the light was bound by nature and her laws to continue moving, annexing the area by degrees as it advanced. It was also obligated to warm the abandoned body, slowly burning off the fug and haze that the violence had coated the man with.

He emerged from his stupor by slow degrees, perhaps wondering if he was indeed dead. The painful stabs of his wounds a hellish demon's spear piercing his body in all places, till at last he summonsed up enough energy to emit a low groan.

His journey from unconsciousness to standing was a long torturous one and even when he was on his feet it was uncertain for a few moments whether he would not turn around and head back to where he had just come from. But he was too weary and disoriented to put up a fight against his instinct to survive, his stuttering movements squeezing the sharp pain out of him by degrees till it sank slowly into a dull throb that engulfed his whole being. His eyes, just slits on a puffed-up face, scanned the dead village, expecting to encounter those who had inflicted the pain on him, but nothing moved. The chickens had been eaten, the wind had not yet woken up and the spirits lived in a world beyond his vision.

With difficulty he hobbled over to where the well was and drew up some water. The salty smell of blood in his broken nose prevented him from sniffing at it to check if it had been poisoned or not, but his mind cared little for that now. He bathed his face, then drank in small sips, wincing slightly each time he swallowed. The water aided his recovery and he limped over to a tree to rest a moment in the shade, his eyes noticing but not realizing the significance of countless wooden crosses that lay around the area, carelessly tossed there, or perhaps kicked from the ground where they had been rooted.

The tree was rough and knobbly against his back, but he rested none the less. His mind, speaking to him in hushed muffled tones, had few things to say. He had been left behind, abandoned for dead, but he was still alive. Alive and free. The second word echoed in the fuzz filled chamber of his head. 'Free'. He was no longer a slave to the war god. He could go where he liked, when he like. He had been so long with the army that the concept of freedom was alien to him, as if some sort of reverberation in his brain was distorting the message, making him hear what he wanted to hear. But his eyes played witness for the defence. There was no one around. He could leave and no one would stop him. They must think him dead or they would not have left him behind. And if they thought him dead, they no longer had any hold over him.

But with these thoughts came the realisation that he was abandoned and badly injured. He would struggle to fend for himself and needed to find help somehow. Not from the rebels, they would only enslave him again. He reached into a pocket and found a small stash of herbs. They would deaden the pain, hopefully long enough for him to find someone who could nurse him back to health, take care of him till he recovered his strength. He began to chew, feeling his senses slowly capitulate to the drug. Then, as the pain subsided, he pushed himself to his feet and began to hobble along a small path that he hoped led in a different direction to that which the army's tracks told him they had gone. He was not long into his journey when his fried mind registered that he was following a trail as an adult's footprints alongside those of a child's lay clear in the dust next to the tracks of a donkey. He smiled and spurred himself on.

Sister Constance did not look back, her nose picked up the smell of burning wood that came, soft fingers on the breeze, tapping her on the shoulder, urging her to turn around and look. She felt the pull of the scent but knew that she must not give in to it. Within the smoke that played around her, she knew, rather than identified, that her saviour's likeness mingled with that of the pews and her mind struggled with the image of the cross and crucified burning in a man-made hell. Christ was too good, too pure for this. His image should not be subjected to such blasphemy.

As they hurried away from the village and the smoke, she wrapped her thoughts up in the familiar words, *Father, forgive them for they know not what they do.* Surely if a flesh and blood Christ could utter those words while enduring a torture so vile, his wooden likeness, which could not feel the pain of a human body, must be able to forgive. Still it did not feel right.

The boy tugged at her hand to make her move more quickly, bringing her back into the moment, her body starting to whisper reminders of her recently diminished nourishment. She would not be able to maintain this pace for long and it frightened her, not so much for her own sake, but for that of the boy. If the army were to capture her alone, she could, she thought, endure whatever they dealt out, but she could not, she knew, forgive herself if she were responsible for the boy's capture. She had heard the stories of boys as young as him 'drafted' into these gangs by force and held there by fear and drugs. She would not allow herself to be responsible for that. When they rested, if they rested, she would tell the boy, no not tell, command the boy, not to let himself be captured for her sake. He was to ensure that his liberty was a priority. If they rested.

The gloom of dusk was slowly folding itself around them, it would not be long before it was completely dark. The sun always seemed to be in a hurry to disappear once it had made up its mind to leave, unlike back home where it would take its time, strolling slowly away from the day. Here it had business to do on the other side of the world and had no time to loiter.

'We must stop for the night,' she said, pulling back on the hand that tugged her forward, as if drawing in the reins of a horse. Whitearm looked back, startled, his face questioning the command, but then a slow acceptance came over it as if he realised that the white lady was right. They needed to find a place to rest safely before it got too dark. Somewhere that, should the war god's men come this way, they would not be seen.

The track that they followed had been well travelled. Before the war god's men came to the village, those who lived there used it frequently to move between home and the larger mission station a week's walk away. They needed to be off the track. If the war god's men were to come this way, they would surely follow the route of least resistance.

About fifty paces into the bush at the side of the track they found a small ditch which would hide them from anyone passing along the track. It was not overly comfortable and was made less so by Whitearm throwing a few stones in first. 'To frighten away the snakes,' he told Sister Constance.

She looked dubiously at the ditch, then at the gloom gathering around her. There was no other obvious place to spend the night. She let the boy go first, in contrast to her earlier decision to make sure he did not put her safety ahead of his own. He was good, he rearranged the twigs and leaves so that by the time she climbed down the small incline, there was a relatively comfortable bed waiting for her.

'I will be the lookout,' he told her when she questioned where he was going to sleep, his young face as serious as an adult's. She turned the corners of her mouth downwards in an attempt to smile her encouragement, but there was not enough energy to light up her eyes. In the near dark, Whitearm did not notice.

'Let us share guard duties,' she said, feeling grateful that he had volunteered to take on the role, but aware that he was just a kid and she should pull her weight. 'Wake me up when you get tired and I will take over so you can get some sleep too,' she explained to his puzzled look.

He nodded slowly but she could see that he was offended. He was the man, he needed to look after the woman. He would take care of her and he would keep watch all night. He did not need her help. She was at once grateful and concerned. He was too young to carry such responsibility, yet she was glad of the opportunity to rest.

Her prayers were said quickly, fingers automatically searching for the beads of her rosary which her mind knew had been left in the in the village as they scrambled for safety. The fingers faltered, fumbled then fidgeted, finally falling into a familiar rhythm on unseen beads while she raced through the words that accompanied the motions. She settled into the rough bed and was soon asleep.

Whitearm watched the track till he could no longer see it in the dark. He could hear the sleep rhythm of Sister Constance's breath and the reassuring breath of Oddsock who had settled himself nearby, not wanting to climb into the ditch with them. The rush of adrenaline that hit when he first realised that the war god's men had come back, now spread itself thinly throughout his body, slowly losing its identity as it merged with all else around it. He closed his eyes and rested his head on his arms. There was something he should be doing his tired mind told him, but sleep was becoming too powerful a narcotic.

The bird swooped down in the grainy charcoal light of dawn to snatch an insect out of the air, then gained altitude again. The human young had not moved much since finding its mother, always staying close, never wondering too far from her. The food around their habitat had been good, so the bird stayed, feeling a connection with the boy.

She had, from her vantage point, seen the approaching herd. It was the same one that she had followed, hoping that the young would catch up with. It moved with the same rhythm, the same purpose seemed to move them. She had tried to raise the alarm, chirping sharply to warn the mother and young. Strays are seldom welcomed into a new herd and it would be best that the mother and child moved off before the herd caught their scent.

Her urgent tweets did not alert the humans, the mother ignoring her while the young merely looked up, smiled and nodded. Fortunately, the donkey understood the urgency and they were soon moving off, out of the path of the large group that rumbled towards them.

There was another stray now, an adult male. But he was injured and the bird was not sure if he would ever move again. She had gone close to investigate, sensing the light rise and fall of its frame as it breathed ragged breaths. The herd had moved on, leaving this one to die, but, if the mother and young came back, they could care for him and just maybe he would survive. It would be good for the two strays to join with this one. It was one of nature's funny rules that, while one herd would not tolerate another moving into its territory, strays, wounded, outcasts, could join up and co-exist, often forming a tight bond, stronger than that affiliation to the herd, sometimes going on to build a herd of their own, their ostracization bringing them together in a closer community.

She swooped again, this time narrowly missing her targeted insect. The morning light was moving across the landscape, an advancing line that split the plain into cool grey-brown and warm red-brown.

The rebels had not come their way. Waking with the light of dawn, Sister Constance's first prayer was one of thanks for being kept safe during the night. The track from the village they had left was deserted, a calm silence hung over the road, coating it with an inviting texture.

Whitearm still slept, his head on a dusty mound for a pillow. The quiet of the morning gave solace to the nun and she lay back in her 'bed', waiting for the boy to wake. She would have to pretend to be asleep when he did, allowing him to avoid the embarrassment of having fallen asleep on guard duty. Her heart ached with pity for the child, for he was still a child, but one on which adulthood had been dropped heavily, an ill-fitting garment that should take years to grow into, a premature hand-me-down. She prayed for him, prayed hard and earnestly, hoping that he would be kept safe in these dangerous times. His nature was good, but she knew how this land could corrupt or destroy that.

He looked pleased when he shook her gently to wake her from her false slumber. 'Look,' his face said, 'I did keep watch all night.' Sister Constance hoped that her acting was good enough to fool as she feigned surfacing from sleep, then expressed surprise that she had not been woken for her shift.

'Why didn't you wake me?' she asked, 'Did you stand guard all night?'

He shrugged at the first question and nodded to the second without a moment's hesitation. It was as if he believed that he actually hadn't slept, but had kept a watchful eye on the path the entire night.

Sister Constance winced at the lie, but busied herself with dusting down her clothes and straightened her hair, a foolish vanity, she knew. She looked back up the track towards the village, the story of Lot's wife jumping into her mind. 'Do not look back,' the Lord had commanded them, but Lot's wife could not resist a last peek. Was it with regret that she turned, a certain sadness that she was leaving? Was she going to miss the sin of the city or was it just a home that, no matter how bad things got, was still home?

Perhaps her punishment came because she turned full of her own piety, relishing the destruction of all those evil people. God would not like someone gloating. Was it just that she had disobeyed a direct order? With the exception of the first explanation, that she regretted the destruction of an evil that she enjoyed participating in, the others seemed to make the punishment harsh. But that was the God of the Old Testament, a God that showed little leniency.

How different this scene was to that story from way back. Unlike the cities of Sodom and Gomorrah, the village had not been full of evil. Yes, they were resistant to accepting the Gospel that Father Slater and the other nuns had brought, but they were not bad people. Their ways were gentle, a respect for each other and the land in which they lived pervaded their lives. They had welcomed her into their midst, always showing her a respect that verged on love.

It seemed so unfair that they had been destroyed and in such a brutal manner. The people of Sodom and Gomorrah had it coming, they laughed in the face of God, in the face of goodness. One could not feel pity for them, but the village, while not believing in her god, at least followed his ways. The destruction that came though was not from God, but from man. This explanation, while not in any way easing the pain or diminishing the savagery of the event, made it easier to accept. Man's inhumanity – 'they know not what they do' – is far easier a notion to take on board than to put the blame at the door of a god who loves.

There had been no instruction from God about looking back when they left the village. Lot's wife had been warned, they had all been warned, but she, perhaps just out of curiosity, had looked and paid the price.

God cannot turn me into a pillar of salt, Sister Constance told herself, because he did not tell me that I couldn't look back. Despite this reassurance, she felt heavy and unmoveable, as if she had been changed into a statue of sorts. The village when it was still alive, with all its ups and downs of life, and all the harsh brutality of its destruction, would remain etched in her mind. Despite those horrific images, it had been home and she now felt a terrible tearing of emotions as she stood staring down the road that led to it.

'Come, it is safe to go back,' Whitearm took her hand and helped her out of the ditch. But once she had scrambled up she did not move, standing staring down the path.

'Come,' the boy said and gave a gentle tug on her arm, 'the fighting men will have gone, they do not stay in one place for too long.'

Sister Constance did not hear, she stared a moment longer, then smiled her upside-down smile, the humour in her eyes a muted pastel to the usual Day-Glo brightness.

'No,' she said softly, 'we cannot go back.'

He looked up at her, his eyes questioning.

'There is nothing left, no food. We were running out and I am sure those men took whatever was left. God has given us a sign that the time has come for us to move on.'

'God our father?'

'Yes, God our Father,' she nodded, her eyes brightening as the corners of her mouth pulled down further. She reached over and gently removed a twig that had caught in his hair, then brushed some dust from his cheek.

He nodded slowly, understanding the need to move on because of food – he had eventually noticed her diminishing portions – but was not sure about the God our Father bit. 'Where will we go? To the ocean?' he asked hopefully.

'Maybe we will get to the ocean one day, but there is another village, like that one, but bigger. It is along this way. They will have food.' She tried to sound hopeful, the fear that the other mission had suffered the same fate as hers gave a rough edge to her voice, but she kept the words as smooth as she could.

The boy nodded again, his brief childlike excitement as he mentioned the ocean, quickly replaced by the mature seriousness she had come to almost despise, not the wearer of the expression, but the garment itself.

'It is about a week's walk down this way...' she stopped, the boy's facial expression causing her to turn quickly. A man, was he a soldier, was stumbling along the track towards them.

'I know, Oddsock, I know, but Sister Constance says we must do this. She says it is what God our Father wants. I still don't know if God our Father exists, I have not seen the ocean and until I do, I will not know for sure. But Sister Constance wants us to do this, so I am sorry, but you must.' The boy spoke in a soft whisper, his mouth close to the donkey's ear, his white hand stroking the beast's neck gently.

The donkey stood quietly listening to the hushed voice. The fuss around the newcomer was dying down. The strange man sat propped up against a tree, his eyes barely open but unseeing. The woman had been the first to react when he collapsed on the path. Whitearm still showed a suspicion of the newcomer that kept him from running to the man's aid, only moving reluctantly when the woman had called him over a second time.

If his friend did not trust the newcomer, then Oddsock could not. But his twin trusted the woman and she, if not showing trust, certainly displayed a care for the man, fussing over his wounds, gently letting him drink some of their water even though they did not have much for themselves.

Despite falling in with the boy's distrust of the newcomer, he recognised that this was a human in need and somewhere in his programming, he could not deny the injured man the help he was being given. He stood patiently, watching the woman, listening to her soft voice reassure the man just as Whitearm's voice reassured him.

The heat of the day was beginning to build and, although it was still cool in the shade, he could feel the comfort of this being slowly peeled away. He swung his head back and forth as if trying to bat the encroaching heat away.

The boy reached out to pacify him, wrongly assuming that the movement related to his unease with the man's presence. Oddsock relaxed to the touch, preferring the petting to the need to banish the growing warmth.

The woman called the boy over and they spoke in quiet voices, occasionally glancing back at him, the woman with questions and urgency in her glance, the boy with uncertainty and a slightly haunted look of one about to betray another. The humans spoke again, in low conspiratorial voices, kept hushed by the boy who would cast anxious glances at the donkey whenever the woman's voice grew a little too loud.

At length they seemed to agree on a point and the youngster came over to him, a certain reluctance to his gait.

'She wants you to carry the man on your back, Oddsock. She says that he is too hurt to walk and that he needs help that she cannot give. She says that she has friends, more of God our Father's people, pale people like her, who live about a week's walk away. She wants you to carry the man there. She says it is what God our Father wants. We are not to leave him here to die. God our Father would not like that, even though this man is one of the war god's slaves. Sister Constance says that if we take him, he will be free of the war god and can become one of God our Father's children.

'I said I will ask you. It is not for me to say if you will carry the man on your back. It is your decision. I know that it will make Sister Constance happy and I must try and make her happy because she took care of me. But it is your decision. What do you say Oddsock?'

The donkey turned its head and looked over its back for a few seconds then slowly returned his gaze to Whitearm, an answer in his eyes. Slowly he nodded.

The stranger was heavy, his barely conscious weight crying out in pain each time they tried to move him.

'It's no good,' Sister Constance said as they gently laid the man back against the tree. His eyes, partially opened slots in a puffy face, twitched to indicate life, but not comprehension and his chest rose and fell in time to the rattling breaths. Low moans slipped out of his lips, bruised purple and thick.

It is best to leave him here to die, thought Whitearm, he is a man of the war god. Why should we help him? He has done nothing but destroy others. He watched the nun as she cast glances around, desperately looking for something to help their plight. What was she looking for? He was restless, wanting to move on now that the decision to go had been made. The ocean was out there somewhere, it had to be. This man with his injuries was just a trick by the war god to stop him from getting there.

He had no way of knowing if the other slaves of the war god would follow the man, either in pursuit of him to finish what they started or just because they wanted to go in the same direction. He shot nervous glances back up the road, intermittent fire, reminding the enemy that he was there, but not wanting to waste too much ammunition.

Sister Constance still fussed over the man. She had torn a strip off his shirt and was wetting it, sparingly, with their water. God our Father would not let her leave this slave. He was a tough old god, Whitearm thought, demanding such things.

He made a decision, acting to save the precious water supply rather than the man, he placed his discoloured limb on Sister Constance's busy hand, stilling it with his quiet gesture.

'Wait. I will fix,' he said, 'we cannot waste water.'

She did not seem to understand, but he firmed his grip on her hand, pulling it gently away from the man's face. 'I will fix. Wait,' he said again, then when he was sure he had her agreement, he moved off quickly between the trees, returning a few minutes later with various leaves and roots which he proceeded to mash into a poultice, his young face wearing the mature look which, Sister Constance noticed with despair, was fitting too comfortably on his features these days.

He is only a child, he deserves a childhood, she prayed, a sense of uselessness creeping over her as the boy took control of the nursing, grinding roots and leaves with a stone and adding spittle till he was satisfied with the mixture. He then indicated that they should lie the patient down, making the groaning man as comfortable as possible before he applied his bush medicine to the man's eyes and then to all the bruised parts of his body that could be exposed within the realms of decency.

She wanted to stop him from applying this 'voodoo' treatment, her mind yelling that this was all primitive mumbo jumbo, it could not possibly help, but the boy worked with such confidence and conviction, and she could not think of anything else she could do to save the man apart from trying to get him to the mission station, so she sat back and let the young doctor do his thing while she did what she did best and prayed to God our Father.

The sun was at its hottest when the man stirred. The poultice, once applied, had almost immediately relaxed him, a serene air descended on his prone body. Sister Constance was unsure if he had been anaesthetised or had just fallen asleep, worn out by the pain which seemed to recede. Could the boy really know what he was doing?

Whitearm renewed the dressing as the mixture already applied began to dry, scurrying off to replenish his stock of raw materials when required. When the man began to wake, Whitearm leaned closer to examine his work, then gently scraped the mulch off the man's face. The swelling round the eyes and lips were drastically reduced, enough so that the bloodshot whites and dark pupils could stare out, bewilderedly.

The boy set about clearing the rest of his medicine, dusting it gently from the man's body while the patient began to revive. Oddsock twitched slightly nearby and moved to graze on some leaves a little way off, looking back at the prone figure warily.

Whitearm finished his work then also moved away, finding Oddsock with his pale hand and patting while not taking his eyes off the recovering man and only inclining his head slightly when Sister Constance stared up at him, indicating that she should take over. He had cured, she must now nurse.

She hesitated, not sure what she had just witnessed, but as the man's movements became more pronounced, she turned back to the task at hand, the need to be doing something a convenient excuse to stop her wondering if she had just witnessed an actual miracle or not.

She helped the man sit up, then shuffled him till he was propped up against the tree again. He was still in some pain, but markedly less so than he had been. His eyes, just slightly puffy now, looking around, gathering information, his mind awash with a soldier's caution. He had to establish a position of safety against...against what?

He blinked, trying to convince himself that the biggest threat to him was a white woman, a bewildered child with what looked like a white glove on one arm and a donkey which eyed him suspiciously.

His fear and anxiety crumbled like a clod of mud, sun dried and crushed in a large fist. He breathed slowly, waiting for words to arrive while his nose leaned across to his brain. 'You know this sweet smell of herbs and roots, don't you?'

The memory of the scent arrived slowly, limping and battle scarred from wars with drugs and conscience, exhausted from its long journey.

He exhaled slowly, a slight smile playing on his lips and his eyes began to focus slowly on the two people who watched him, one with caution, one with awe.

'You know the old cures?' his voice emerged slowly from underneath a layer of haze and fuzz. It was as if he had just discovered his voice for the first time. He was looking at Sister Constance as he spoke, a disbelief coating his words while a hint of doubt in his tone asked if she understood his language.

The nun shook her head, not trusting herself with the words that swirled in her mind. Then in response to the quizzical look her unspoken reply evoked, she pointed to the boy, a strange pride rising within her.

The man's eyes limped slowly from the nun to the boy, resting on him for a second before the eyelids blinked a languid thank you then, after a moment staring, closed again and his breathing fell into a sleep pattern.

Sister Constance stared at him for a long time then looked at Whitearm for guidance.

The man

Oddsock was happier, one could see it in the way he walked. There was a lightness to his step and, one could almost swear, a smile on his face as he would trot to catch up with the rest when he lagged behind them, taking a few moments to enjoy some juicy leaves he had spotted.

He was still wary of the man, that large weight he had borne on his back for the previous two days, his suspicion arising perhaps from some sort of animal instinct, or maybe a hand-me-down from the boy who kept a distance between himself and the newcomer.

He had accepted his burden with good grace, his eyes seeking the boy for reassurance as the woman had helped the man to mount, the large soldier feet hovering just above the ground once the passenger was seated. The boy looked on, his face showing no emotion, a stoic acceptance that this must be so, whether he liked it or not and the donkey accepted the message, his eyes blinking this response back to the boy in their secret code while he pawed the dusty road with his 'odd sock' leg.

He had watched the boy apply the mashed-up leaves and roots to the man's wounds over the last few days, the sweet scent of the poultice tickling his sensitive nostrils, but offset somewhat by the unwashed funk of the man. He could smell the battles and devastation in the man's sweat. The blood and terror buried deep in his pores was bubbling to the surface and seeping slowly out of him.

The man had tried to break down the invisible barrier that lay between him and the boy. He smiled, kindly it should be said, and asked non-threatening questions in an attempt to connect with Whitearm, but the boy remained distant, answering politely with an economy of words, saving what he could for more important conversations, most of which he had with the donkey.

Sister Constance also tried to lure him out of his withdrawn state, throwing subtle comments his way, trying to bait him into joining in, but even her sway over him seemed to have vanished as he remained separate and quiet.

The man was a good hunter and they never had want for food as each evening he would disappear for a while, returning with a small animal or bird which he would roast over a fire that he built quicker than Whitearm could ever manage. His movement became more confident as his limbs were slowly released from the bonds of injury and the prison of drugs. His smile grew and the cloudiness of his eyes cleared like a blue sky re-establishing itself after a storm.

He would share the food out, giving a good portion first to Sister Constance, something contrary to Whitearm's experience. In the village, the men always ate first, taking the best portions for themselves and leaving lesser cuts to the women. Even when it had been just himself and Sister Constance, she had always ensured that he got fed first and, as custom dictated, got the bigger and better portion. He could not understand this disruption of the order of things.

They talked a lot, Sister Constance and the man. Mostly about God our Father with the nun explaining and the man interjecting with questions, but Whitearm paid scant attention to the conversation, lagging a good number of paces behind, sometimes letting the distance between them become so great that it smoothed the sharp crispness of their words into rounded mumbles, as meaningful as weather-worn stones.

He would watch the two adults from his vantage point behind them. The man – who had a name but Whitearm refused to use it – was becoming stronger each day, his limp and pained movements dissolving slowly and falling from his body. Sister Constance, animated in her talk of God our Father, was also growing stronger. The nourishment of the first serving combined with the slowly reducing use of her as a crutch, seemed to straighten her back, and the downturned corners of her mouth brought a greater brilliance to the smile in her eyes. She would cast occasional glances back to ensure that he still followed, but her attention focussed more on the man. He felt like a child again, he was no longer looked to for companionship, nor was his ability to provide held in any regard, being completely outshone by the newcomer's skills.

Eventually Sister Constance, who initially put it down to the boy being shy, realised that perhaps the youngster was feeling put out, the newcomer usurping the boy's 'adult' role. She tried to draw him back in, tried to re-assert the lost masculinity but with little result. If anything, it seemed to push the boy further away. He was reluctant to even take food from the man, accepting the proffered morsels with a begrudging look on his face and then sitting some distance off to eat.

When the man slept one afternoon as the sun's heat made walking impossible, she went and sat with Whitearm, two trees' shade away.

'You don't like him, do you?' She was not sure why she did not use the man's name, an instinct that perhaps it was not welcome in the discussion.

The boy shook his head, looking into the distance, deliberately avoiding her and the man.

'Why not?' She wanted to add that he was helping, providing for their needs, but again thought better, trusting her intuition that this was the issue and to re-iterate it would not help the conversation.

The boy shrugged, but his eyes told a different story. His shoulders may not have known, but his eyes did. However, they also had a determination to lock her out of the reason. Unconsciously she picked up a pebble, her hands moving through the routine of the magic trick she had first bought Whitearm's confidence with, the movements detached as if another force controlled her limbs. It was more a nervous restlessness that brought about the action rather than a pre-meditated attempt to win him back. She finished by brushing her hand against the boy's ear, giving the illusion that the stone had somehow materialised there.

Her eyes, however, never left the boy's as she searched for a way into his mind, a key to unlock the unhappiness that was clearly there.

'You must know why you don't like him,' her voice was soft, soothing.

Behind him, Oddsock, who had been chewing on some leaves, sensed something was happening and nudged the boy gently in the back.

Seeming unaware of the donkey's attention, he smiled, whether from the show of affection from Oddsock, or the trick, Constance could not tell, but he reached out and took the stone from her palm and, with surprising adroitness, performed the same trick, producing the stone from Sister Constance's ear his smile, introspective, arising it seemed, from some private joke.'

Sister Constance decided to risk a defence of the man.

'He needs our help, he has suffered much, but we can help heal him by showing him love, like God our Father shows us love.'

The boy stared at her for a moment, then turned his head away, his words barely audible. 'He killed my father.'

The afternoon air bore the warmth of the day with grace, like the woman of the village would balance a load on their heads, their bodies seeming to glide across the land, hips gently sashaying, necks making minute adjustments in complete rhythm with their burden which would feint left and right in a playful attempt to escape. But the backs of the women remained absolutely straight, the dignity of their deportment resting entirely on the spine. The heat moved through the air as if suspended on it, carried on its head with care and love.

The bird sat atop of the warmth, wings stretched out lazily, letting the currents take her. Occasionally she would dip a shoulder to either swoop or climb as the fancy took her. The scene below intrigued and puzzled. The female had found a mate, one that did not appear to reject her adopted young, although there was no apparent acceptance either. Unlike other mammals, the elephant, for example, where the adults would keep wary eyes on the young, protecting them from every perceived threat, the human adults did not concern themselves with the small one to the same degree.

Occasionally the female would turn to check that the young was still following while the male seldom looked back. Perhaps they trusted the donkey to keep an eye on the young. It was obvious that there was a close relationship between the beast and boy. The bird liked the donkey. She had spent time on its back, picking at the insects that lived in its hide. The donkey had turned its head and nodded a thanks before continuing with its grazing.

This afternoon though, things changed. The female was not so close with the male and kept checking back at the young, making sure it was there. A strange tension seemed to exist between the two, as if the female wished to walk with the young, but something kept her from doing so.

The male was unchanged, his strength since his injury continued to improve and the bird felt more wary about him. She was a tiny bird, prettily coloured, and with barely enough meat on her to count as an *hors d'oeuvre*, but she didn't want to risk becoming a small snack and kept her distance from the male, especially when he wandered off in search of food. He did not seem to be affected by the change in the relationship between the female and the young, walking with confident steps and still not caring about the child's presence.

The man, despite his apparent rejection from the war god's army, was awash with blood in the young boy's eyes. In the beaten form that he had staggered into their lives, he was not readily recognisable, but as the swelling subsided, the face slowly morphed into one that had seldom been far from Whitearm's nightmares. The slightly dreamy smile that played across his lips as he pointed the bang stick at Whitearm's father, remained an ugly gash across the boy's memories.

The explosion, puff of smoke and grunt of his father as his chest burst open, were loud and cacophonous, drowning out the calm and melodic images Whitearm had had of his father.

His emotions troubled him. Before recognising his father's killer, his distrust was based purely on the fact that the intruder into their world was associated with the war god and he wanted nothing to do with that. But he had recognised that somewhere within the battered body lay a soul, a person and this prompted him to help, despite his feelings.

Then the disguise of injury had slowly melted under the influence of his medicine, falling away from the face like a snake shedding its skin, revealing a shiny mamba, the dreamy smile returning to his lips.

Whitearm had caught his breath the first-time recognition struck him, stumbling back and only catching himself from falling by his miss-coloured hand finding Oddsock for support. The donkey gave a low bray, as if it too had just made the connection between the damaged human and the devastation of the village.

Whitearm's dreams – which had slowly sweetened as Sister Constance massaged the knots of the destruction and his hunger-wracked journey from the muscles of his memory – turned quickly back to the confused clatter of violence and mayhem that had so haunted him in those first days after the war god came.

He continued to prepare the poultice needed to complete the transformation of the man from his unrecognisable beaten state into the grinning killer of the war god slave, but left the application of it to Sister Constance, watching from a distance the relationship building between them. He did not feel excluded from them, the natural order of adults sticking together had been restored and he, as a child, had to find his own company. Oddsock was there for him, so he did not feel lonely, however, he did miss the maternal attentions of Sister Constance.

There were moments when the man went off hunting, when he and Sister Constance were alone together, but since his revelation about the man, she had seemed a little distant, unsure of what to say. He did not have the words to express that he in no way held her accountable for the actions of the man, nor for her wanting to heal him. He had heard enough about God our Father to understand that this was her way. She had only spoken with sadness of her companions, as if the memory of her Father Slater would be defiled should she harbour anger towards those who had taken him away. The man on the hands-up tree in her building, the one she called Jesus, he too had told her not to be angry with those who wronged her.

Their conversations, when they could have private ones, tended to be about everything but the man, yet his presence haunted their small talk. He was not going to go away.

How do I talk to him about it? Sister Constance found that the more she pondered the right words, the further they seemed to run from her, always visible, always out of reach. She needed to connect with the child again, needed the right words to re-establish her rapport with him, but she could not find them.

Ever since his death, she had carried Father Slater in her mind, trying to recall everything he had taught her and now she hoped that this memory would offer up some pearl of wisdom to cope with this situation. He had been a very wise man and knew how to react appropriately to any situation. If only he had been here instead of her, how much better for the boy. But God, in his wisdom, had seen fit to let her survive and had taken Father Slater. She could not understand the ways of God in this one. She had barely coped with the instruction of the boy on God's ways when they were still at the mission station, when the soldiers were not around. How did God expect her to up her game now, throwing this wildcard killer into the mix?

She was not afraid of the man, she knew that he had been press-ganged into service at a young age and, from what he had told her, was only too pleased to be free from the rest of the group. His addiction to the herbs that he spoke of had all but disappeared with the beating he had received, as if the part of his mind that depended on the high had been killed off. Or perhaps knowing that he no longer had to rely on the mind-numbing effects of it to block out the violence that betrayed his nature as he killed indiscriminately, his inner core of values locked up and coated in a protective wall of steel for safekeeping, perhaps that gave him the strength to quit the drugs.

It was as if the man had been born again, his release from the grips of that band of guerrillas, freeing him from having to perpetrate the gruesome acts that had become almost second nature to him. He was so receptive to her good news of God and Jesus – the messages of love thy neighbour and forgiveness – that her words almost tripped over themselves as she rushed to tell him everything about her religion. It was only when she slowed down that she felt a pang of guilt about how she babbled on now, yet had been slow in delivering the message to the boy, feeding the greed with which the man devoured her words, yet only dropping crumbs to the boy whose hunger was more physical than spiritual, but whose need of the spiritual feast was no less important.

'You cannot force feed,' she told herself, but this did not help.

Progress was slow. The days threw the heat in their faces with such force that it took a physical effort to walk and they usually surrendered to the demands that they find shade and rest, using the early mornings and late afternoons for walking. The air was a hot wet facecloth wrapped around their faces, a relentless suffocation that they carried with them, a private burden.

The man, despite his remarkable recovery, was still slow when they walked, but he maintained a steady pace, speaking little, conserving his breath which had to be sucked out of the humid air.

They followed him, his muscular build giving the illusion that he knew what to do and, when he halted them suddenly one day, indicating silence, his eyes searching the bushes, they obeyed completely. Even Oddsock froze, his ears alert, his nostrils flaring, trying to catch the scent of the danger the man had sensed. It turned out to be a small herd of elephant moving slowly through the land, ripping up the trees as they went.

The quartet watched the beasts, letting them pass a respectable distance away, grey hulks – born to bring meaning to the word 'lumbering' – which moved across the land like great ships on an ocean. The old bull leading the herd tossed his head in their direction, his long trunk snaking through the air, ears flapping and grand tusks swinging high, a warning to the man, a respectful bow to the nun and a warm greeting to the boy and the donkey all wrapped up in that one movement. The baby of the herd, barely tall enough to graze the underbelly of the bull, paused to emulate the bull before rushing to catch up to its mother, falling in stride behind the tree-trunk like legs and hiding within the herd.

'This is not their normal path,' the boy whispered into the long ears of his friend. The donkey nodded, perhaps also sensing the elephants' unease with the territory, or perhaps just an indication that it too wanted to move on.

The boy shook his head. 'The war has made them move, like me and you.' He stopped short and scratched the donkey's head, fearful that the man who had turned around to look at them would hear.

The man smiled, not the dreamy debauched smile that he had when he was killing, but one that was trying hard to be friendly. Whitearm shrunk away from it though, looking back at the elephants in order to avoid looking at the man.

'Why does he not like me?' The man tilted his chin towards Whitearm who sat eating his supper two trees away.

Sister Constance choked slightly on the meat she was eating. The man had caught an Egyptian goose for their dinner that night.

'I...' she swallowed, thought for a minute, her mind fumbling around for what Father Slater would do, then said, 'He does...' again she faltered. She could not deny it, pretend that maybe the boy was shy or something. 'I think...' she paused, took a deep breath then on the exhale said quickly, 'I think that he does not trust you.' She let the sentence hang in the warm evening air for a few seconds then went on, 'You are a soldier.'

'Was a soldier,' he corrected quickly.

'You were a soldier,' she nodded to confirm his assertion, 'but he does not trust the soldiers, he is scared of them and I think that even though you are no longer one, he still sees you as one.'

The man nodded and tore a chunk of meat off the duck carcass, shoved it in his mouth and chewed.

'There is more, it is not just because I was a soldier.' It was a question wrapped up in a statement.

Sister Constance looked away, across at the boy who sat innocently next to the donkey, stroking its fur. It was not as if what the boy had told her about the man had been a confession or anything, although even if it was, she was not qualified to accept it as such, but it was a sort of confidence he had shared. She thought for a moment about what Whitearm had told her, then looked back at the man, trying to place him in the scene that the boy had painted, but she could not. She could not even place him at the imagined scene she had carried in her mind, one that haunted her dreams, one where men mowed down the villagers, Father Slater and the other sisters.

'He lost his family, his whole village to the soldiers,' she said without looking up at the man, her words so soft and light that the slight breeze that carried the heat around picked them up, played with them as it would a feather, then in a sudden burst of energy slapped them against the man's ears.

Instead of being surprised, he just nodded, scratched his ear and looked into the distance that lay in the opposite direction to the boy, the evening gloom slowly closing this down.

He was silent a long time. Eventually he shook his head slowly, turned back and tore himself another chunk of meat.

'We have all suffered with this war,' he shoved the meat into his mouth and tilted his chin in a dismissive gesture. His voice and his demeanour suggested a hardening, the unspoken phrase, 'he should just get over it,' danced a taunting jig in his aura.

Had Sister Constance been aware, the way Father Slater would have been, she would have picked up within the steps of the jig another unspoken sentence, 'I had to get over my own family's murder, why should this one be any different?' But she was Sister Constance, not the wise father and an anger flared suddenly within her. Her words, hot lava, shot out of her mouth.

'You killed them! You killed his father! He saw you do it!'

The boy's head snapped up as the outburst reverberated around the bushes, his eyes wide.

The man tracked him down. He had crept off quietly when the adults were asleep, gently leading Oddsock who sensed the need to move soundlessly. They headed out into the darkness, the finger-nail moon exposing the bare minimum detail of the landscape to allow them to move with relative confidence, but was not sufficient to aid the boy in avoiding a few scratches from the thorn bushes that dotted his way.

The heady funk of the land that the heat stirred up during the day had settled into a semi-sweet scent that was almost alluring, pulling the boy and the donkey further into the magical darkness. He muttered as he went, the sense of betrayal by Sister Constance that he carried in his breast was tempered only by a fear of the man, uncertain if this soldier felt the need to finish off the last survivor of the village.

He had resisted the temptation to run as soon as Sister Constance's outburst reached him. Shock at first rooting him to the spot then, as he had tensed his muscles, preparing to move, Oddsock had shoved his big nose in front of him, momentarily cutting off the line of sight between him and the two adults and in those few seconds it occurred to Whitearm that if he was to run now, they would easily catch him. He had to be patient. He thanked Oddsock for the advice and then looked away from the adults, trying to act as if he hadn't heard.

Sister Constance had come over soon after the outburst while the man sat staring in the opposite direction. She did not mention the breach of confidence, just checked that he was okay, as she had done every evening since they had fled from the village, but this time she seemed to fuss a little bit more, asking if he was fine a few times and ending by putting a finger under his chin to lift his reluctant eyes to hers and say, 'He is not a bad man, he really is not.' But then she looked away, unable to maintain eye contact. She did not believe what she was saying, he had thought, his eyes suddenly gaining confidence and staring into the space that hers had just vacated.

He waited till the two adults settled down, giving sufficient time for them to fall asleep, then crept off into the darkness, moving as quickly as he could till exhaustion forced him to find a hiding place and rest. The thick darkness of the night was just starting to soften as the growing grey of dawn began to colour the black and white of the night. He lay down in the gloom and was soon asleep.

The shadow that passed across the sun woke him. At first, he was disoriented, not sure why the sun was so high in the sky. In the village they had always woken as dawn crept across the compound and even when he and Oddsock had set out after the war god's men came they would wake at first light and get moving. His tired mind remembered the routine, but was slow to recall the disruption to it.

The remembrance of the late-night walk hit home at the same moment he realised that the shadow was a figure standing over him, blocking the sunlight from direct access.

Oddsock was late arriving, the man had approached from down-wind and had given no scent as a warning. The donkey trotted quickly between the man and the boy, causing the man to give a snort of humourless laughter, a not entirely unpleasant sound.

'You have a good friend in that donkey,' he said calmly before Whitearm could react to the panic that rushed through him.

Oddsock stood firm, his muscles tensed, ready to kick out if required.

'Come,' the man said, 'you will find no safety that way.' He turned and began to walk off, the presumption that Whitearm would obey written clearly in his posture and the way he did not turn back to check.

The boy took a moment, then began to walk behind his father's killer, driven partly by an inborn instinct to obey orders from adults, and in part by a realisation that the man, for all his faults was right, fragments of memory of the trials of his journey from his village still rattled in his head.

Worry and guilt mixed with relief flooded through Sister Constance. She made to go and hug Whitearm when she saw him approach, then checked herself, smiled a thanks at the man, the down-turned corners of her mouth failing to ignite enough light in her eyes to counteract the concern. 'I am glad that you are safe, Whitearm. I was so worried,' she said softly.

A prayer of thanks tried to scramble over the pile of emotions that littered the forefront of her mind. She had fretted over the boy's absence when they awoke, her concern for his safety and well-being splashing against the feelings of guilt at her blurting out his confession as she had. The latter feeling, which sloshed around her head till she had gone to sleep, and pervaded her dreams, stabbed her in the guts the moment she realised that he had run off.

Doubts then crept into her mind, slinking into a far dark corner and sitting sulkily, surveying the scene, not saying anything and putting the other emotions on edge. What if the man was still a killer? Despite his words, his eyes still carried the bloodshot tattoos of his addiction to the herbs. She had told herself that the menacing effect of this was just the scar of an old battle wound, that beneath this, things had healed. But as she waited for their return she did not know.

Her suspicions were not allayed by the safe return of Whitearm, despite her telling herself that they should be. If he wanted to harm Whitearm this would have been a perfect opportunity. He could have returned telling her that the boy had been mauled by lions and she would be none the wiser.

It's the disorientation, she told herself. I am not used to this rough travelling, I am scared and I am confused and am seeing enemies where there aren't any. If this man were truly still caught up in his old ways, why would he travel with us? We would only be baggage for him to drag along. He no longer needs us, he is well enough to function on his own. Whitearm's medicine is one that he knows and he could prepare it himself if he needed to, so why keep us around?

It is only natural that Whitearm is scared of him. Who would not be when you had witnessed him kill your father with a seeming lack of emotion? But Whitearm is too young to see the change. This man did not want to be a soldier. He was forced to become one, a fate that Whitearm has been lucky to escape so far. There is a decent man inside that outer shell. Decent, but damaged. He does not know how to behave in company other than amongst other soldiers, where revealing your emotions, or even expressing a desire to get out of the business would cause isolation or worse.

She settled down with her justification, a slightly smug feeling just tickling her senses. She was in Father Slater territory with these thoughts. This, she was sure, would have been how he would have thought if faced with this situation. He would have seen the man's side of the story. Her role now must be to help him on his journey away from the uncaring way of life he had suffered and to gently lead him to God and into the way of love that Jesus Christ had taught.

She would also have to lead the boy, show him how to forgive, show him that people can change. She glanced back at Whitearm, checking that he was in his customary position about one hundred yards behind them, with the donkey a few feet away. She would begin work on him when they stopped to avoid the heat of the day. In the meantime she hastened her step to catch up with the man.

He had managed to catch a dik dik. Whitearm seemed quite happy with the meat from the small deer, but Sister Constance had to make a concerted effort not to grimace at the thought of eating such a cute animal.

'Tell him it is ready,' the man glanced up from the fire.

Sister Constance dusted off her dress and walked across to Whitearm to announce dinner. During their midday break she had realised that before she could start coaching the boy to forgive the man, she needed to work on getting Whitearm's forgiveness for blurting out his 'secret'. Whitearm remained polite but a gap had opened between them. She could have taken him some food, saved him from having to be in close proximity to his father's killer, but it was important that there be contact between the two, however minimal, if they were ever to be reconciled.

She had also sensed a reluctance in the man to have the boy around. He had clearly been distressed by the news that he had turned the boy into an orphan, but was unsure how to act.

Whitearm got to his feet, gave Oddsock a quick hug and then began to walk across to get his food. Sister Constance could almost see the conflict between hunger and distrust of the man, flashing across the youngster's face and her heart wept for him.

He accepted the meat the man offered, dipping his head in a polite thanks, a reflex movement that carried no real emotion behind it.

'Sit with us, Whitearm,' Sister Constance said quietly, her tone almost expecting him to turn the offer down. But it was a command. She had not, in the words she chose, given Whitearm an option, the omission the result of a mind too tired to search for the necessary additional words to provide the boy with a get out clause. And Whitearm, despite his mischievous nature in happier times, had been brought up to obey his elders, so he sat down, ensuring that Sister Constance was between him and the man, close enough to obey the command, yet with enough distance to register his disapproval of his orders.

The man glanced up, his face taking on a sharp edge of surprise before settling to one of blunt resigned indifference and he tore some meat off a bone and chewed, his eyes looking off away from Whitearm while the boy nibbled at his morsel, his appetite seemingly suppressed by the adult intervention in his meal.

Sister Constance sighed inwardly. She felt like a mother trying to reconcile two siblings after a spat. But she knew this was no trivial disagreement.

And yet...

She sensed within the two a willingness, almost a desire to be reconciled, as if they both could see a world beyond the barrier that lay between them, as if perhaps peace in the land and an end to the war depended on them being able to find a way round this obstacle. But neither could work out a route to get there. She looked from one to the other, the meat in her hand forgotten as she studied, first the boy, then the man.

Where to start? Again her mind turned to the absent Father Slater, trying to visualise him sitting there with them, hoping that the vision, should she be able to conjure it up, would give her the words she needed to say to help them break down the barriers. But the dead priest was not open to being summonsed up, he had disapproved of séances in life and would have no part of them in death.

'You are not hungry?' The man was looking at the untouched meat in her hand.

She shook her head to clear it while her mouth said that yes, she was hungry, just thinking. The man shrugged and continued to eat, but seemed to attack the meat with less vigour, as if he felt that in order to be polite, it was necessary for him to think as well.

Whitearm's stomach got the better of his thoughts and, while the adults began to pick at their food, he started to eat his with some relish, finishing off his piece and gratefully accepting the next one Sister Constance offered him. There was plenty to go around, the man's ability as a hunter and a cook meant that they could afford to leave whatever they could not eat to the scavengers.

The light took a final look round the land before bowing and exiting, leaving the small fire as a place marker so that it knew where to return to the next day. The heat settled down for the evening, the work of the day done and it could put its feet up and be a pleasant father, home from a busy day in the office.

They finished eating and sat back, the man leaning against a tree, Sister Constance, a respectable distance from him, had found a rock to support her back. Whitearm sat cross-legged where he had first planted himself. He had not been dismissed. Somewhere, not too far away, they heard the grunt of a warthog and then a snuffling in the bushes nearby, giving them just enough time to tense up before Oddsock appeared in the gloomy circle of light that the fire and slither of moon had teamed up to bring them. He was on the other side of the group to Whitearm and he paused, as if deciding whether to walk past the man or retreat into the dark again and reach his twin via a more circuitous route, then just before the man could reach out and pet him, he moved quickly on, ignoring the nun and settling himself behind the boy, allowing the youngster to lean back and use him as a kind of pillow.

The man stared after Oddsock, watching the beast settle, a quizzical expression playing across his face.

'You have a good friend in that donkey,' he echoed his words of the morning when he had found Whitearm, but this time there was no sneer in his voice, more a feeling of regret that touched his words.

Whitearm nodded, reluctant to have to communicate with the man and gave Oddsock a protective pat, saying with the gesture, 'he is mine. Hands off!'

Sister Constance sat up slightly, glad that one of them had reached out, although she could not be sure where this would lead to.

'I used to have a donkey as a friend,' the man's eyes left the boy and beast and stared off into the gloom, perhaps watching some mental film that flicked on the black canvas around them. 'He was all grey, not like Oddsock with his,' he paused as he thought, 'special leg. We should have called him Nosocks,' he gave a humourless laugh and continued to stare out into the dark, staying silent for a few moments.

'We called him Spotless because he did not have a mark on him.'

The memory of his friend cast a melancholic air about the man and he soaked in it for a good while before going on, almost oblivious of his audience, the nun who stared at him, willing him to continue and the boy who feigned non-interest.

'The soldiers killed him when they came.'

The boy looked up sharply, his mouth opening in preparation to utter the words that wanted to tumble out, but his mind pulled them back at the last second. His sympathy for the donkey without blemish could not extend to the man.

The nun leaned forward, her hand starting to stretch out to touch the man, a gentle reassurance that she felt his pain, but then realised that he sat too far away to reach and she eased herself back, wriggling her bottom on the dusty ground to feign an adjustment to a more comfortable position to cover the unfinished gesture.

The man did not notice either reaction and continued to study the darkness which was thickening around them. The loss of his family and his subsequent involuntary drafting into the army that had ripped him from his normal life, jostled in his mind for space, but tonight was not the time for that story, tonight it was the donkey's turn.

'I remember we used to go down to the ocean and collect coconuts. I would load them onto Spotless' back and carry them back to the village. I would then swap them for eggs or bananas, sometimes even a small piece of meat. We would eat like kings then,' he went on, oblivious to the reaction this had provoked in the boy. The youngster sat up, alert, studying the man.

'You have seen the ocean?' he asked when the man paused. Unlike the words of sympathy for the murdered donkey, there was nothing to hold these ones back, his whole being craved information on this issue. The man was startled, not only by the fact that the boy had actually addressed him, but also by the eagerness in the voice.

'Yes, I used to live a morning's walk from the ocean before…a long time ago.'

'Is it really as big as the sky?'

The other side of the night sky is where the daylight goes to sleep. Whitearm remembered his mother telling him this. There is a big wall in the sky made of branches and mud and in the day time, the light is on our side of the wall, but at night it goes to sleep behind the wall. The sky is so old that the wall has worn in places so little bits of light shine through and we call those little lights, stars.

'What about the moon?' he asked, his excited eyes staring up at the bright round light that punctured the sky.

His mother laughed, 'that is a hole that the daylight has made in the wall so that he can look through and make sure that everyone is sleeping when they should be. Now it is your bedtime.'

He stared at the sky a moment longer, then obediently went inside and curled up on the floor next to his sister, his eyes wide open in the dark.'

'Mother?' he whispered.

'Yes, my son, what is it?'

'The hole in the sky that the light looks through, why does it change shape? Sometimes it is round and sometimes it is like a fingernail.'

His mother chuckled quietly, 'because, my son, sometimes the daylight does not want to look down because people are being so bad, so he will close his eye and that is when he thinks, will I come back round the wall tomorrow or not? The people are being so bad, I don't know if I want to make a day for them, maybe they should only have the night.'

He thought for a long while, then asked, 'Mother, what bad things do people do to make the daylight not want to come back to our side of the wall?'

'Well, it could be anything, people fighting with each other or stealing someone else's eggs, or even a boy not going to sleep when his mother has told him to.'

Whitearm shut his eyes tight, 'Goodnight mother,' he said and tried very hard to go to sleep.

'Goodnight, my son,' his mother's voice was filled with love.

He stared up at the night sky. The daylight was not wanting to look, the moon just a slither in the dark sky, but he knew that was just a story his mother had made up to make him go to sleep, a story for small children. He was grown up now and he had big things to think about, like the ocean.

The night sky reminded him of his mother. He missed her, but not with the sharpness that had bitten into him as he had struggled alone in his search for the ocean. Rather it was with a dull warmth that he felt her absence. Sister Constance's care for him had blunted the sting of loss. And the ocean, its mystical allure, its exotic coconuts, had kept him going.

The man had seen the ocean. He had eaten the sweet coconut fruit that only grew there. It was not a story of a story that the elders had heard from someone who had heard from someone. This man had seen the ocean.

Questions that had been floating in his mind came flooding down, only to be damned up by his mouth, suddenly made shy by his initial outburst.

'Yes, it is as big as the sky. If you stand next to it, you cannot see where it ends.' The man seemed pleased that he had asked but then went on to speak about his village and the people who had lived there, people had different names, but as the man described them, Whitearm could name in his mind the equivalent person from his own village.

The man spoke of a pretty girl in his village who he had liked, and Whitearm thought of his sister and the young man who was always round their place. In his village that he now spoke of the man was certain that the girl liked him. Whitearm's sister did not take to her suitor.

The man laughed as he spoke of the woman who could never find her chickens. Whitearm recalled the woman from his village who was always misplacing her children.

'There was one young boy who went swimming in the river and nearly got killed by a crocodile. Twobites popped into Whitearm's mind.

The man seemed happy when he said goodnight. Sister Constance was happy, she had kissed Whitearm's forehead before settling down to sleep. He lay awake, listening to the man's breathing turn slowly to a low snore while the nun's settled into a slow contented rhythm.

Whitearm felt a happy warmth as he watched the night sky. The ocean did exist, the man had seen it. With that thought he knew that he could not continue to hate him. He would have to talk to him to get more information and you cannot do that if you hate someone. He resolved to walk with the man and Sister Constance the next day. Maybe he would speak again of the ocean.

With that decision made, he closed his eyes and snuggled up to the thoughts of his mother, looking forward to sliding into sleep with those pleasant memories on his brain. He let out a contented sigh, then suddenly threw his eyes open. If the ocean did exist, then so too would God our Father. He recalled his decision to wait until he saw the ocean with his own eyes before he would believe in Sister Constance's god and a small thrill ran through his body.

Mamba

The bird sat on a low branch near to where the young lay. The adult humans slept closer to him than they had been doing. A kind of serenity clung to the young's small form and the bird tilted its head in approval. It was too early to chirp, the darkness of the night was just starting its routine morphing into the day, shedding its dark skin with a slow shudder, then emerging with bright colours splashed over the landscape.

The male and female humans also slept fitfully, the peacefulness of the young seeming to cover them too in a contented blanket. The male lay next to a tree, his head, resting against the folds of the trunk, lolled slightly to one side, his mouth open just enough to allow a low whistle of air to pass between his lips.

The female was curled on the dusty ground near the remnants of the fire. Her hands, together as if in prayer, served as a pillow. A few feet away from her, the boy was cradled by the donkey, lying sideways against the beast, his back just touching his friend's side.

The slightest movement along the branch startled the bird and it launched into the air, an involuntary chirp escaping from its beak as it did so. From the safety of the air, it watched the snake ease itself back into the shadows, its dead black eyes watching the lost snack with an impression of mild amusement created by the strange line of its mouth. The bird hovered for a moment, then sought safety in another tree, peering into the dark branches first before settling nervously.

The male had awoken and was staring at her, then its eyes moved across to the tree she had just vacated. There was a tension in the human, but the bird was busy calming her own nerves to take much notice. She preened her feathers in quick, jerky movements, her eyes constantly returning to the human, making sure that it posed no threat. The female human stirred and took the male's attention.

'What is it?' Sister Constance whispered, her eyes immediately registering on the man's state of alertness. Her heart, responding to the sudden alarm, sent the blood out at pace to wake the extremities of her body.

The man looked round slowly before relaxing noticeably. 'It is nothing,' he said, 'just a bird.' He rubbed his face with his hands and then stood up slowly and stretched.

Oddsock had also been disturbed by the bird and was on his feet, but unnoticed by the adults, did not relax. He gently nudged Whitearm with his knee and once the boy was up, jostled him away from the tree that he had been sleeping under and in which the mamba lay draped deep in its branches. Whitearm was drowsy, his sleep had been deep and relaxed and his body was not ready to move on from that state, but by instinct he obeyed the donkey's urgings without question or really registering on the fact that he was being manoeuvred in such a manner.

Once relocated, he set about waking up properly. The stories of the man's village life mingled with the memories of his own, like old friends meeting after a long time and talking of the old days, remembered from different viewpoints, but having sufficient reference points to appear as one recollection. He smiled quietly and unconsciously reached out and patted the donkey.

He would walk with the adults today and force his shy tongue to ask about the ocean. 'And the coconuts,' a corner of his mind reminded him and he smiled again. 'Yes, and the coconuts.' He felt the saliva gather in his mouth as the description of the exotic fruit crashed like a wave over his thoughts. The man must know about coconuts if he had lived by the ocean.

Then another thought struck which bubbled up inside him, warm lava of excitement looking for a route to the surface. The man must know the direction to the ocean. He must know how they could get there. He wanted to blurt out the question, his small body shaking with excitement at the prospect of getting a first real steer towards his goal.

'Are you okay, Whitearm?' Sister Constance had just noticed his excited state. 'It was only a bird.' She pointed at the colourful bird in the nearby tree.

Whitearm nodded, forcing his limbs to relax. It was not the right time to ask the question, it must wait until they were walking. It would help pass the hours as they travelled.

Sister Constance watched him a moment longer, a strange questioning look on her face which disturbed him. She would draw his secrets out of him if he looked at her too much. He was not ready to tell her that at some point in the future he would have to leave her so that he could go find the ocean. But he was not ready to tell her that just yet, so he turned his attention to Oddsock in order to avoid her gaze and to draw on the donkey's calming effects.

Oddsock, however was still tense, keeping a suspicious eye on the tree where the mamba hid while still watching the boy to ensure that he was not going near it. Whitearm followed his gaze, too wrapped up in his own thoughts to properly register the beast's unease.

What would a coconut tree look like? he thought. The elders had only said that they grew on a tree by the ocean, but had not explained what those trees looked like. The tree that Oddsock was staring at was a squat ugly one, an umbrella canopy constructed of dusty leaves and dull brown branches, thin and twisted like snakes that bobbed and bowed to the wind. They could not kill the wind with their bites so they had to bow to it to keep favour.

A coconut tree would not be like this evil and bent one, a nasty servant to the wind. A coconut tree would be tall and proud. Its leaves would not be dirty and dusty, but shiny and green. And it would not have to bow to the wind, it would wave to it like one does a friend.

He smiled to himself as the imagined proud tree grew up in his mind. Yes, a fruit as good as the coconut required a tall and proud tree. They would have plenty of water to drink from the sea so it would grow, not like the short thorny ones here where the water is scarce. He stared at the tree which Oddsock had moved him away from. The morning light was beginning to wiggle its way through the tangle of branches, creating yellow flecks on the dusty floor beneath the umbrella branches.

The man stood under the tree where the snake hid and felt the warmth of the day began to build. He liked the heat, the way it would grip his body and squeeze out the aches that accumulated in his bones and muscles while he slept. The boy's poultice had done its miracle working and the mornings were not as fraught as he began to move, but there were still aches where he had been kicked and beaten, echoes that rang through his body as he began to move. But now those aches were friends, reminders of the price he had paid to gain his freedom. He stretched, enjoying the dull pain that moved lazily through his muscles.

They all heard the hiss, Whitearm catching the movement of the branch a moment before the snake struck, his warning cry sucked back in the gasp of horror. The mamba moved with incredible speed. Its head shot forward, mouth open, fangs bared, venom in its eyes and potent poison in its bite. The recoil was as quick as the attack, the snake disappearing into the branches, becoming one with the tree. Had the man actually been bitten? It was so fast, Whitearm could not tell if the fangs had made contact, but the look on the man's face gave him the answer.

'Quick!' the boy rushed forward, grabbed the man's arm and pulled him away from the tree. The man was staring at his hand, a stricken look struggling through his bewildered features.

The boy led him gently to another tree some distance off and eased him down against the trunk. In Whitearm's mind he traced the procedures the elders had gone through with Twobites, his eyes already searching for something to use as a tourniquet as he helped the man settle.

'Has he been bitten?' Sister Constance's tone answered her own question, but the boy nodded anyway.

'We need to tie,' his hands filling in the details that his young grasp of language could not, then added, 'quick!' in response to the nun's shocked inactivity. The urgency of the situation overriding his natural instinct not to bark orders at adults.

The sharpness of the command breathed life into Sister Constance's paralysed body and she looked round desperately, then down at her shirt, paused a moment to dispose of the modesty that threatened to well up in her and began to unbutton it. She tore at the sleeve, her panic fighting with the stubborn stitches before they gave way and she passed the boy the ragged material.

The man was still staring at the bite while the boy tied the tourniquet tightly over his forearm, his young features straining with the effort. Sister Constance took this moment to give in to her modesty and quickly buttoned her one-sleeved shirt while Whitearm began to suck at the small puncture marks on the man's wrist, spitting out the blood and poison.

'What are they putting on the bite?' He recalled the question he had asked his mother as the adults crowded around the prone body of his friend Twobites who at that time was called Survivor. He needed to recall in absolute detail the necessary plants that he would need to make the potion to entice the poison out of the man's body.

'Hold his hand,' he commanded the nun. Whitearm was not sure if this was part of the cure, but the adults had done that with Twobites and he couldn't take a chance.

The ingredients of the medicine were slowly filtering into his mind, his mother listing them one by one while her eyes had not left the bitten boy. At one point she had turned to him highlighting an important distinction that he should make sure to remember if he ever had to prepare the potion.

'Green or black?' he asked the man whose breathing was already beginning to take on a rough edge.

The man shook his head, 'black.' The word, spoken in the local language, held all the darkness and fear that its English cousin could muster.

Whitearm clicked his tongue and shot a glance at Sister Constance. Green was bad. Black was much worse. She would need all the power of God our Father to help her and even then that may not be enough. He looked round and saw Oddsock standing a few paces off, his nostrils flaring with distress at what had happened.

The boy stretched out his pale arm towards the beast and it came to him.

'Stay with the man,' Whitearm whispered. 'Sister Constance will be here and she will talk to God our Father to help, but you must help too. It was black. With Twobites it was green. This man may not even live to become Onebite. Stay with him and help him.'

He took the man's free hand and placed it on the donkey's neck, then said to Sister Constance, 'I must go get things to help. I will return.'

Twobites' ordeals had come from green mamba attacks which, Whitearm knew, were deadly, but, his mother had told him that the black mamba was more lethal. He needed to get the required ingredients quickly if the man was to stand a chance. His efforts to gather them though were hindered by the thought that the mamba's mate may be nearby, so he had to check bushes and shrubs carefully before picking what was required.

The whole time a part of his mind was fretting that he may lose this one connection with the ocean.

The man's breathing was becoming more fraught as the poison slithered slowly through his body, conquering his muscles which began to freeze with fear at the onslaught. He held Sister Constance's hand tightly, his eyes pleading with her to do something.

She prayed hard, her mind racing through the ones she knew by rote and fumbling over those that she was making up, trying to get the specifics of the situation crammed into the words, informing her God of things He would already know, needs and wants that He would already understand.

And still it did not feel like she was doing enough. The enormity of the problem at hand seemed too big for words, too big for prayers, too big even for God.

She tried to calm herself, tell her racing mind that she was being stupid. Nothing was too big for God. Father Slater would be telling her that, if he were here now. 'But sometimes,' he would have gone on, 'our will and God's will do not coincide. We want things that do not fit in with God's plans.'

The thoughts of Father Slater calmed her racing mind and her prayers became less frantic and more focused. At the same time, a part of her subconscious realised that the man's hand had become disconnected from Oddsock and, without thinking, she gently placed the loose hand onto the rump of the donkey who sat close by, blinking slowly. She laid her hand over the snakebite and, dusting the last vestiges of panic from her mind, she began to pray earnestly without the angst and fretfulness of her earlier babblings.

The man relaxed under her touch and his breathing, while still ragged round the edges, held a steady rhythm, his eyes expressed gratitude although it was not clear whether it was for the gestures of kindness, trying to make him comfortable as he died, or for the fervent prayers being offered, trying to stop him dying.

The calmness of the man reflected in Sister Constance as her shocked being began to accept that maybe the man would not survive. He had fought many battles and now that he was free of the fighting he would succumb to a different enemy. But he would have died a free man and that was important to him. She smiled a reassuring smile.

Whitearm's mixture was applied to the bite without question from the nun. The man's eyes were closed by the time the youngster returned and his breath was coming in spasmodic gasps, his body stiffening by degrees, a slow coming to attention at the command of the poison.

The spare hand, the one not being held by Sister Constance, had once again become disconnected from Oddsock, who had shifted at one point, letting the limb flop to the dusty ground. The boy immediately corrected this situation as if hooking the man back up to a life support machine. Sister Constance could not be sure, but it did seem that this small procedure smoothed the edges of the jagged breathing.

The boy applied his herb mixture, gently prising Sister Constance's fingers from the man's wrist first, then rubbing the odd smelling potion over the puncture marks and was about to sit back and watch, then remembered and guided the nun's hand back to the stricken man's wrist.

'Ask God our Father to help,' he said and sat back, checking again that the man was in touch with Oddsock. This was serious and Whitearm knew that they needed to call on everything they possibly could to try and overcome the poison. He hoped that he had remembered the ingredients for the medicine correctly, but there was nothing more he could do. They had to wait, just as the village had done when Twobites had lain in his bed, his body stiff and lifeless, only hope, a thin thread, connecting him to life.

He reeled out that thin thread again, feeling the expectation of his village that it would be able to hold the weight. He sensed his mother's pride at his ability to remember the medicine and the way he had gone about putting it together so swiftly. They were there for him, the whole village, his mother and father, his sister, Twobites and all the elders and he knew then that no matter what happened to the man the spirits of the village would all nod and agree that he had done well. He settled down, cross legged near the man to watch.

The day moved languidly through its usual steps, heat building up throughout the morning, distorting the air and making breathing feel like sucking hot water through a face cloth. The morning blue of the sky, now blanched to a white-hot silver by the sun, seemed almost to press down on the land, threatening to collapse on top of everything like the burning roof of a hut.

The dust, made lazy by the heat, did not rise from the floor, preferring to stay where it was rather than move around. And the animals respected this, most choosing to lie in whatever shade they could find and leaving the dust for later when things cooled slightly and their feet could stir it into action.

Only the insects seemed to enjoy the heat, their beating wings adding a buzzing throb to the one that already pulsed around the land, a steady drumming of hot air on the plains. The flies and mosquitoes rode the currents of this rhythm, playing gleefully in it.

The bird watched the insects swoop and settle on the donkey, only to launch themselves again when the beast's skin would twitch in irritation at the invasion. The male adult lay still with his hand touching the donkey, while the female and young sat close by, the female holding on to the male and the young watching them.

The bird looked back at the tree where the mamba still sat curled around a branch, barely visible to the eye. It would move off when the night came, it did not like being close to the humans, but at the same time it liked to travel at night when its dark colours would make it almost invisible. For now though, the humans would be safe from further attack unless they provoked the viper again.

The bird looked back at the male and gave a muted chirp of encouragement. The mamba was an enemy to the bird and she did not like seeing the human suffering from its bite.

Time ticked over slowly, the seconds, bogged down in a muddy quagmire of heat and anxiety, bubbled to the surface of the thick porridge of the day, a growing dome on the surface taking an age to plop! and let out its sigh of expiration.

Sister Constance's lips still moved as silent prayer followed silent prayer, her devotions slowly wrapping her in a protective blanket, cutting her off from the reality around her. In her heart she knew that the man would die. This was a harsh, untamed world. It had no conscience. If someone survived an attack from their fellow man, it cared nothing if that same person would fall prey to one of its animals. It was not a vindictive thing, it was just a cold fact. The land could not be held responsible for something that just was.

Whitearm sat quietly watching, waiting. He could not ask for God our Father's help as Sister Constance was still busy talking to Him and God would not be able to listen to both of them at the same time. So he hoped, as he had done with Twobites, especially the second time when he had dared his friend to pick the snake up. His hope was a selfish one. He did not care for the man, only for that knowledge that was in the man's head, precious knowledge of the ocean. He could feel the poison creeping slowly through his patient's stricken body, paralysing it by degrees, locking those secrets of the ocean up in tightening muscles and failing organs.

The poultice fought a tug-of-war battle with the poison, trying to drag it out of the man's blood stream, pulling back at the toxins as they in turn tried to bury themselves deep into their new home.

The connection the man had with Oddsock had stabilised as if both man and beast realised the importance of it, yet neither aware of the way this touch linked the man with the god to whom Sister Constance prayed. Had the healing powers of that man, who lived so long ago and who had ridden Oddsock's ancestor into Jerusalem, had those powers passed through the ages and generations of donkeys?

Whitearm was the first to notice. It came gradually so was not readily identifiable, but the man's breathing seemed to be losing its raggedness and was edging itself by small degrees towards normalisation. If that was the case, then they had hope. The boy remembered the excited ripple that ran through the village when they realised that Twobites was slowly regaining control over his breath.

But it was still too early to tell. After the initial excitement of the recovering breath, there had been a long nervous wait to see if Twobites would eventually wake. It had taken days before his friend had opened his eyes, as if the fight against the poison had worn him out so much that he needed to sleep forever.

Still, Whitearm sat forward slightly and studied the man closely. Somewhere hidden behind those closed eyes and guarded by slowly recovering breaths, lay the secrets of the ocean. They were too big and too important to stay locked up in that tomb. He concentrated his thoughts on everything he could recall that the elders had said, hoping that those secrets the man clung to would feel the presence of other thoughts of the ocean and that they would fight to escape from their prison and unite.

'Is he breathing more easily?' Sister Constance, distracted by Whitearm's slight movement, temporarily put aside her prayers and, following the boy's gaze, she too sensed the change.

Whitearm shrugged. 'Maybe,' he kept his voice low, not wanting to frighten the secrets away. 'It is difficult to say, but I think so.'

Sister Constance leaned forward, eagerly wanting a sign that her prayers had been answered, but the man continued to struggle with his breathing, his eyes closed and face stretched tight.

She eased herself back, fighting her disappointment and doubts about her prayers. Maybe she was not praying hard enough, or was it her faith that was not sufficiently strong? She glanced at the boy, hoping that she was not displaying her feelings, she did not want him to see the frailties of her faith.

But the boy still watched the man closely, a kind of stoic faith etched on his face. Again she was acutely aware of the unwanted maturity that clung to his features. 'There is still hope,' the man in a child's body seemed to say with his demeanour. Or was there a desperation in that look? Sister Constance was not sure, but there was more than just measured hope and this puzzled her. Why would the boy be so keen that the man survive? A small thrill ran through her. Had Whitearm actually forgiven the man to the extent that he now wished him no harm? For a second shame flashed through her at her own lack of faith, then, as she realised that this was what she had prayed for, before the mamba had attacked, she relaxed and luxuriated in the joy of an answered prayer. Then remembering the man, she closed her eyes and continued to ask God to spare his life.

Oddsock moved quietly away from the humans. They were all asleep and he had grown tired of lying with the man's hot hand on his rump. The leaves, dry and dusty as they were, were calling and the worst of the midday heat had been soaked up by the land.

As he chewed on his late afternoon snack, he began to miss the hand that had lain on him for the most part of the day. There had been something peaceful about it and he had felt useful lying there. The boy with the white arm had made sure that the man's hand was in contact with his grey body, so there was something important about it for the boy and if that pleased his friend, then it pleased him.

But needs had forced him to abandon his post temporarily. He would go back as soon as he had relieved his hunger. Events were taking yet more strange turns for him. It had started with the horror of the bang sticks followed by the long journey where he had worried for his friend. Then came the time of peace when they had found the woman, only to be thrown back into turmoil by the re-appearance of the men with their bang sticks. The arrival of the man in his beaten state had spooked them further, but he had, despite Whitearm's initial wariness of him, ingratiated himself into the company, providing food and companionship for the woman and bringing an element of peace to them.

Now, nature had conspired to overturn their peace again. The panic that ensued after the snake struck had settled into nervous waiting that had exhausted the boy and the woman. Oddsock had wanted to go to his friend and comfort him and to seek comfort from the unease he felt, but the boy had insisted on him being close to the man. He did not understand this sacrifice that the boy appeared to be making, foregoing the closeness and friendship so that the man could be comforted. The boy knew best and once he had settled down beside the man, he knew that the boy was right. There was something about the contact with the man that felt essential. He could not quite work out what it was, but there was definitely a purpose to it. He tore a few more mouthfuls of leaves quickly and then trotted back to his post.

Whitearm woke when the donkey returned and resumed his position next to the man. The strain of keeping his hopes alive and the heat of the day had taken their toll and, despite his brave effort to fight it off, sleep came pulling at his eyelids.

He rubbed his eyes, looked round to take in his surroundings and took a moment to recall why they were all arranged as they were; Sister Constance, still asleep, lay curled up a few paces away from the man while Oddsock sat at his post near the hand of the stricken ex-soldier. As he recalled what had transpired and the importance of the information about the ocean locked up inside the man, he moved quickly to re-establish contact between Oddsock and the hand that lay in the dust nearby, looking almost as if it had been carelessly discarded there.

Once he had hooked his patient back onto the life support machine, he examined him. The breathing was definitely getting better. The wheezing, choking gasps still there, but there was a smoothness to them that had been lacking earlier. Whitearm checked the puncture marks on the man's wrist and decided that there was nothing more that his medicine could do. It had sucked as much of the poison out as it could, it was now down to the man to fight what was left.

'How is he doing?' Sister Constance sat up slowly and, like Whitearm, had taken a few moments to bring herself up to date with what had happened.

Whitearm shrugged. 'His breathing is better, but he is still sleeping. It is good about his breathing, but he is not safe yet. The elders...' he paused. The elders were all dead. Could what they had said, when the village waited to see if Twobites would eventually wake up, still have validity? As soon as that thought struck, another also arrived which said that the elders had spoken of the ocean. So those words must still hold meaning despite those who had said them no longer being around, Whitearm concluded.

'The elders in my village said that we could never be sure until someone had woken up after a snakebite.'

Sister Constance nodded and looked at the man, then smiled her upside-down smile at Whitearm, her eyes giving out a message of encouragement to keep the faith. Whitearm sat still for a moment, his eyes flicking between the man and the nun, then he got slowly to his feet. They were going to need some food and the man was not going to be able to do any hunting. He told Sister Constance what he was off to do and left with her nod of blessing. As he moved out from the shade of the tree, his eye caught the circling birds high in the blue sky, an easy energy keeping them floating on the currents. Nature, that gossip, had sent the message round quickly. He expected nothing less of the land, but the sight shocked him somewhat. It flew in the face of Sister Constance's smile. It said nature knew something that even God our Father did not.

He paused in the sun, squinting up at the vultures, an anger at their message starting to build up in him. They could not take the man. They were birds, they had no use for the ocean. If the man were to die, then those secrets about the sea would pass on to these scavengers as they went about their work. The only way this could be prevented would be for the man to live.

He looked round the bush slowly. Nothing moved. The air was still, as if holding its breath, waiting for something to happen. The trees, squat, ugly and dusty, watched him and in the branches, a small solitary bird cocked its head as if asking the question, 'What now?'

The boy took all this in, acknowledging the bird and its question with a small nod then, making certain that Sister Constance had not followed him, he went down on his knees as he had seen her do and began to pray.

'God our Father,' he said, his words barely disturbing the stillness around him, 'God our Father, I need the man to live. He has the secrets of the ocean locked up in his head and I need to know them otherwise I will never get there. I have done all I can to stop the snake poison and Sister Constance has asked you to help and Oddsock is there, but we can do no more. We can only hope. All I am asking is that you too do everything that you can to help. I cannot ask for more than that.'

He finished his prayer and moved to stand, then remembered and made the sign of the hands-up tree as he had seen Sister Constance do so many times.

As he started to move on, a guinea fowl walked out from the bushes and began pecking at the ground near him. It seemed oblivious to his presence, only realising that the boy was there when quick hands grabbed at it and only moments to realise what had happened before the click of its breaking neck reached its ears.

What was it about the donkey? Sister Constance tried to fathom out this question as she watched the man's breathing even out again. It had suddenly regained its rasp as she sat quietly next to him, her eyes closed with exhaustion from the heat and stress of all that was happening. Startled from her reverie, the first thing she noticed was that the man's hand had once again disconnected itself from Oddsock and without thinking she had restored the touch, only then realising the effect it had on the stricken man. He had sighed, almost in relief, and the breathing became more natural.

She sat back and studied the donkey who blinked at her, his expression was also one of puzzlement, as if he too did not understand what was happening. She tried to tell herself that the quizzical look Oddsock gave her was mainly questioning why they kept putting the man's hand on his back, but she could not shake the feeling that there was more to it.

Father Slater could have offered an explanation if he had been here. Or could he? She shuddered slightly at the doubt. She had never before considered that he was anything but invincible. The 'Father' in his name went much further than a religious title. She suddenly felt that she had betrayed him, daring to doubt his ability to explain the unexplainable.

And yet...

As her thoughts settled themselves, she found that it was neither a crime nor a sin, nor was it even blasphemous to harbour thoughts that her mentor was anything but human. He was a very knowledgeable human, but one, like every other one, who had limitations to their abilities. He had not been some superhuman, his vulnerability to the bullets had proven that. She gave a small sigh, her body relaxing as the thoughts moulded themselves around her and she became comfortable living inside them.

This still did not resolve the riddle of the donkey, but it was somehow not as important as it had been a few moments earlier. Father Slater would have admitted if something was beyond his grasp, he was not a vain man. This did not stop her asking the question, 'What is it about you, Oddsock? How is it that you have a calming effect on this man, that you can turn his breathing from sharp to smooth?'

The donkey looked up, but looked past her, nodding a greeting to Whitearm who had returned triumphant, dinner in hand.

The hours of waiting, watching the man, stretched themselves lazily over the days, oblivious to the heat and dust and unaffected by the slow creep of hunger that began to settle on the boy and the nun. As with his first journey, his early luck in hunting had quickly faded and he would spend hours each day trying to find food. They were luckier with water as, before he had been bitten, the man had discovered a small river nearby that, against the odds of the heat and the dryness of the land, still managed a small trickle.

They would drip water into the man's dry mouth where he seemed to absorb it in a sponge-like way, but the lack of food was causing his body to slowly deflate and crumble in on itself. If the poison didn't kill him, the hunger would.

Whitearm fretted. The added burden of not finding food worried him, not so much for himself and Sister Constance's sake, but he knew that if the man woke up, he would need to be fed otherwise all his attempts to foil the poison would have been in vain. The desperation to find food made him over anxious in the hunt and he often found himself launching his attack too early, or in moments when he forced himself to be more patient, he would over compensate and be clutching at the space his prey had just vacated.

Sister Constance did not say anything. She would give him a sad smile each time he returned empty handed, the corners of her mouth barely moving down, the sympathy-laden smile confining itself to her eyes.

He could not hold her look for long, acknowledging her concern, but it served more as a reminder of failure then as encouragement to continue.

Oddsock became restless too. He sensed the growing despair in his twin and wanted to help, but had no idea how. Whitearm and Sister Constance found themselves reconnecting the man with the donkey more frequently as the beast would move restlessly, uncomfortable with its helplessness. When in contact with Oddsock, the man's breathing had become almost normal, resembling a sleep rhythm, but it still took on an edge, although in diminishing intensity when the donkey insisted on getting up to feed and attend to its comfort.

'Why does he not wake up?' Whitearm wanted to scream out his impatience, but he restrained himself, trying to exorcise the frustration by pacing up and down when the air was not too hot. When he was not pacing he began to wander further afield in his attempts to find food, causing Sister Constance to worry about his whereabouts and pray more fervently for the youngster, that he be delivered from these monstrous adult responsibilities and he be allowed the freedom to be a child again.

But the gamble of wandering further began to pay off and he brought home food on three consecutive nights. The following night, however, he returned quickly, his eyes wide and his legs trembled.

'Soldiers,' was all he said when asked by Sister Constance what was wrong.

She crossed herself quickly, barely aware of the action as she felt her body turn cold in the balmy evening.

'Where?' she asked.

He flapped his hand to indicate a distance off.

They huddled together, not daring to light a fire that evening, but the night passed without event and, as the following day drew on, they both began to relax somewhat. But the sight of the soldiers had spooked Whitearm and he narrowed his hunting area, moving with greater caution. Despite this, his luck held and he was able to bring back some small prey on two of the following three evenings.

They were busy preparing their meagre meal on the second of these occasions when Oddsock snorted, stood up and shook himself, then began to sniff inquisitively at some leaves on a nearby bush. It was unusual for the donkey to move around at this time of the day and they both stared at Oddsock before they became aware of a hoarse whisper coming from the man.

Sister Constance was at his side first, while Whitearm stood a few feet off. The man's eyes were open, but not yet seeing. There was a cloudiness that fell across them and his face had a look of someone clutching for a memory to grab hold of with which to pull themselves out of their confused quagmire.

'It's okay, we are here,' Sister Constance's voice was gentle and she took his hand. The man's eyes searched for the source of the voice, settled on her for a moment, but showed no signs of recognition, then moved on to Whitearm before finally settling on Oddsock. A puzzled look passed over his face, then he smiled and relaxed.

'Water, bring some water,' Sister Constance commanded and Whitearm hurried to obey.

Oddsock remained a nagging question in the back of Sister Constance's mind, but her time was now filled with nursing the man and giving thanks to God for his recovery. She seldom left his side, fretting somewhat each time he fell asleep that he would return to his coma state. But this fear slowly diminished with each awakening and the length of the sleeps shortened as strength trickled into him.

The man's body began to re-inflate slowly as Whitearm doubled his efforts at hunting, the re-awakening of the holder of the secrets of the ocean, gave him a focus and he was quickly learning the ways of his prey.

He would pause each time he passed the spot where he had knelt and prayed to God our Father for the recovery of the man, wondering if he should say a prayer of thanks. Sister Constance still prayed fervently even now that the man was recovering. He could not understand her prayers as she spoke softly and in her own language, but the urgency and desperation was replaced with joyous expressions that mixed with awe and there seemed to be a sense of discovery, or rediscovery in her eyes.

Despite pausing at the place of his prayer, he felt too shy to thank God our Father for granting his request. He would still not be sure that Sister Constance's God existed, not until he had seen the ocean. That was his promise to himself. But also 'thank-you' was not a word in his language. You expressed your gratitude by how you treated the giver of the gift. He resolved to make the hands-up sign each time he passed that spot and hoped that God our Father would understand.

The soldiers who had passed by had left their mark on the land. Fires had been carelessly covered over, animal bones lay strewn around the area where they had camped and they had not made any effort to cover their toilet. Whitearm gave the deserted camp a wide berth, attaching a sense of evil to the place.

Their tracks showed that they had headed off in a slightly different direction to that in which Sister Constance had been leading them, but it did nothing to ease the nagging sense of unease in Whitearm's mind. He wondered where the war god's men were headed and hoped that they had not discovered the route to the ocean. If the man knew of the ocean, then surely the war god's men would too. Until now he had not entertained the thought that there could be war god slaves at the ocean.

Safety

When they started to move again, the man was slow. His strength was returning by degrees, but the first day's travel proved too much and they scaled back the next day. He refused to ride on Oddsock's back, keeping a distance from the donkey as if frightened by the beast.

Oddsock treated him with a quizzical aloofness, neither shying away from him, nor deliberately moving towards him. If the man accidentally found himself in close proximity to the donkey, he would stumble drunkenly away before looking nervously round to see if his companions had noticed.

'Why is he suspicious of Oddsock?' Sister Constance asked Whitearm one evening when the man had fallen asleep early. They sat a short distance off and kept their voices low.

The boy shrugged, but his eyes showed that he understood more than he let on. 'It is very strange,' Sister Constance pushed gently, hoping that the boy would trust her with his thoughts.

'I don't know,' he answered, 'maybe...' he stopped, unsure whether to open up his answer to possible ridicule.

Sister Constance smiled gently, her eyes conveying the message that, if was all right, he could trust her, while the corners of her mouth tugged downwards.

'Maybe, I am not sure how to explain this,' Whitearm went on, 'maybe he is now scared of Oddsock because he has the power to cure.' He looked up at the nun, scratching his discoloured limb nervously, expecting her to be angry that he would attribute the recovery of the man to his twin rather than crediting her God our Father.

But she did not show anger. Instead she looked troubled. 'Yes, that could be,' she said, almost to herself, her words betraying the conflict that raged within her. She thought for a long moment, then asked, 'has Oddsock healed anyone like that before?'

The boy shook his head, then thought about it. Where had Oddsock been when Twobites had lain so ill. Like the man, his friend had survived against the odds. He remembered how some of the villagers had begun to treat Twobites and his family with suspicion, especially after the second recovery. He concentrated, calling back to mind the hours he had sat close to his friend as he lay struggling against the poison. Had Oddsock been there too? He was not sure. His donkey twin had never been far from him, but he could not recall if Oddsock had been near Twobites or not.

'I don't know. It is possible that he was,' he answered the questioning look from Sister Constance who had sensed that perhaps there was more to be heard. 'I cannot remember properly.' The answer satisfied neither of them and they both turned to look at the donkey who had wandered off to find some tastier leaves, oblivious of the attention.

Eventually Sister Constance sighed. 'We are not too far from the mission station,' the English words for their destination clashed with the rest of the sentence in her stilted way of using Whitearm's language. 'We will be safe there,' she said, explaining the strange words.

Whitearm nodded because he knew that that was what Sister Constance would want, but he felt ill at ease about this 'mission station'. Not that he doubted the nun's assurance that they would be safe, but rather he wondered if he would eventually be able to get away from this safe place and find the ocean.

'There will be lots of people there, I think, lots of children. You will be able to play with them. And lots of food, you won't have to go hunting every day,' she smiled now, her eyes lighting up.

He smiled back politely, not wanting to offend, but these promises did not offer him what he really wanted.

'And what about Oddsock? Will he be able to stay there too?'

The smile dimmed as Sister Constance's eyes returned to the donkey and the mystery surrounding it.

'I am sure he will.' Her eyes betrayed the element of doubt she had in her answer.

They sat quietly again for a while as the hold the donkey's supposed healing abilities had on her thoughts slowly waned. *The Lord moves in mysterious ways* was all she could take comfort in and she pulled that thought closer to her and tried to snuggle into it.

'What will happen to him?' Whitearm asked, lowering his voice and tilting his head towards the man.

Sister Constance was unsure what answer Whitearm wanted to hear. She had still not worked out how the boy felt about the man.

'He is no longer a soldier. They will accept him at the mission station, feed him and look after him. The people there follow God's way, God our Father's way,' she corrected, remembering the boy's way of referring to her deity. 'We are told by Jesus that we must take care of anyone who needs our help, so we will look after him.' She smiled her upside-down smile.

Whitearm nodded at this news, although he was not sure why it took a God our Father or a Jesus to tell Sister Constance's people that they should do what would come naturally to his village. The land they lived in was a merciless one. It would not deliberately cause a person harm, but it was not one to readily help out when trouble struck – whether unwilling to or unable to, Whitearm had not yet fathomed – but he knew that should a person find themselves in need, the village would do all they could to help because they never knew when it might be them who was in need. Helping others earned them the right to receive help should they ever need it.

And that was what had made the attack from the war god's men so hard to accept. If they were in need of food or medicine, or just a place to rest, they only had to ask. They did not need to take by force, the village would have done all they could to help if the slaves of the war god had just asked.

He had tended the wounds of the man when he first arrived in their company and he had done all he could when the mamba had struck. He had not needed a God our Father or a Jesus to tell him that this was the right thing to do.

Still he was glad to accept the news that God our Father knew what was right, it would make it easier to accept Him as his own god should he ever get to the ocean. He looked again at the man who slept near them and wondered about the ocean and coconuts and if he would ever get to see them.

These soldiers seemed different. Not like the war god's slaves. They still had bang sticks which they held with some menace, mostly trained on the man, but some pointed at Sister Constance and some at him. Yet Whitearm felt they were less likely to make the bang sticks shout than those men who had come to the village. They froze at the sight of the soldiers as they appeared suddenly out of the bushes on the side of the road. Even Oddsock pulled up, but did not bolt.

These men all wore the same clothes, the colour of dust flecked with leaves. They wore heavy boots and strange hats that looked like badly shaped and flattened pots. But they were neat and tidy where the war god's men were shabby and bedraggled. There was an air of uncertainty about them which, so it appeared to Whitearm, stemmed from Sister Constance's presence. One of them was dispatched down the track with a mumbled command in a language that Whitearm did not understand. They waited. The sun, which was beginning its afternoon descent, still burned hot on their backs as the soldiers searched the man, then him but not

Sister Constance, their hands, firm yet gentle. Once satisfied with the search, they indicated for the trio to move into the shade and sit down, but still kept the bang sticks pointed at them. Oddsock, who had followed them, was given a strange look before being allowed to bring up the rear. No one took any notice of the small bird that swooped and flittered from tree to tree at the side of the track.

'It is okay,' Sister Constance told him in a hushed tone, 'these soldiers are on our side.'

Whitearm nodded to let her know that he was not concerned, but he did not like the idea of soldiers, no matter whose side they were on. They carried bang sticks and he hated those. And if those men who carried bang sticks for the war god were slaves to that deity, then were these men who carried bang sticks on 'our side' the slaves of God our Father? Sister Constance had never spoken of her god as one who had slaves.

He watched God our Father's men intently, looking for clues. They were relaxed now that they had searched him and the man, but still kept a few bang sticks pointed in their direction. One or two were staring at his discoloured arm in a strange way and he began to feel uncomfortable. He moved closer to Sister Constance, trying to hide his arm behind her.

The men laughed and Sister Constance, mistaking his action for fear, wrapped her arm around him, pulling him closer to her.

'Don't worry, it will be okay,' she whispered to the top of his head and then kissed him gently and he became a child again, basking in the motherly love and protection of a surrogate.

'Do not laugh at the boy,' the man who had docilely obeyed these new soldiers so far, suddenly spoke up. 'He cured me of a mamba bite.'

The men of God our Father stopped laughing, some of them lifting their bang sticks slightly higher to point at the man's head.

The man slowly held out his arm, showing the two neat puncture wounds that were slowly healing.

One of the soldiers leaned forward for a better view.

'Black or green?' he asked.

'Black,' the man said.

The soldiers looked at the bite marks, then at the man, then at Whitearm, a sense of doubt passing through them.

'Black? Are you sure?' The most menacing of the soldiers asked roughly, his bang stick twitched a warning to the man not to lie.

The man nodded slowly, 'Definitely black. I was walking close to death, but he pulled me back. Him and...' he glanced at Oddsock, then thought better of it, '...and the sister helped with her prayers.' He smiled at her and the corners of her mouth moved down in acknowledgement.

The soldier eyed the man, then passed a puzzled glance over at Oddsock before settling on Sister Constance for an uncomfortably long moment. Finally, he shrugged and turned to his men, mumbling something in their language and they seemed to lose interest in their captives without letting their guard down.

Whitearm stared at the man. No one had ever stood up for him before when they made fun of his pale arm. And certainly no one had praised his ability as a healer with such passion.

And yet...

It was not him who had healed. Yes, he had prepared the poultice, but it would have been that medicine, the secret of which lay inside the leaves that had helped. There had also been Sister Constance's prayers, Oddsock's presence and even his own selfish prayer. It could have been any one or a combination of those that pulled the man through. There could even have been something about the man himself. The man's praise, though well meant, was hollow in what was said, but meant so much in that it was said.

He had still not asked the man about the ocean, finding himself unable to frame the questions in his mind and, more frustratingly, had been given no opportunity to ask even if he could have found the words. He wondered now if he would ever get a chance to do so. What would these soldiers do with them despite seeming more relaxed? He reached out with his darker arm and found Oddsock, seeking the antidote to the growing unease inside him, that peace which only his donkey friend could offer.

'Constance!' The man came running and held her in his arms almost before she could recognise him. 'Thank God you are alive!'

'Father,' she half stumbled over the word, the emotional wave that struck her as the man in his clerical collar suddenly appeared from a building as they were escorted into the compound, threatening to take the strength from her legs. She was safe. All that had gone before was a dream that she could wake up from now. All the killing, all the worrying about how she could survive, the long journey with all its deprivations and unexplained happenings, all this she could hive off in her mind, partition a part of her brain where she could seal it off and let it gather mould, never looking at it again.

And yet...

She felt the boy's eyes on her as she scrambled around for the name of the priest who was greeting her with such enthusiasm. She would never forget Whitearm or Oddsock, but she needed to recall another name now. Alphonse. It came just in time, just as the welcoming priest held her back to look at her.

'It is so good to see you, we have been praying for you ever since we heard that the rebels were in your area. We tried to get a message to you but...' he didn't want to speak of the messenger.

'...but what of the others. Father Slater? Sister Rose? Sister Rebecca? Sister Shannon?' Each name was spoken with less enthusiasm as Sister Constance's eyes answered his question. He let go of her to cross himself, once for each lost colleague.

'But how did you...' he started again, then looked at her. He took her arm, 'Come, you must be tired. We will get you something to eat and you can freshen up, then we will talk.' He guided her gently away, her tired mind telling her that there was something she was forgetting, but her body, suddenly feeling its exhaustion and griminess, screamed louder and she bowed her head as Father Alphonse led her into one of the buildings. As they entered, she turned and saw Whitearm standing staring after her.

'The boy...' she began, but Father Alphonse pushed her gently on.

'Someone will take care of him, don't worry.'

They had marched the man off in one direction and Oddsock had been led firmly in another. Now the pale man had taken Sister Constance and he stood alone on the dusty ground outside one of the buildings. This was a big and busy village. A lot of people walked around, all looking busy and no one took any notice of him. Even the soldier left to guard him seemed uninterested. There were a lot of soldiers, but many more people, mostly women and children. The soldiers carried bang sticks and were telling the people where to go, but they were not angry like the war god's slaves. He even saw a soldier help a child, who had stumbled, to get back on her feet.

He watched the movement around him and it made him dizzy. He put out a hand to try and find Oddsock to steady him and felt acutely the absence of his friend. His eyes looked round, scanning the camp for any sign of the donkey, but the buildings hindered his view and the tide of people confused his brain. A tremble began in him that seemed to start in his feet and slowly work its way up his legs. The confusion and sudden wrenching from his companions stabbed at him with a stinging sense of loneliness.

He wanted to run away, but fear of the bang sticks kept him rooted and he struggled to bring the shivering in his legs under control. The people seemed friendly, but there had been uncertainty in both the man's and Sister Constance's faces as they were led off. He wondered about his own fate.

He did not have to wait long to discover as a door nearby opened and a woman in a white coat nodded to the soldier who indicated that Whitearm should go inside.

He moved nervously, unsure what would happen. The room was neat and clean in an almost unnatural way that seemed to defy the dustiness that pervaded everything else in the land. It was as if this room was not of the earth, it was clean and white like the surface of the moon.

A pale man sat behind a table, but he did not look up. At another table to the side of the room the woman was busy with some dishes and things that Whitearm had never seen before. She turned and smiled. Her skin was dark like his and when she spoke, the words were in his language.

'Come in.'

She came over to him when he did not move and bent down to look at him more closely. 'It is all right,' she said taking his hands gently in hers. 'This man is a doctor. He is going to see that everything is okay with you. He won't hurt you. Okay?'

Whitearm nodded but did not move, his eyes moving continuously between the doctor and the woman, waiting to see what would happen. The doctor eventually stood up and came over to him. Then with firm hands began to look into his eyes and ears using strange lights and one of the funny things that the woman had been tidying up when he arrived.

The doctor prodded and poked him while the woman, responding to the odd comment from the pale man, would pass on instructions in Whitearm's language. 'Take off your shirt', 'Open your mouth', 'Cough'. It was a strange experience, neither pleasant nor particularly unpleasant. If anything, Whitearm found it slightly amusing. No doctor in his village would deal with a sick person this way and besides which, he wasn't even sick. He wanted to tell the woman that, but shyness paralysed his tongue and he submitted himself to the examination with wide-eyed wonder.

When he was done, the doctor left and the woman sat him down.

'What is your name?' She asked and he told her, his darker arm trying to cover the lighter one as she stared at it for a moment. She then asked the name of his village, but he did not know, it did not have a name other than 'the village'. He could not even tell her where it was.

'What about your mother and father?'

'They are dead, the men with the bang sticks came.'

The woman smiled, but he could see no humour in the fact that his parents were dead. Realising her *faux pas*, she quickly discarded the smile and an embarrassed look passed over her face.

'I am sorry,' she said kindly. I have never heard them called bang sticks before. Tell me your mother and father's names,' she hurried on. She was writing his answers down as he spoke, but he could not understand why.

At length the questions stopped and she said, 'Someone will take you to a place where they will give you some food and water. The doctor says you are in good health but that you need some food. You can then rest.'

'Can I see Oddsock then?' he asked as politely as he could.

'Oddsock?'

'My donkey. They took him when we got here. I would very much like to see him.'

The woman shook her head, 'I don't know anything about donkeys. You will have to ask the person who takes you to the food.'

He nodded, then a thought occurred. 'What about Sister Constance? Would she know where Oddsock is?'

Again, the woman shook her head. 'You do ask a lot of questions,' she said, 'I don't know any Sister Constance. There are many nuns here, but you will not get to see them much. Now that is enough questions.'

Whitearm nodded, feeling aggrieved that the woman who had asked him so many questions which he had answered as best he could, was now telling him off for being too inquisitive when all he wanted to know was the whereabouts of Oddsock. But he waited patiently, the promise of food helping him to sit still.

Eventually a soldier arrived and he was taken to a large thatch-covered shelter. The area teamed with people. They jostled and bumped into each other as they slowly moved forward to a large table where Whitearm could see big steaming pots. A faint smell of food, good food, soaked in the air around the place, mingling with the sweet funk of the human mass.

'Food,' the soldier said and pointed with his bang stick towards the crowd, then left before Whitearm could ask about Oddsock. He looked around, trying to find Sister Constance or even the mamba man, but the people swarmed in front of his eyes, making him slightly dizzy and the smell of the food seemed to be luring him into the crowd with unseen vaporous tentacles.

Without being conscious of having moved, he suddenly found himself in the midst of the swaying push-and-shove of the sea of bodies and slowly being edged towards the tables. Those around took no notice of him, their eyes fixed, trance-like, on the tables ahead, an edge of panic settling on them that the food would be finished before they got any, a wave of relief greeted the arrival of a large fresh pot.

He was handed a bowl with rice and a watery stew, a single lump of meat sat on top of this, the fatty gravy glistening on its surface. He found a spot away from the worst of the crowd and ate quickly and quietly, those few sitting near too engrossed in their food to take much notice of him. As people finished eating, Whitearm saw that they would take their bowls to a separate area where large baths of water were used to clean them. Feeling better for his food, he followed the queue to wash the dishes, then looked round, awaiting instructions on what to do next.

Since arriving at this camp everything had been ordered and he had been told what to do, directed by soldiers pointing their 'bang sticks', the phrase that the doctor's woman had found so funny. But now he was left to do as he pleased. He felt tired, but could not rest until he had found Oddsock and was assured of his friend's safety. He began to explore this strange busy village, finding that entry to certain areas were barred by soldiers, or gates or doors, but generally he was free to go where he pleased within the confines of the perimeter fence.

Towards the far end of the village he found another fenced off area. Inside a good number of men, some very young, barely men, sat huddled around whatever shade they could find. Most studied the dusty ground, their heads hung between knees. One or two would occasionally glance up and give an imploring look at the sky as if begging for some relief from the heat before the futility of the action hit and the head bowed again.

One man noticed Whitearm staring through the wire and gestured angrily for him to leave. The sudden movement caused a fellow prisoner to glance up while Whitearm began to back away, then he realised that the one who had been disturbed by the angry gesture was the man, the one they had travelled with. A quick rebuke and a strong hand stayed the one who would dismiss Whitearm and the mamba man gestured for the boy to come closer to the wire while he stood and moved across to speak.

'So, they trust you, but not me,' the statement, as cryptic as it was, was said with no bitterness, rather mild amusement.

'That is good. You deserve to be free, my friend.'

Whitearm stared, not sure what to say.

'You are a good person, Whitearm. You will grow to be a good man, strong and wise. I may not see you again. They are saying that we will be taken away somewhere else tomorrow. We are all from the enemy's side and they don't want us here. I am glad that I have seen you. I want to thank you for all you did for me, you and...' he paused, wondering whether to say it, '...you and Oddsock. You saved my life and I will never forget that. I took the life of your father and yet you still saved me. There can be no greater deed than that. You are so young and yet you have already done something greater than men older than me have done. You are a special person, Whitearm, and I cannot begin to thank you, or even repay you. But if we do ever meet again and I am able, I will do whatever I can for you.'

Whitearm stood quietly listening, then almost before his mind could send out the shyness signals, he said, 'There is something you can do for me now.'

'What?' the man said eager to repay his debt.

'Tell me the way to the ocean.'

Sister Constance fretted as Father Alphonse talked. Mostly he reminisced about his time spent with Father Slater before they came out here. His memories were fond, and his grief sharp, as if recalling and grieving a blood brother. But Sister Constance had already gone through the initial stages of shock that the death of Father Slater, her surrogate father, had brought and all she could do was sit quietly, a physical connection between this grieving priest and his lost friend.

Her thoughts of her departed mentor were, however, not stoked by these memories being expounded to her. She was thinking of Whitearm and of Oddsock. She was still unable to explain to herself with any degree of satisfaction what part, if any, the donkey had had in healing the man of his snake bite.

There was something else though, something about the boy that held her thoughts. She could not quite lay her finger on why, but she feared for his safety, even now that they had reached the mission. She knew that he would be taken care of and would be protected from the rebel armies and all that the wild land could throw at him.

And yet...

She smiled and nodded at a comment from Father Alphonse that struck a chord with her memories of Father Slater, then returned to her thoughts. The way Whitearm had reacted to coming to the mission still irked her. It was not that he disbelieved her when she said they would be safe here. His mature child face had shown her this, but there had been another look, a glance to either side, as if searching for somewhere else to be. There was a frustration in the look, as if this place of safety was just getting in the way of where he really wanted to be. She worried that he would try and leave, try and get to wherever it was he wanted to be. This was not a prison, he was free to go if he wanted, they could not force their charity and protection on him, but she knew the stories of child soldiers and how the peace keepers had sometimes been given no option but to kill them. It was kill or be killed situations which, unpleasant as they were, she could understand. But now she worried that should Whitearm decide to leave, he may be mistaken for a child solider trying to escape and be shot by an overzealous guard.

She wanted Father Alphonse to stop talking so that she could go out and find Whitearm, check that he was all right and warn him against doing anything rash. But the priest was too busy trying to gather information about Father Slater and his last days. It did not seem to cross his mind that she cared for the orphan she had brought with her, a care that went beyond just a wish to see him to safety. To Father Alphonse, Whitearm was merely another refugee, praise the Lord, and the job was done. There were others to care for them now. He did not need to do anything more, so why should one of the nuns care beyond that point. She sensed that if she asked to see the boy, he would berate her, in a kindly manner of course, for showing favouritism when there were so many in need, or worse yet, accuse her of getting 'too involved'.

'We can't afford to give individual attention, there are too many of them,' he would chide gently.

She wondered too about Oddsock. There would be no way the authorities would allow the boy to keep the donkey with him. But what would they do with the beast? She wished it was Father Slater she was talking to now. He would have understood the questions, even if he couldn't answer them.

'But my dear, you must be exhausted and look at me keeping you from food and rest.' The priest finally realised that he was not welcome, but did so for the wrong reasons. 'We must let you wash and have something to eat. We can talk again in the morning.'

She felt guiltily clean and fresh as she stepped outside into the murky heat of the late afternoon. Across the compound the mass of refugees milled around looking tired and dirty. Her freshly washed body seemed to mock these poor souls. She took a deep breath to try and shake the feeling, then walked slowly across the compound, wondering how she would find Whitearm in the throng of people.

The camp's rubbish dump suited Oddsock. After all the dry and dusty leaves, the pickings here were sweet and tasty. Discarded orange peels, corn husks and cabbage leaves littered the place and he gleefully set about devouring them as quickly as he could. There were a few other donkeys already there who had nodded a brief welcome to him before they returned to their own grazing. There was plenty to go around so none was overly concerned with the newcomer. They gave him space and – a trained eye would have noted with some puzzlement – seemed to nudge him towards the best pickings in the dump. A strange feeling of reverence moved among the other beasts, as if there was an air of authority about this stranger.

Oddsock ate quietly, his thoughts constantly on his twin. The men had separated them, but they were not evil men. Despite their bang sticks, he sensed good hearts and so he let the boy go with them without fuss. Instinct told him that they would be reunited soon and for the moment he relaxed, enjoying the tasty food and companionship of his fellow donkeys.

Once he had satisfied his hunger, he joined the others in the shade of a large tree and watched the life of the camp bustle around. The local people, those of his land, huddled together, a stagnant pool of patience awaiting a fate that they had no idea of, yet submitted themselves fully to it.

Then there were the outlanders, those whose smells marked them different. Some carried bang sticks, others wore the uniform of the woman whom they had travelled with. As he watched, he became aware of a restlessness amongst these strangers in his land. There was something happening. They moved too quickly for the heat, a sense of purpose in their actions and it seemed to be rippling out from some hidden centre. He watched this for a few moments then nodding his head to his companions as a thank you for their hospitality, he set off, knowing that he needed to find his friend, and do so pretty quickly. Already he could hear the rumble of large man-made beasts heading their way. He could not tell if they were friend or foe, but he knew that burbling bass note that he could barely perceive in his long ears would bring about change to the camp and he needed to ensure that his twin was safe.

'Ah, there you are.' She had moved awkwardly through the crowd, most parting to give her passage, some staring dumbfoundedly at her, too in awe to move and she would have to delicately manoeuvre round them. Some children fled in terror, seeking refuge in their mother's arms while others would shyly reach out to touch her as she passed, grinning with pride at their courage.

Whitearm stood aside from the crowd, his eyes searching for something.

'Are you okay?' she asked and he shook his head.

'I cannot see Oddsock,' he replied without looking at her, his gaze still moving around the camp as he looked for his friend.

A twinge of emotion ran through Sister Constance. She had searched the whole camp for him only to find that he was more interested in finding his donkey than showing any sign of pleasure at seeing her, a friend in this throng of strangers. She quickly quelled her feelings, reminding herself of the strong bond between the boy and the donkey. She understood in that moment the pinpricks of pain a mother would feel each time their child chose a favourite toy over a cuddle from their mum. It was natural for a youngster to look elsewhere for comfort and companionship and it heartened her that in this respect he was acting his age.

And yet...

There was something different about this boy's search for his friend. Something that went deeper than her young niece's preference of a doll over spending time with her aunt.

'I am sure he is fine. He must be around somewhere.'

The boy nodded, but continued to scour the camp.

'Have you had some food?' she asked, still trying to illicit something more from him. She so wanted to engage with him. Her conversation with Father Alphonse had left her feeling rather cold. He was a good man, yet he was unconnected to this land, to these people. He had lived among them, not with them. As they had talked, she began to feel that he viewed the people as necessary cogs in the machinery of his own self-worth. They were objects that he could care for in order to make him feel good and take pride in his good deeds. It was more about self than others.

She did not judge him too harshly for this. He was a good man, wanting to do good yet somehow not quite getting it right.

Whitearm smiled at her. 'Yes, the food here is very good.' There was a 'but' hiding in the shadows of his answer, however it did not reveal itself, just hinted at its existence.

'You are safe here. You do know that, don't you?'

He nodded, then looked away, his eyes searching again for Oddsock, but something in the look betrayed his thoughts.

'You don't want to be here?' Sister Constance asked gently then, when only a look replied, went on. 'Where would you go? There are rebels all over the country. They will catch you and kill you, or turn you into a soldier. Where could you hide from them? You would not be safe.' She put her hand gently on his shoulder and knelt to look him in the eyes as she spoke.

He did not look away this time but rather searched her face with his strange maturity. Then, as if finding the answer he sought, he said, 'I must go to the ocean. I cannot explain why, but I must go there. It is something I have longed to do ever since my family was killed. The elders in our village spoke of the ocean with its coconuts and I could see in my father's face that he wanted nothing more than to see the ocean and taste the coconuts. I would watch the way he listened to the elders' stories and I knew that he desired this more than anything in the whole world. He will never see the ocean now, so I will have to do it for him so that when we meet again in the spirit world, I can tell him all about it.' He stopped and waited for Sister Constance's understanding to catch up with his words, then repeated, 'I have to do it for him.'

Sister Constance began to nod slowly as the meaning seeped into her brain.

'But I cannot go without Oddsock. I will not make it without him,' he looked round again as the rumble of trucks began to grow louder.

Sister Constance heard the noise too. 'We will be moving on soon. The rebels have become too strong here for us to be safe much longer.' Father Alphonse's earlier words explained the sound of the trucks to her.

She took a deep breath then said, 'Come, I think I know where Oddsock is. Then we can go to the ocean.'

'We?' he looked at her.

'Yes, I will come with you.' Saying it out loud brought as much dread as it did relief.

When she thought of Father Alphonse, the guilt washed through her like the blood that rushed around her body, circulating round and round, finding no rest in its rhythm, or direction. He was a good man she told herself again, a man perhaps misguided by the repetitiveness of his life, but a good man. He would be worried sick when he discovered that she was not on one of the trucks as they left for safety. Her heart ached with the pain she was going to cause. She could imagine the good priest trying to persuade the peace keepers to go back and look for her. He would plead, emotional at first, then anger would take hold and perhaps the wrath of God would be threatened as his dark eyes would fire up. Then at last he would slump back, resigned to the situation, too caught up in his own guilt at not ensuring she was on one of the trucks to even think of offering a prayer for her. His own sense of well-being and worth battered to a point where he could not acknowledge the religion that had moulded him to care. And at last, when he had moved through the gamut of emotions, then maybe he would remember his God and offer up a prayer, the words of which focused on her and her safety, but the real request would be around his need for forgiveness for not taking care of her properly.

And then she thought of Father Slater. The man who had so fashioned her life with his quiet voice and gentle actions. He would be praying for her, his whole being focused on protecting her from all that was evil out there beyond the perimeter fence, all that was evil and that which was neither good nor evil, but just followed a natural instinct which could result in harm coming to her – wild animals protecting their young, or looking for food, snakes feeling threatened, or just the land itself, harsh and inhospitable, the land not made for man. Father Slater would know why she had to go with Whitearm even if she herself could not really articulate the reasons in her mind.

This was not a mind thing though, the reasons were fuzzy, their meanings a blur and hidden from thoughts. This was more a heart thing, a thing that sat cocooned within her breast, driven merely by a sense that it was the right thing to do.

She could not deny that curiosity about Oddsock played a part in her sudden decision, but how could you explain to your religion's superiors that you would be sneaking off and causing much consternation because you felt closer to God in the presence of a boy old before his age and a donkey.

At least they had found Oddsock. She had marvelled afresh at the bond between the donkey and Whitearm, the beast trotting over quickly when called and nuzzling the boy with clear affection, its head nodding excitedly.

Even the other donkeys around the rubbish dump looked up and studied the boy with a sense of wonderment, as if Oddsock had been boasting to them about his friend. 'Is this the one?' their look seemed to ask. Then they began to nod among themselves, sagely agreeing with Oddsock's assessment of the human young. Yes, he had an aura about him that gave him an elevated status amongst the donkey community.

It was amongst this small gathering of beasts and child that Father Alphonse found her. 'Come, Sister, the trucks are here. We must prepare to leave.'

Whitearm watched them walk off, wondering if she would be allowed to keep her promise of going with them. He did not know the white people well, but it did seem to him that Sister Constance would have to go with the white man who wore black clothes. There was authority in him, like the elders in the village. She would have to obey that authority, despite the look that she cast back to him as she was led off.

He stared after them for a while, then gave the slightest shrug of his shoulders and concentrated his attention back on the donkeys, petting each one in turn as if being introduced to them by Oddsock who followed him round as he went through the pleasantries. Once he had done the rounds, he led his friend to one side.

'We are going soon, Oddsock,' he told the donkey, 'we are going to the ocean. I know where it is now. The man told me. "Follow the rising sun," he said, "and you will eventually find it." He said that when I see the coconuts then I will be close. They start growing a day's walk from the ocean and you will see them all the way from then on.' He paused to adjust his image of the coconut tree, removing the large sky of water from the background of the mental picture, uncertain if he could accept this new view. The ocean and the coconuts had been so indelibly linked in his mind that this revision of his ideas did not sit easily in his mind.

'We will go alone,' he distracted himself from these strange new thoughts by continuing his conversation with Oddsock. 'The man is a prisoner here. They told him he was free, but his eyes said that he was not. He is no longer a slave of the war god, but he is now a prisoner of these people,' he gestured with his discoloured arm, taking in the whole camp. 'He will not be able to come with, but he did wish me luck in finding the ocean. "Do not let it swallow you," he said, "It is powerful water. Let it cool your feet, but do not wash your whole self in it for it will take you under and you will not come back. The waves are strong," he said.'

Whitearm paused again making sure that Oddsock was taking this important information on board.

'We will leave soon Oddsock. Prepare yourself.'

Evacuation

The bird flew up over the camp. It was too noisy and there was too much movement in the herd of humans for her to feel safe settling amongst them. Since those large beasts with the hard skin had lumbered in amongst them, there had been a lot of activity. The humans had trumpeted and yelped a lot, the stronger ones in the herd seeming to be imposing their will on the rest.

Unrest was in the air, unrest without violence. So many times she had seen this unrest as one herd of humans attacked another with those loud barks and screams. She would fly high then, her fear of the large predator birds that could swoop down and take her, momentarily overridden by her dread of the noise and pandemonium going on below. But the unease in the camp now was a restlessness as they prepared to move.

She circled round the perimeter of the herd again, trying to spot the young and his donkey. She had lost sight of them in the melee of bodies that pushed and shoved around those large elephantine beasts which stood quietly as the humans loaded them up. She could not understand how such large animals could be domesticated by the humans, but they had been. They stood silently, unmoved by the bustle around them.

The bird moved further round the herd, gliding on the warm air currents and found a perch on the far side of the camp where things were quieter. Most of the humans who were there were preparing to move towards the large beasts and the rest of the herd. Her head turned left and right as she tried to locate the young she had followed here. He never seemed to fit in with a herd so, she felt, he was more likely to be here where things were quieter. She gave a low chirrup and a snort of a donkey replied, then she spotted them.

Sister Constance was not sure how she would do it, but she had to get away from Father Alphonse who, bless him, was fussing over her, making sure she knew where to go and what to do.

'There is just about enough room for everyone on the trucks. The soldiers and the mission staff have priority so you must not be late, they will not wait. Make sure you get up front in the cab with the driver, you don't want to end up sitting in the back, it will be uncomfortable. You want to be up front, it is going to be a long journey.'

The more he fretted about her, the more she felt the clash of guilt and anger within her. His concerns for her well-being, which she knew she would spurn, shot spasms of guilt through her, yet his almost callous tossing aside of those they came to help so that she could get the most comfortable seat, fought a bitter battle with her remorse.

But more so, she wondered how she would escape his attention and sneak off with Whitearm. 'Sneak'. That was the right word for it. She had been shown nothing but kindness by Father Alphonse and yet she knew in her heart that going off with Whitearm on his quest to see the ocean was the right thing to do. She could not explain why it was right, she just knew that it was.

She nodded as his barrage of instructions continued.

'And make sure you have some water and food with you. I don't know when we will stop and it will be hot in the cab.'

He stopped and looked at her properly for the first time since he had started giving her his advice.

'Don't worry,' he said and took her hands in his in a fatherly manner, 'everything will be all right.'

It was then that she sensed his fear. He was very frightened and had been babbling to cover over it, trying to project his concerns on to her so that he could feel justified in having his own.

She did not share his worries. His were of a different world, one that, without disturbing her conscious self, had sneaked away when she had found that boy, barely conscious in the dust. She had entered a world so new to her yet so tied to the past. She barely knew Father Alphonse's world anymore, it felt strange and alien to her.

She still had the sense though to recognise the man's concerns and acted accordingly, giving him a look of thanks for his reassurance, mingling it with a touch of bewilderment at all that needed to be remembered.

He patted her hand, 'Don't worry,' he said again, 'we will be taking God with us.' He released her hands and fingered the cross that hung around his neck.

'Take God with us.' As if dragging the deity along on a journey. He was pulling God along with him, yet Sister Constance had a strong sense that she was being pushed by God to go with Whitearm, but she could not articulate this. She could not show any of these doubt fraught convictions to Father Alphonse. It was better that he just read them as worry about the evacuation.

'I know,' she smiled. She wanted to add, 'He will take care of us,' but couldn't, not after Father Slater. She would feel hypocritical even trying to believe that. God cares for us in His way, not ours.

'Come,' Father Alphonse did not notice her last thoughts, 'it is time to get ready.'

Whitearm sat watching the bustle from his hiding place. There were not many places to conceal oneself in the camp and there was no way Oddsock could join him up here in the tree. He knew he would have a bit of a wait. It would take time for the soldiers to get everyone on to the trucks, especially those who were separated from the others, like the mamba man. He could not see what was happening to that group as the foliage barred his view, but he cared little for their fate.

The man had repaid his debt for killing Whitearm's father. It was almost as if he had sensed the spirit of his victim alive again in the boy with the discoloured arm. He spoke to Whitearm as he would another man, his tone apologetic yet seasoned with a gladness that he could somehow atone for his previous offence against both man and boy. And, as the man spoke, Whitearm himself had felt the spirit of his father moving within him. There was a lifting of the weight that had slowly started to build in him as he began to despair about ever reaching the ocean. In those early days after his father's death, as he had wandered directionless around the land, so familiar yet so foreign, the newness of his hope had sustained him. But as hunger and lack of any evidence of the ocean existing had borne down on him, he had felt acutely the growing disappointment of his father. It was not directed at him, Whitearm knew that. His father in life had never been an unjust man, but rather it was a disappointment that he would be denied something in death that he could only hope for in life. It was death that had disappointed, not life.

But now things were different. If he could just rid himself of this group of soldiers who wanted to take him to who knew where, then he could find the ocean and free his father's spirit.

Movement just below him distracted his thoughts of his father as a mother, herself stressed with the movement of the camp, tried desperately to instil a sense of calm into her two young children. The youngsters clung nervously to her, the tumult of the adult world around them too reminiscent of the recent upheavals, during which, most likely, they had lost their father. Whether they had just been separated in the panic as their village was attacked, or they had lost him to one of those lightning fast stones that fled from the noise of the bang sticks, Whitearm would never know, but he was glad for the children who still had their mother, that they had someone to cling to when scared.

One of the children, a young girl, slightly smaller than him, huddled closer to her mother, the heat of the day no barrier to the comfort she craved. Her small head turned upwards to get reassurance from her mother, but her eyes strayed too far and met Whitearm's. She struggled to sit up properly to get a better view and convince her mind that her eyes were not making things up.

Both panicked slightly by the encounter but Whitearm quickly put a finger to his lips to silence the girl, giving her a calming smile. She stared a moment longer, her young mind unsure of what to decide. The hesitation, however caught the attention of her mother and the woman glanced up.

Her first instinct was the safety of her children as she scrambled to her feet, trying to protect them from whatever evil lurked in the tree. Her fright quickly turning to anger when she realised what was causing the child's distraction.

'What are you doing up there you naughty boy? This is no time to be fooling around, the trucks are going to be leaving soon and you will be left stuck up a tree. Where is your mother?'

She still held her two children behind her, protecting them from this boy's disobedience.

'My mother is dead,' Whitearm answered calmly from his lofty hiding place. 'And my father too,' he added quickly, sensing the next question. 'I have no family. Everyone in my village was killed. I am the only one who is still alive.'

The woman's face softened. 'I am sorry,' she said and shook her head. A moment's silence passed as the dead were given their respects, then, as if moved by the spirit of the absent mother, she looked up again and said in a gentle voice, 'You do need to come down. They are evacuating the camp because the rebel forces are too strong here. They are taking us to a place of safety. You can come with us if you like.'

Whitearm shook his head slowly. 'Thank you, mama, you are very kind, but I cannot go with you,' he paused, wondering how truthful to be, then sensing something about the woman, he went on, 'I have made a promise to my father's spirit that I will see the ocean for him. He always wanted to go to the ocean and to eat the flesh of a coconut and drink its beautiful milk, but he cannot do that now, so I have to go in his place. The people here will take me to safety, but I will never be happy because I will not have fulfilled my promise to my father.'

The woman nodded slowly, understanding Whitearm's need to fulfil the pledge he had made.

'It will be dangerous,' she said after a while. 'If the rebels catch you they will kill you or make you fight for them.'

Whitearm nodded. He remembered well the 'hands up' boy who had saved him from that fate. 'I know,' he said, 'but I will have my donkey with me.'

The woman was unsure of what this meant and without thinking picked up the smaller of her children who had begun to niggle, resting the girl on her hip.

'My donkey, Oddsock,' Whitearm said by way of explanation, reading the woman's concern, yet not sure why she could not understand that all he needed was Oddsock.

As if summonsed by his name being mentioned, the donkey appeared, its head bobbing slowly in time to an unheard rhythm. The shy girl, the one who had initially spotted Whitearm, reacted first, reaching out to pet the donkey's long nose and giggled slightly. The other girl became less restless on her mother's hip and stared wide-eyed at her sister and the beast, her small hand reaching out to join in.

The mother, sensing the change in her children, looked round at the donkey and she too relaxed noticeably and patted Oddsock's flank while the donkey stood patiently enjoying the gentle attention.

'Now they will understand,' Whitearm said to himself as he watched the scene play out below him.

'Everybody to the trucks! Everybody to the trucks! Quickly now!' The command rang out across the compound and a soldier came running past.

'Come on,' he commanded the woman, 'You cannot take that donkey with you, come on.'

The spell was broken and the woman gathered her daughters to her. 'Come, we must go,' she said, the agitation and fear that had plagued her demeanour all but gone now. She paused a moment as she adjusted the position of the girl on her hip, looked at Oddsock then at Whitearm, then nodded a slow blessing on his plans. She would not betray him to the soldiers. Taking the hand of the older girl, she began to move quickly in the direction of the trucks. Only the small girl on the hip looked back as they went and waved a goodbye to Oddsock.

'It is time, Sister,' Father Alphonse said, 'Come quickly.' He found her behind one of the buildings and it was only because of the rosary beads moving between her fingers that he did not chide her for disappearing when it was time to go.

Praying for the safety of the departing convoy had only been a small part of her communications with God. She was more concerned with the guilt of her betrayal of Father Alphonse's goodwill and a request for God's blessing on the journey she was about to take with Whitearm if she could just find him. He must be somewhere in the camp and, she hoped, would avoid getting forced onto the trucks, waiting for the camp to become deserted before making his move. She had to rely on this hunch for she had nothing else to go on. But she too needed some way of getting out from under Father Alphonse's caring yet watchful eye. It was as if he suspected she was up to something. But how could he?

She nodded and shoved her rosary into a pocket, then followed the priest as he made his way through the throng of refugees, the sea of bodies parting to make way for the pale swimmers, then closing behind her as if barring her escape route.

She tried to look round to see if she could locate that one discoloured limb amongst the moving tide, but the jostling crowd banged and bashed her, a panic bubbling just below the surface.

Would there be enough room for everyone on the trucks? The question was a strong undercurrent that flowed with the quickening pace of the people. She sensed it in the push and shove and saw it in the wild, frightened eyes around her.

And yet...

She felt strangely at peace within the turmoil. Her God was with her, her God would take care of her. He would answer her prayers. She would find Whitearm, they would get to the ocean and they would be safe there. Father Alphonse would understand and forgive her eventually. All would be fine. She let herself drift with the tide of people.

She imagined that this scene must be something like the people in Noah's time. They had laughed when he built his ark on dry land in a dry country, but when the rains came and the water levels rose, there must have been a mad panic, everyone wanting access to the only vessel of safety on offer. They would have begged and pleaded to be let on board.

'Why do you save the animals and not us, Noah? We are your kind, throw the animals off and let us come aboard. Have you no heart, Noah?'

Noah had a heart, like Father Alphonse had a heart. Neither would want to willingly see their fellow man left to be destroyed. How it must have troubled Noah to close his ears to the pleas of the desperate. And, she imagined, Father Alphonse would be torn should he have to choose between sailing off in the trucks and leave behind desperate, pleading people looking for safety. But Noah was under instructions from God and Father Alphonse would be at the mercy of the soldiers, the peacekeepers, as they called themselves. They were hardened men, used to making decisions that could affect life and death. They would leave behind a few if it meant that it would save many.

As the tide of people carried her closer to the trucks, she wondered what the soldiers would do if they had to choose between leaving her behind or saving one of those who crowded around her. Already she was a good few paces behind Father Alphonse and she did not want to find out what the peacekeepers would do, she did not want to cause them to hesitate where timing could be the difference between life and death. The rebels could not be far off. She could sense that in the anxiety of the soldiers.

Oddsock was agitated. Along with the other donkeys, he had been shoo-ed out of the camp. They were not invited onto the arks that towered above the mass of people swarming around them and were slowly being swallowed by these great beasts.

It was not the indignity of being moved along that caused his mood. As a donkey being ordered about was part of life. Neither was it the fact that his twin was still in the camp somewhere that bothered him. His friend had reassured him before climbing up that tree. He knew that Whitearm would find his way back to his side. Rather it was the scent that he had picked up, carried lightly on the heat haze that boiled and bubbled slowly across the land, that unnerved him. The bad bang stick men were about again, so time was now crucial. Whitearm needed to move before they came.

He ate some more leaves as a matter of habit rather than from appetite, his dark eyes watching the gate of the camp for any sign of his friend. The donkeys around him had caught the scent too and were restless, yet all looked to him for guidance. They seemed lost without their human masters, nervously picking at the leaves as if expecting to be chided for the act.

In Oddsock though, they sensed something different. His master was different too, almost able to overcome the language barrier between man and beast as the soft whisperings of the boy were met with knowing looks from the donkey with the one black sock. They held both Whitearm and Oddsock in a kind of awe for their abilities to understand each other and they now felt that Oddsock had a message for them from his human friend – they hoped he had a message.

Oddsock felt their eyes on him, felt their questions, but he did not know the answer. Few of these donkeys would survive on their own for long, yet he knew that Whitearm could care for them. Their only other choice would be to follow those big lumbering beasts when they left the camp. They were going to head away from the war god's slaves, it was the only thing that made sense. Why would anyone deliberately head towards those bang sticks. He and Whitearm had been moving away from them ever since that day in the village.

He turned to the other donkeys and flicked his head to try and communicate their choices to them.

The loading was a slow process and Whitearm sat patiently in his hideout, his attention moving between the people getting onto the trucks and the branches around him. He had checked carefully for mambas as he climbed, his recent experience with the man making him extra cautious.

Despite being up the tree for a while now, he could not let his guard down. Mambas did not lie still and may appear at any time, so he divided his attention between what was happening below him and what was happening around him.

Between these two tasks, he could not help but think of the ocean, that long dreamed of thing which was now taking on a level of reality. The direction in which it lay was now known and the big sky on the land, God's bath, had become something tangible, not just words spoken by the elders. The coconut with its juice as sweet as mother's milk and flesh as white as your teeth tingled in his taste buds.

A nervous energy pulsed around his body, his blood carrying excited chatter from his heart to his head, and his head, too dizzy from the onslaught, did not dispute the messages, nor dull them with sensible missives. He willed the people onto the trucks and out of the camp so that he could get on with his journey.

The war god's men could not dampen his enthusiasm now. Despite the threat they posed to the camp, he felt that he was beyond their reach, untouchable. It was as if the ocean, or even the thought of it, somehow put him in a protective custody. It was reaching out to him and its power went beyond that of the war god.

He thought of his father again, that gentle man, and pictured him sitting by the fire in the evening, listening to the elders as they told their stories. His father had loved that time when all in the village would set aside their work and any disagreements of the day and would gather together to share food and stories. His eyes would brighten in the firelight, his face aglow as it would move from the one storyteller to the next, absorbing their words and soaking in the images that the words created.

His father had never said anything, but Whitearm knew that his father's one great wish was to experience enough of life so that he could one day sit by the fire and tell his stories just as the elders were telling theirs.

'One day I will go to the ocean,' he told Whitearm as they worked on his small piece of land, 'I will go there and see it with my own eyes. I will touch the fine sand that the elders speak of and feel the coolness of the water. I will look out as far as I can and will just see the ocean that goes on forever until it reaches the sky. And I will eat the sweet fruit of the coconut. And when I have done that I will load up my donkey with coconuts and bring them back to the village. Then I will sit at the fire in the evening and we will all eat the coconuts and I will tell my story and all will listen with big eyes and hungry ears.'

He had stopped tilling and was staring out across the big brown dusty sea that lay around him. Then a bird or a breeze would stir him and he would look round and down at the ground, then at Whitearm.

'Don't tell your mother of this,' he would smile and rub the top of Whitearm's head, 'She will not understand.'

The trucks were nearly loaded, the dense mass of people squashing round them had thinned and the large beasts seemed to groan with the heavy weight in their bellies. Whitearm studied the branches around him, checking for snakes, before moving deeper into the foliage.

People pressed against her, adding to the dizzy heat of the day. The mild panic of the crowd had slowly squeezed out the colour differential between her and those around her. They no longer made way for the white woman.

Father Alphonse was a good few people ahead of her now and she slowed slightly to help increase that distance. He was sure to look round soon and check on her. Her nervousness was growing as she searched desperately for a way out, an escape route that would let her get away from his protective grasp without alerting him to this.

She thought of ducking down in the crowd, pretending to adjust a shoe or something then, once below the surface of this human sea, swim to a far shore. But the movement and press of people frightened her off this idea. It would not only endanger her, but also those around her who may stumble in the tide.

'Come on, Sister, this one is nearly full.' The priest had noticed that she was lagging behind and tried to reach out to her.

'I am fine,' she shouted back over the noise of the people, 'you go on, the next one still has space.'

She could almost feel God opening up a way for her. The truck they were headed to was showing signs of becoming overloaded and it was likely that Father Alphonse would make it on that one just before the soldiers began directing people to the one behind which was already beginning to take passengers on board.

The sea that she bobbed in had already sensed this and the tide was taking her away from the priest's reach and nudging her towards the next life boat.

'Make sure you get on it,' Father Alphonse shouted, resigning himself to the inevitable. She nodded and waved.

'See you when we get there,' she smiled to reassure him, then moved with the crowd towards the next truck, fighting with the tide just enough so that she would end up being hidden from Father Alphonse's view behind the next truck.

The large interior of the truck was dark and a hot funk of people squashed together blasted out of it like bad breath. Already it was almost full and the soldiers who were helping the people aboard gestured for her to hurry up. One was already preparing to lift the tail flap.

She hesitated and felt a nudge in her back and a small hand grabbing gently at her hair. Turning, she saw a mother with a child on her hip and another young girl holding her hand. A desperation and fear clouded the woman's eyes as the realisation that she would not be getting on this truck began to seep through. The child's hand reached out again to touch her.

'This one is full, use the next one,' a soldier barked and pushed the crowd away as he closed the flap. 'There will be enough room for everyone,' he said in a slightly softer tone when he noticed the nun.

Constance turned and directed the woman and her children towards the cab of the next truck. As the white person, she would most likely be given the privilege of sitting up front, so she headed for the door of the cab, gently guiding the family in front of her. She was right, the throng instinctively headed for the back of the truck so she was able to get to the large door and help the woman and her children up into the seat. The woman looked down as she adjusted the child in her arm to make it comfortable. 'What about you?' her face asked and she tried to squeeze further along to seat to make room, but Constance shook her head and smiled then pointed to the back of the truck.

The woman nodded her gratitude and as Constance started to heave the heavy door closed she just caught the girl asking her mother, 'Will that boy in the tree be okay?'

'Hush, my child. We are safe now. He will be too.' She looked round to see if the nun had understood but Constance ignored the thumping in her heart and closed the door.

'There is only one more truck,' the soldier said and he motioned towards it, 'you must go quickly.' He turned to sort out those in his care.

The crowd around her was already thinning and she knew she should act quickly while the soldier still had his back to her. She pushed gently through the crowd, then turned and ran from the trucks, ducking behind the first bush she came to.

Whitearm nodded a greeting to the small bird that came and perched on a branch nearby. The bird watched him closely, then in a few jerky head movements, re-checked her surroundings to ensure her safety.

She could not fathom this young out. She had realised that he did not feel comfortable with those earlier herds that he had followed, not all groupings accepted outsiders and the humans were no exception to that rule. She had learnt this much, but now the young was with a herd that had taken him in, yet still he did not want to move on with them.

She cocked her head to one side and gave the small human a quizzical look. 'Why don't you want to go with the others?' it asked. She wanted to chirrup, but sensed that the boy would not appreciate this. It would attract attention and give away his hiding place. She preened herself, checked that her safety had not been compromised, then studied the human young again. He was re-laxed, sitting on the branch, a look of serenity on his face. There was something about his manner that answered the bird, some-thing that said everything would be alright or at least that he deeply believed this.

The herd below had just about all clambered onto the backs of the large rumblings beasts. One or two were running around like those she had seen controlling the cows, guiding the strays back into the pack. They would move on soon. She gave a low, almost whispered tweet, then checked the sky above for signs of predators, before launching herself off the branch and up into the air to get a better view of what was happening.

The big beasts were getting impatient, their growling was grow-ing and those running around them were doing so with greater urgency. She banked and swooped round the camp. Her alert eyes nearly missed the other stray and she had to circle round again to confirm what she thought she had seen the first time around.

It was the female, the one that the young travelled with. She was hunched down between a building and a bush, anxiously peeping out at the large beasts as they began to move slowly forward in their rumbling, bumbling way. The bird landed on the roof of the building and studied the female. She did not have the same relaxed air that the young had. She was nervous, uncertain of herself.

And yet...

There was a strange determination about her. She was not going with the others if she could help it.

The bird gave a low chirp and cocked her head as she had done with the young. She could not understand this behaviour. It went against the usual rules of the herd, but both the female and the young seemed convinced of their actions. She wondered where this breaking with the norm would lead to.

The trucks juddered and slowly began to move. So far, her absence from them had not been detected. It would only be Father Alphonse who would notice, he was the only one in the camp who knew her. Despite not being completely in the clear, she felt herself relax slightly, the realisation that she may actually have pulled off her 'escape' lifted her spirits. Then, as suddenly as this positive-ness arose, an equivalent force of dread entered her as the reality of what lay ahead struck home.

Her time travelling with Whitearm had been hard. Food was difficult to find, as was drinkable water. The fear of the rebel army and the thought of the mamba had played on her mind as she travelled through this wild land.

And yet...

She had never felt as close to her god as she did then. The god that was out there in the wilderness amongst the thorn bushes and dust, that god was a real one to her, one that was in every thought, every step, a protective force that gave her the courage and ability to continue.

But once they had reached the safety of the camp, he had faded. No, he had not left her, she could still feel his presence here, but it lacked the intensity it had out there. Perhaps, she thought, God is more concentrated where need is greatest. Like a true parent, His care and attention was focused where it was most required. A mother will not leave her new born alone for a minute, giving constant attention to this helpless newcomer to life. Likewise, God, that great parent to mankind would surely keep closer watch on those who needed it most.

From her hiding place, she watched a soldier do a brief sweep of the camp before climbing on the last vehicle as it began to roll slowly out the gates, dragging all the unnatural and protesting noises with it. She could almost see the silence falling on the camp, fine as dust and as welcome as rain. She let it soak into her body, relaxing her muscles, feeling her way through this new, evacuated environment.

The rumble of the convoy slowly faded, becoming one with the pulse of the heat and she cautiously peered out from the bush where she hid. On the roof of a nearby building, she heard the cheerful chirping of a bird. She turned and, shading her eyes, spotted the small creature and smiled.

Oddsock and the other donkeys watched the trucks trundle by. They stood a little way off the dusty road, heads facing the departing vehicles, unmoved except for eyes which blinked away the dust that the wheels threw up. One or two of the beasts tossed their heads to emit a sneeze. They made a solemn guard of honour as they stood, their heads slowly following the last of the trucks.

Then, as the noise and dust of the departure faded away, they began to stir, one by one, a sense of 'what now?' pervading the group. Instinctively they turned to look at Oddsock, awaiting a sign from him. But their leader still stared in the direction the trucks had gone, his nostrils flaring as if trying to pick out a certain scent in amongst the hundreds that had just passed by. He stood a long time before he lowered his head, scratched at the dust with a hoof, then began to jog back to the camp, the twenty or so other donkeys instinctively following.

Oddsock found Sister Constance first. She was just emerging from her hiding place, her upside-down smile at giving Father Alphonse the slip, tempered only by her concern that somehow Whitearm had ended up on one of the trucks. The corners of her lips pulled further downwards and the light in her eyes grew when she saw the small herd of donkeys coming toward her.

'Oddsock!' she greeted him, throwing her arms around his large neck. His presence meant that the boy must still be in the camp.

Oddsock accepted the greeting with mild amusement, but his eyes and nose were searching the camp, this was a distraction which was more necessary for the woman than for him.

The threat of the rebels hung in the air and Sister Constance knew that she could not spend too much time enjoying this reunion so when Oddsock stirred, she ruffled his mane and said, 'We must find Whitearm, we cannot stay here too long.'

'I am here,' a voice behind her said as the donkey politely released himself from her attentions and trotted gleefully over to the boy.

The upside-down smile which had dimmed momentarily, lit up again. She wanted to go and hug the boy, but the premature maturity of him held her at bay.

She stood for a moment, smiling at him, then said, 'I told you I would come with you to the ocean.'

The boy nodded, then a broad smile spread across his face. His discoloured arm still stroked Oddsock. 'You did say that you would, and you are here now.' He bowed his head slightly, a thank you that his language did not let him verbalise.

They stood looking at each other, an awkwardness falling between them, like long lost friends wondering if they still had anything in common. Whitearm was the first to move.

'We must find food if we can. And water.' He looked at Oddsock's friends, 'I think we can carry quite a lot if we want, but we cannot take too long, the bad soldiers will be here soon.'

Sister Constance nodded and silently chided herself for being 'out-matured' by the boy. She should have been the sensible adult talking about getting food and drink and moving on, not standing there all emotion and no sense. But she nodded and said, 'Come, I think I know where we may find some supplies.'

Whitearm was still not sure he wanted Sister Constance with him on what he hoped would be the last leg of his journey to the ocean. He hoped that she would not slow him down. He was also unsure about all of Oddsock's friends. They would be good for carrying their supplies, but they were something extra to worry about. And what if they needed to hide from the war god's slaves? It would be easy to conceal himself and Oddsock, but with Sister Constance and this herd, it would be more difficult and he was not sure if the donkeys would be used to hiding. Any one of them could give their hiding place away.

But he could not leave them. They would be slaughtered by the war god's men if he left them behind.

There was not much left in the camp by way of supplies, the departing soldiers had ensured that very little remained for the rebels to use. But they managed to scrape together some food and a fair bit of clean water which they loaded on to the donkeys. The beasts stood patiently letting the humans tie the packs to them.

Whitearm took care not to overload them, gently correcting Sister Constance each time she tried to add something extra to one that was already carrying its fair share. The temptation to not put anything onto Oddsock's back was great. If they should encounter the war god's slaves, he wanted his friend to have the best chance of escape, but every time he tried to give a little of Oddsock's share to another donkey, his twin would nudge him as if to say, 'I am here, I want to help.'

He worked quickly, the threat of the rebels pushing him almost as much as his destination was pulling. At one point he stopped and listened. What was that sound? He was not sure, as it was muted by the heat which had its own buzzing sound.

'What is it Whitearm?' Sister Constance picked up on his distraction.

'I don't know. I thought I heard...' he stopped, listened again, but the sound was gone, the light wind seemed to have scooped it up and thrown it away.

'It's nothing,' he said at length, but quickened his packing efforts.

Soon they were done and he looked round the camp. He had no feelings for it, unlike his village, or even Sister Constance's village. Those had been homes, places of peace and laughter. But this place was a clinical one. It offered shelter and some food, but little else. Even the tree that he had hidden in had felt like it was only doing so because it could not uproot itself and be somewhere else.

He would not be sad to leave this place, it had been too busy. There were too many people here, and too many soldiers, even if they were supposed to be good soldiers. They still carried bang sticks and he knew that as long as he lived, he would never feel comfortable around bang sticks. They caused too much damage to people to ever be something he could accept, whether they were in the hands of good soldiers, or those of the war god's men.

Sister Constance was also looking round the camp and he wondered what it meant to her. She seemed to have found someone she knew amongst all the people here and yet she had not gone with her friend when they had all left. She had chosen to stay with him, or had she, like him, just wanted to get to the ocean. He remembered his decision to believe in her God our Father if he ever got to the ocean and the thought crossed his mind that maybe God our Father was sending her with him to make sure that he got there. He smiled at the thought. If he was right, then there was a lot more to this God our Father than he had imagined.

He double checked the last of the packs on the donkeys and then said, 'We had better go.' An urgency was injected into his voice as the faint whisperings of the noise he had heard earlier brushed his ears again.

Shaken faith

'Follow the morning sun,' the man had said. But the morning sun had long since changed from that fresh brightness that dispels the darkness of the night and was now wearily trudging along the hazy home straight towards evening. Its heat making one last effort to keep the land interested and engaged, but the land was too tired to respond with much energy. It lay flat and exhausted, the movement and life of the morning squashed by the weight of the heat that the day had laid upon it.

But they could not wait for the morning sun to reappear and bring a new life to the land. There were threats that lurked which had their own oppressive heaviness, so as soon as they had packed everything, they walked quickly through the gates of the deserted camp, Whitearm out front, Oddsock at his side and Sister Constance a few steps behind already struggling a little with the pace that the boy was setting. The small herd of donkeys followed, their flanks swaying rhythmically in unison, like drilled soldiers, but their ranks were haphazard and better reflected their freedom.

Whitearm turned off the main road as soon as the scrubland allowed, the bushes closing quietly behind them. Once a suitable distance into the bush, they turned and walked parallel to the road, picking their way cautiously round the low trees. The donkeys spread themselves out, instinctively aware that bunching together would create an attention seeking dust cloud. They trod lightly, their hooves barely disturbing the fine sand on the ground.

The boy led the way, walking with a confidence older than his years. The nun followed in a semi-dazed state as if on some sort of automatic pilot, caught up and dragged along in the slipstream of the boy. Yet, despite her apparent daze, there was an underlying determination to her steps. She was being driven as well as pulled, the boy's energy just part of the engine that propelled her forward. Her eyes, which kept a wary watch on all around her, returned again and again to the donkey with the one black leg.

A small bird flittered alongside the group, twittering quietly as it landed and took off again. A curiosity clung to its tiny frame as if it were just following the story, wanting to see how it ended. It swooped down and alighted onto the back of the leading donkey, hitching a ride for a while before lifting off again, then, catching an air current, rose into the sky to get a good view of the land.

Off to the right of the small band, she watched a large herd of humans moving towards the settlement that her wards had just vacated. Even at that distance, she could sense the menace in the group and she instinctively banked away from it, swooping down and re-joining her group, chirping her warning about the other herd. She did not tell them what else she had seen from her vantage point.

Despite the determination and hope that he had set out with from the camp, Whitearm was unsettled. There was something in the heavy air that did not sit well with him, a scent of something amiss. He kept his shoulders up and refused to alter his pace, he did not want Sister Constance to pick up on his unease, nor did he want this feeling to spoil his good spirits. He was going to the ocean, he told himself over and over. He now knew how to get there and he was going to see the sky on the land, he was going to taste the sweet milk of the coconut and eat of its brilliant white flesh. Nothing should be allowed to spoil that.

And yet...

There was the smell again, just the slightest hint of it, a feather light disturbance in the usual natural odours, something man-made and not pleasant. He breathed out heavily through his nose, trying to exorcise it and everything it could mean, but it was a part of the air around him.

Oddsock could sense it too. Whitearm noticed his twin's nostrils flaring, a quizzical look of distaste in his docile eyes and an unease in his gait. This feeling was slowly transmitted to the other donkeys and they watched the human's friend closely, awaiting a signal or a command from their leader.

Only Sister Constance seemed unaware of the unease of the others. She walked as if in her own world, perhaps just concentrating on keeping up with him, but Whitearm suspected that she was too busy talking to God our Father to notice what was happening round her.

He had learned much about God our Father in the short time he had known Sister Constance. He knew that you could talk to Him without making a sound, God could hear your thoughts. He knew that you could ask God for things such as requesting that He would keep you safe, that He would keep others safe, that He would feed people who are hungry. But Whitearm also knew that God our Father would not always give people what they asked for. Maybe that was why He was called Father. Whitearm remembered the times he would ask his own father for things. Sometimes he would be given them, and sometimes not.

He wanted to talk to God our Father, ask him that his fears be unfounded, that what he feared had happened, had not. That it was his imagination conjuring up the scents and unease in the air. But he didn't need God our Father to tell him not to waste his time on that prayer, his nose was not lying to him.

His eyes rose above the low bushes that they walked through, looking for clues to back up the story that the smells were telling him. He became aware of the warning twittering of the small bird that swooped down near him as soon as he spotted her. It chirruped urgently and tried to steer him further from the road. He nodded his thanks for the warning, but continued on his path, casting glances to the side where a dust cloud told him that the war god's men were moving along the road that he and his small band were travelling parallel to. The dust cloud did not worry him. There was sufficient distance between them and the road. What was disturbing him was the spire of black smoke that was growing a little way ahead.

Her prayers had been deep, troubled ones. She immersed herself in them. The steps her dusty feet took had faded as did the dull ache in her legs and the sting of the heat of the sun on her back.

She prayed fervently for the success of their journey. She did not know what, if anything would happen once Whitearm reached the ocean, but she hoped and prayed that things would turn out all right. The un-thought prayer was the one that asked that she too be included in the 'all right' part, but she skirted round that prayer, fearing that if she dared give this selfish request thought time, it would somehow conspire against her. She had to concentrate on the needs of others and leave her own fate in the hands of God.

She prayed too for the man whom they had encountered on their journey, the snake bite survivor. She had seen him being herded on to one of the trucks and there was no doubt that he, and those going on that particular vehicle, were prisoners. Quite what their fate would be was unclear. She had heard talk of 'rehabilitation programmes' but she had her doubts. So she prayed hard for his well-being.

She prayed too for the souls of Father Slater and the sisters who had died in the massacre. Her own survival still clung to her, a choking emotion that twisted her innards painfully, constricting her thoughts. She could still not work out why God had chosen her to survive that ordeal and taken someone as good as Father Slater. Surely God must have preserved her to help Whitearm, she could think of no other reason for her survival and that was why she now trudged behind the boy and his donkey. There had to be some purpose to this.

And she spared a prayer for Father Alphonse and his misguided kindness. She still felt the guilt at abandoning him, abandoning his concern and kindness which had stifled her. She knew that he had not meant it to be so, that he was led by his heart and that his intentions were good. One could not begrudge that, especially in a time when the world around one rages with anger, hatred and destruction.

The gradual change in the rhythm of their steps drew her slowly from her prayers, like someone waking from a deep sleep, moving by degrees from meditations, across a series of slopes and plateaus, her conversations with God cross-fading with the clammy warmth and cloying dust of her surroundings. At last, she looked up, her stuttering steps coming to a halt behind Whitearm who had stopped walking.

The cloud of smoke rose lazily into the sky, oblivious of the message it sent. Blue sky, bruised black as the cloud expanded, a living thing that slowly spread itself across the horizon.

Sister Constance stood beside Whitearm, both staring at the growing menace, a sickening horror grabbing at their hearts. Even Oddsock and the other donkeys stopped and studied this unnatural sky. Overhead a small bird swooped in tight circles, a sense of distress orchestrating the movement. It would bank violently each time the cloud appeared at her side on her circuitous route, as if an invisible barrier was suddenly changing her course. A harsh cry, unnaturally loud for the smallness of the animal, emitted from her in stuttering bursts.

'What is it?' Sister Constance's voice was barely a whisper, the answer she dreaded but did not want to verbalise, coating her words in fear. Neither looked at each other, their eyes firmly fixed on the cloud.

'I don't know.' The falseness of Whitearm's answer was betrayed by his tone. His discoloured limb sought out his donkey friend, working independently of his mind as it slowly stroked Oddsock's back, seeking solace and strength in the action.

All of them had witnessed the destruction that the war god's men could sow, even the donkeys were orphans of such attacks, so they all knew what the black cloud portended. But none had seen it on this scale. Their minds – fixated as they were on the cloud – were also mentally trying to count the number of people who had climbed aboard those trucks and rumbled slowly out of the camp.

It was Sister Constance who broke ranks, moving slowly at first, trance-like steps giving way to determined strides which in turn broke into a panicked run. The low scrub, tried to grab her as she ran, slashing viciously at her legs, scratching angry criss-cross cuts across them, but she ran on, oblivious to their attention.

Whitearm was slow in starting after her, his own abhorrence at what he believed the cloud signified distracting him at first, then the shock of the nun's sudden action delaying his reactions. But he was not far behind her and soon grabbed at her, sending them both tumbling on to dusty ground. 'Constance, Constance,' his voice a sharp whisper, the 'Sister' lost in the urgency of the moment. 'They may still be there,' he panted out the warning, the words coated in desperation, hoping they would have an effect. She could not just run over, they had to be cautious. He held on to her, pinning her gently to the ground, his skinny young limbs showing surprising strength. His eyes sought hers as if his urgent message could be better transmitted through them than with words.

But she shied away from those eyes, a vain hope that if they did not get the message through then it would not be true, the news that the cloud sent out would not have any substance. Her head thrashed from side to side, trying to avoid the truth, but it was losing the will to fight. Her jerky movements slowed and Whitearm, feeling the relaxing of her body, eased his grip on her. At last she fell quiet, her head still turned away from him, her eyes staring along the dirty ground, her chest rising and falling to the rhythm of the emotional fall out. 'Father Alphonse,' she whispered.

The other donkeys obeyed his command to stay. He glanced back and saw them huddled closely around Sister Constance whom he had left propped up against a tree. He could barely make out the nun between the legs of the beasts that crowded round her, forming a protective fortress to both keep her in and others out.

Oddsock walked quietly beside him, head bowed yet ears erect and alert for danger. Whitearm kept one hand on the donkey's neck as he walked cautiously toward the smoke cloud, his confidence waning then waxing as if topped up through a store that the donkey carried.

The smell of the smoke and destruction began to itch in his nose and scratch at his eyes, disturbing the memories of the devastation in his village which he had pushed to the far recesses of his mind. His father's chest exploding in that bright red flower of blood, flashed in his mind as the stench of death assailed his nostrils. A mechanical note within the scent jarred against the human tones of the funk, a metallic thread that prevented his mind from totally replaying the scene from his village.

He slowed his pace further as he drew near to the source of the cloud, moving carefully from bush to bush, peering furtively around them, his eyes alert for signs of danger.

'Wait here,' he told Oddsock, the animal's bulky size becoming a problem as he attempted to reach the scene undetected. He did not know if any of the war god's men would still be there.

Bodies lay strewn along the dusty road, most face down with blood covered backs. Already the flies gathered hungrily around this banquet suddenly laid on for them. The burnt-out hulks of the vehicles exhaled their dark breath as flames still danced gleefully around them, taunting those great beasts. 'You're so big and menacing, but what can you do now?' the flames chanted, 'Look at you, you are nothing.'

The flames were the only things that moved, except for a small bird that swooped down close to the bodies then veered off as if repulsed by the scene, only to return again, drawn by a morbid curiosity at what lay about. Occasionally it would fly towards Whitearm then turn back, realising that she may give away his hiding place should she fly too near.

Whitearm waited, crouching behind a low bush. He knew that the war god's men had caused the carnage. They had ambushed the convoy and slaughtered everyone mercilessly, the soldiers who Sister Constance called 'good', the prisoners, the old men and women and the children, all of them had succumbed to the insatiable appetite of the war god. His hand reached out to touch Oddsock, but the donkey was a hundred yards or so further back, waiting as he had had been commanded to do.

'Oddsock,' he called, his voice loud enough, yet still hushed.

The donkey came, obedient to the call, and after gaining his strength from contact with his twin, Whitearm stepped out from behind the bushes and began to move quietly among the bodies, his eyes quickly ascertaining that they were all dead.

The truck, the one that the mamba bite man had been herded into, still burned with some ferocity, the flames seeming to gleefully attack those who had been trapped inside, as if their crimes against mankind required a particular intensity of punishment. The wall of heat that protected the truck from any sort of vain rescue attempt, stood solidly in front of Whitearm as he tried to look past the brightness of the flames, trying to see the departing soul of the man. A soul would not lie to him, a soul would tell honestly if the man was truly sorry for killing Whitearm's father.

But there were no spirits to be seen, just the thick billowing black smoke that reached heavenwards.

He moved round that truck, and on to the one ahead of it. The flames had not feasted on this one, but its belly seemed full of the hard stones that the bang sticks threw. The holes in the door were barely held together by scraps of metal, twisted painfully in all directions. A vicious red smell poured out through the holes, screaming a silent plea for the blood from which it arose. But Whitearm could not help and started to move on to the next truck when a small whimper that rode on the back of the odour returned his attention to the door.

It opened with a loud protesting crack, the bloody smells tumbling out behind the noise, rushing past him in search of the freedom that the hot air offered. A body of a woman lay in the squashed space between the seat and the dashboard, the top of her head facing the opened door. She had curled herself, foetal like, around something but all Whitearm could see was her back, a dark red sweat soaked her clothes and still oozed slowly from her. The dim light in there compared to the brightness outside took a moment to adjust to, but then he noticed a pair of eyes looking at him over the prone figure. He had seen those eyes before, staring up at him as he hid in the tree waiting for the crowd to depart. He reached forward slowly and eased the girl out of the protective cocoon of her mother's body. Then he heard the scream.

Sister Constance stumbled backwards, her hands grabbing at the air for support that did not come. Instinctively her body swung round to prevent itself from falling and she staggered forward, eventually falling to her knees and retching at the side of the rough road.

'No, no, no, no, no,' the words left her reluctantly as if their being set free reinforced the positive that their meaning fought against. She retched again and repeated her mantra, but this time the words were already beginning to resign themselves to their opposite meaning.

'Not again, Lord. Please, not again.' She crossed herself now, a hurried, jerky motion that was too quick to have meaning, then as she calmed herself, she re-made the sign of the cross, her hand moving slowly to the four points on her chest, each light brush of her fingers bringing a sharp pain like the thorns in the crown, the nails in the feet, the nail in the left hand, the nail in the right. She winced at each one, yet accepted the punishment despite wondering why she was being dealt such a cruel lot.

She did not want to turn around. Her eyes could not take the sight of Father Alphonse's body. It was as if looking at him in death were as much of an intrusion as if she were seeing him naked. His wounds seemed as private as those parts of him that lay beneath his clothes. She felt his death as a heavy weight bearing down on her, pushing her into the dusty ground and she longed for her turn. The pain when Father Slater and the sisters had been taken from her had felt like a burden too great to bear, her only solace then had been to bury herself in burying her friends.

She could not go through that pain again. Her body did not want to move, the shock paralysing her as it had done when she had crawled out of her hiding place and returned to the scene of destruction in the village. She would never know how long she had wept over Father Slater's lifeless form, those were minutes, or hours, days even, that were a black hole in her life.

And yet...

As she now wept over the body of Father Alphonse that hung halfway out of the door of a truck, a surprised look on his face, she could already feel her senses returning to her, as if strength were being drip-fed into her system. Her first thought was that this land and all her experiences in it had hardened her, that she was no longer the young nun who had arrived full of innocence and wide-eyed awe. The land had dealt her a large dose of reality and she had grown through these experiences.

But then she felt the light touch of Whitearm's hand on her shoulder and saw his other hand on Oddsock's neck and she could not help but wonder where her returning strength was coming from.

The boy waited till she had fully returned from her grief then said softly, 'We must go.'

She fought against the notion that they had to bury the dead. While her upbringing screamed at her that this was the decent thing to do, she calmly tore herself away from everything that had been drummed into her. She accepted Whitearm's helping hand and regained control over her shaking legs.

She could not, however, leave without saying a quick prayer over the body of the priest, bowing her head, her lips moving quickly over the words, letting their meaning do the hard work, her one hand unconsciously resting on the back of Oddsock who stood patiently beside her. She finished and crossed herself, then looked up. 'I am ready,' she said.

They walked in silence, Oddsock leading the way. Even the bird accompanying them did not flit or chirp, but rode on the back of one of the donkeys, its head slightly bowed. The destruction that they had seen lay heavily on them.

The small girl sat on Oddsock's back with Sister Constance walking at her side, ensuring she did not fall. She clung steadfastly to the animal's mane, her eyes wide yet not seeming to see anything. She had not spoken a word since Whitearm had found her and, it seemed, had not blinked, a bewildered aura clinging to her.

Whitearm walked slowly, his own thoughts keeping him pensive, but he followed the instructions the mamba bite man had given him. 'Go in the direction that the sun rises.' It was setting now and its cooling light threw long shadows out in front of them, stretching towards the ocean, as if they were trying to get there first.

They walked on the road, Whitearm beyond caring about possible danger and Sister Constance too shell-shocked to notice. Oddsock, however, moved his head slowly from side to side as he walked, his docile eyes on the lookout for any danger, his ears alert to the noises around him and his nostrils flaring as they searched for any odours at odds with the world around them. But he gave no sign that he had detected anything of concern. The sun sank slowly into the horizon behind them and a red and orange light spread across the sky while the heat of the day began to retire. They would need to rest soon, but his friend was showing no signs of stopping.

He put his head down and quickened his pace slightly till he was beside Whitearm, then gently veered sideways till the boy found himself amongst the bushes and under a tree perfect for shelter for the night. They were far enough from the road, just in case more of the war god's men came along it, and the tree would give them something to rest against. The whole group followed and, like Whitearm, seemed unaware of having done so, but all went about settling into their makeshift camp as if it had been a well-planned stop.

The girl was the only one who seemed unsettled by the stop, not wishing to be taken off Oddsock's back. Sister Constance had to gently pry her hands from the donkey's mane, soothing words pouring out of her as she applied a gentle yet firm touch. It was only when Oddsock turned his large head to his load and nodded it in his bobbing, dipping way that she relinquished her hold. Even then she would not let Sister Constance put her down.

'You sit with her, I will sort out the food,' Whitearm said, guiding the woman and child to the tree where he helped them to settle before he began to look through the supplies they had managed to salvage from the camp. Sister Constance held the child close, rocking her gently. A lullaby, relying on its tune, for the words were meaningless to the child, flowed from the nun's lips, a soft susurration that floated gently on top of the quiet whispers of the land. Slowly a peaceful calm settled on the group as the other donkeys found some leaves to chew on and Whitearm sat to eat after sorting out some food for Sister Constance and the girl. The small bird returned from its swooping for insects and landed on Whitearm's shoulder, the first time it had done so. Whitearm smiled and offered a few crumbs in the palm of his hand. The bird hopped down and began to peck gently at them. The girl watched this with her wide eyes and when the bird began to feed, a soft smile touched her lips.

While walking, Whitearm had pushed all images of the attack from his mind. The effort of putting one foot in front of the other had monopolised his thoughts, making it easier to ignore what he had seen. But now that they had stopped and he had eaten, his mind succumbed to the seductive lure of the terrible memories.

The scene had been grimly familiar. The only difference between the destruction in his village and what he had witnessed earlier on their way from the camp was that there had been trucks today. But the effect had been the same. Sister Constance's cry when she had seen her friend's body still pierced his soul. The anguish in that scream seemed to carry with it something more than just shock. It went deeper, as if she were crying out against her god, the God our Father she had spoken of with great reverence. He cast a glance over at her, wondering what effect, if any, this had had on her faith. But she was engrossed in the girl, rocking the child gently on her lap. He could not tell if there were prayers or curses going on in the nun's mind.

The girl took his attention. She looked so small and vulnerable, her eyes were heavy with the tiredness of grief and shock, yet she refused to close them. It seemed as if she believed that were she to lose eye contact with Oddsock, something terrible would happen. He felt a sudden pain in his heart, a sadness mingled with anger at the war god that it could cause so much pain and distress. What right did the war god have to take away loved ones in the way it did? What right did it have to chase people from their homes and families?

His family, his village and all the surrounding land had been wrenched out of his life. The girl too had lost family and a village. The mamba man had talked of his home and family as something in a life before the war god. Even Sister Constance, the woman with the pale skin, the woman with a family of hands-up trees, even she had had that taken from her. No one was safe from the war god. What sort of a god was God our Father that he could allow such things to take place and not seem to care, or to try and help stop the carnage that went on around them?

This did not fit in with the image of God our Father that Sister Constance had spoken of. Her god was one who cared, one who looked after those who followed him. That god had not helped the man whom Sister Constance had cried over at the trucks. He thought back to when the other man had been bitten by the mamba and remembered Sister Constance and his own prayers for the recovery which had come. But why would God our Father help him then but not when the war god's men came? And why had the girl been saved, but not the girl's mother? Did the girl know God our Father but her mother did not? He could not believe that that would be the case.

He watched as Sister Constance's gentle rocking slowed. The girl's eyes had eventually closed, the exhaustion of the day was finally winning that battle. Sister Constance's head rested back against the tree and her eyes closed too, but Whitearm was not sure if she was asleep or not.

He put his hand out and found Oddsock, the contact with the donkey, despite all his doubt, made him feel a link to the God our Father of Sister Constance and the link felt good.

Even in her dream state she knew she would wake and smile and carry on as if nothing had happened to shake her faith, but her sleeping self knew that she could never wake again with the same intensity of faith as when she had arrived in this land. Father Slater's death and the death of the other sisters had dented her belief, questioning why her loving God had allowed this to happen to those who had devoted their lives to doing His will.

Father Alphonse's death had further damaged her relationship with God. Her prayers for his safety had been fervent, scented with an aching wish that this other priest to whom she had felt less attachment than she had to Father Slater, would come to no harm. Yet harm, horrific harm, had come. Not just to him but to all in the convoy. Where was God in all this? She felt her body outside of her dreams shudder at this rebellious thought, then a strange sensation took hold, as if a weight had been lifted from her.

She stirred, climbing slowly out of her dream, almost reluctant to face what lay beyond the cocoon of her slumber. But the unexpected lightness she felt despite her thoughts intrigued her and she battled on towards consciousness, an image of a donkey and a young boy floating alongside her on her journey.

The girl, waking in the nest of Sister Constance's lap, lay still for a while, her young eyes searching the makeshift camp, re-orientating her mind with her circumstances, before she slowly started to move her head round to widen the scope of her search. When she saw Oddsock, the confusion faded and a small smile glowed in her eyes. The gaze lingered for a moment on the donkey, then she turned her head, asking the question with a look, but her protector was still asleep, the pale arms of the woman hung loosely around the small body on her lap. They were protecting, not restraining arms.

The girl assessed this, then, moving as gently as she could so as not to wake the nun, wriggled off the lap and tottered over to the donkey. Her small arms stretched out in front of her as if they were pulling her along.

The other donkeys grazing nearby turned to watch her progress, a few bobbing their heads, approving of the scene.

Oddsock sensed the approaching figure and turned to greet her, lowering his head to allow the girl to pet him and nuzzling gently against her, recognising the frailty of the small body and allowing for the clumsiness of movement in the young hands. The girl giggled quietly, her eyes wide, echoes of the emotional turmoil she had experienced still evident in her stare, yet it had already been softened in the short time that had elapsed.

Whitearm watched the scene play out. He had sat with his face towards the rising sun, his eyes watching the horizon slowly assert itself in the murky gloom of dawn. The stirring of the donkeys caused him to turn. He had not smiled much since the day in his village when the war god's men had come. Despite the salve that Oddsock had brought to ease the pain, the hardships he had endured had sucked the joyfulness of youth from him, leaving in its stead a hardened maturity to his face and he looked out on the world with a mixture of watchfulness and seriousness.

But he smiled now, seeing the girl interact with his friend, Oddsock. There were still moments in this world filled with war gods and bang sticks and hyenas and mambas where you could see pureness and happiness, where you could sense something of the goodness of the God our Father that Sister Constance spoke of. He was not in everything that you saw, he was not in the destruction and devastation that the war god's men brought. Nor was he in the paralysing poison of the mamba's bite and you could not go looking for him there, Whitearm could see that now.

God our Father was in the good things, the things that made you smile, the things that made you look forward in life, waiting for the next moment like the one playing out in front of him, scenes where what happens to others, or even to yourself, fill you with indescribable joy. They did not have to be big things like an ocean, they could be small, almost everyday things like the joyful interaction between a little girl and a friendly donkey.

He still wanted to see the ocean, sensing now that if he felt the way he did about this small good thing here under the trees, how much more the feeling could be multiplied by seeing the great big and good ocean. He let out a small laugh and jumped to his feet to help the girl climb onto Oddsock's back.

The sound of children's laughter greeted Sister Constance as she awoke, a sound that had become alien to her and it took a moment for her waking mind to understand what it was she was hearing. She opened her eyes, a blur of sleep still floating across them, and searched for the source of the sound.

The girl sat on Oddsock's back, clinging tightly to his mane, a broad grin across her face. Whitearm was leading the donkey slowly round their impromptu camp, sweet childish laughter coming from him. Oddsock's head bobbed excitedly as he was led, as if he too were joining in the joy of the moment. The small bird swooped and dived in and around the group, adding to the girl's excitement.

The heaviness and philosophy of her dream fell from Sister Constance like a large cloak dropped to the floor, discarded and forgotten. The joy of the girl and the excitement of Oddsock buoyed her spirit immediately, as did the playfulness of the bird. But it was the look on Whitearm's face that released her from the shackles of her dream. He looked like a young boy. It was the first time she had seen him like this. His adult mark of seriousness had been tossed aside and he was a child again, as he should be.

She watched as he led Oddsock while at the same time holding out his white arm to be there should the girl need support. His eyes, alight with the pleasure of the moment, concentrated on the small child on the donkey's back. Sister Constance could sense the emotions piled up behind that gaze, but was not sure how to read them. There was a kind of brotherly affection in his actions, his protective arm seeming to give off a message that this was family. The soft laugh that he shared with the girl contained secrets that were usually only privy to siblings and his voice, as he spoke quietly in his own tongue, contained, or so Sister Constance felt, the tone of familiarity.

She moved her attention to the girl now, the young smiling mouth displaying the gaps of lost milk teeth, her eyes jumping between Oddsock and Whitearm as if drinking in the joy their company brought her. With a slight shock, Sister Constance suddenly recalled the bewildered tear-stained face she had first seen on the child when they had rescued her at the scene of the attack. The girl's grief and confusion at the loss of her family had had a sobering effect on the nun's own emotional turmoil at the devastation they had seen.

It was just yesterday that the girl had suffered such a catastrophic loss.

And yet...

The joy the child displayed this morning was not natural for one who had gone through such an ordeal. Neither, for that matter, should Whitearm be in such good spirits. Surely the memory of his own family's destruction would have been stoked up with the scene from yesterday. But the two did not display any signs of having been witness to the horrors.

Even the donkey, she thought, should be showing some sobriety and solemnity at the occasion, but Oddsock was there at the centre of the scene, his presence seeming to be the epicentre of the joy. Sister Constance stared harder at the donkey. Yet again a strange aura surrounded it, a mysterious mist of unanswered questions clung to the beast, impenetrable, yet at all times radiating a goodness that she could not fathom. She began to wonder if she would ever work out what it was about the donkey that made it have this effect on people. She no longer doubted her thoughts that the beast was not your average run of the mill donkeys. There was something about it that set it apart from the others.

But just as her thoughts turned serious, Oddsock snorted which set the children giggling again and she could not help but smile, things suddenly made lighter either by this unnamed power that the donkey had, or purely a chemical reaction brought on by the smiles of others. Either way it did not matter much. The warmth of the morning had not yet turned to the oppressive heat of day, a soft breeze keeping the mood of the weather buoyant.

She moved to stand, hoping to join the children in their frivolity, but her stirring caught Whitearm's eye and his child-adult look fell like an executioner's axe across his features. The girl, quickly sensing the change, let out a last giggle before letting a wide-eyed, sombre stare take control of her face. Oddsock pulled up and gave the nun an accusing look.

Her heart sank. Her adulthood burned crimson with shame at being the cause of this sudden change in the children, especially that of Whitearm whom she so desperately wished to see have a chance to be a child again. Father Slater would have told her that it was neither her, nor her status as an adult that had caused the youngster to be a grown up caught in a child's body. It was war that did that. War robbed people of their rightful positions in life, turning settled people into refugees, docile people into killers bent on revenge and children into adults before their time.

She wanted to turn away and run, leaving the children to be children, but she could not. She had chosen, had been chosen, to go along on this journey. She had to be there to take care of them, but the pain inside her left her immobile. Going with would just force this adult world on them.

Oddsock moved restlessly within the awkward moment, and accidentally, or so it seemed, nudged Whitearm who suddenly grinned and held out his hand to her.

'Come,' he said, inviting her to join them. The girl giggled again and began to pat Oddsock lightly.

Sister Constance felt the heaviness lift and she moved over to join in the fun.

The ocean

The small herd of humans looked tired. Their steps were slow. Even the donkeys alongside them moved with a lethargy that only the heat of the land could induce. Despite the slow movement of the group, the bird sensed a lightness of spirit as she flittered from branch to branch alongside them. The land and heat had taken its toll on the physical, but she could feel the determination within them, especially the young whom she had followed for so long. Their goal, whatever it was, was achievable in their minds.

The other donkeys, the ones who had joined later, could sense it too. She watched how they kept a close eye on the male young, followed his lead, drawn along by the drive his small frame had.

The insects were out and the bird swooped, climbed and dived through the air, catching them expertly as she did so, but her mind was not on her food. She concentrated on sharing in the positiveness of the group, dipping low to fly close to them between snacks.

Evening was drawing near and they would stop to rest soon, this was their routine. The male young would go and hunt or forage. He had become good at this now and hardly a night went by when the humans didn't have a small animal of sorts cooking over the fire. Then they would sit and chatter to each other, or the two young would play, the older male always with a cautiousness, as if the smaller female were fragile.

As she rose again into the dusty blue sky, the bird suddenly became aware of a change in the air. It had been there, building, but a faint trace, buried beneath the weight of the heat and dryness of the land. But a breeze heading in the right direction alerted her to a slight saltiness and there was just a hint of moisture spreading itself thinly across the evening sky.

She looped a couple of times to confirm the message her senses were giving her, then dived down to tell the donkey in her excited twitter chatter voice.

The girl lay curled up in the dust, a small arm stretched out, just touching his hand which hung loosely next to him. Whitearm looked at the sleeping form, watching the small frame rise and fall with hurried breaths. The little lungs, still developing, had to work twice as hard to collect the air needed for survival. The girl's head rested on the outstretched arm while the thumb of her other hand hovered close to her mouth which was slightly opened, waiting to receive it. A small moustache of crystallised snot glistened beneath her broad nose and Whitearm smiled when he saw it. Sister Constance had not noticed that this evening. She would have tried to clean it off. But this was more natural, this was how children were supposed to be.

The guinea fowl he had caught earlier lay comfortably in his stomach. It felt good to not have that hunger devil pricking its sharp claws into his gut all the time. He felt a certain sense of pride in his ability to hunt now. Since they had left the camp, there had only been one evening when he had come back empty handed. He wanted to take all the credit for this, but a small part of his mind told him that his task was being made easier by a greater abundance of wild life around them. In the last few days they had had a troupe of baboon walk alongside them for a while, they had

disturbed a family of warthog grazing and the herd of impala and
zebra they had passed was the biggest he had ever seen.

The landscape was changing too. The ubiquitous brown of the
land he had travelled through was giving way to a greener environment. It was only a matter of time before he would see a coconut
tree. The mamba man had said they grew a fair distance from the
ocean and that he would encounter them long before seeing the
sea. He studied each new tree he saw, looking for the big brown
balls that, so he had been told, hung high in the tree. He wanted to
ask Sister Constance about them but couldn't bring himself to do
so, a strange pride preventing his tongue from betraying his lack of
knowledge.

He sat back against the familiar roots of a baobab and looked
around the small band of travellers. The donkeys stood a few feet
off, some testing and tasting the greener leaves while others stood
staring at the last flecks of light that floated around on the horizon,
seemingly lost in thought, or perhaps just enjoying the beauty of
the sunset.

Oddsock was closer to him. He too watched the sun going down,
but would swing his head round every now and then to check on
Whitearm and the girl, his wise donkey eyes sending a peaceful
message despite his nostrils being ever alert for the scent of the war
god's slaves.

Whitearm watched the donkey for a while, his eyes focusing on
the one dark limb that had given the beast its name. This was the
thing that tied them together, the mark they both had. He looked
again at his own discoloured arm. The dark hairy leg of the donkey
could be the hard shell of the coconut and his arm the white flesh
inside. He and Oddsock were two parts of the whole. They were
meant to be together. And soon he would see the real thing, a real
coconut that he could touch, smell and taste. A small bubble of
excitement rose up in him for the first time in a long while. He
would, he knew, see a coconut tree soon and not long after that he
would reach the ocean. He looked again at Sister Constance, then
at the girl. The latter so calm and relaxed as she slept, but the white
woman still had an unsettled look about her. He did not like this.
It brought doubt to his mind about the ocean. She knew God our
Father's will. Maybe she was getting messages about the ocean

from her god that made her unsure. He stopped looking at her, not wanting her misgivings contaminating his hopes.

The boy's confidence unnerved her. She did not think she could cope with his disappointment should they fail to find the ocean. Despite her concerns though, she still could not dismiss the role the donkey seemed to be playing in all these events and she could not say for sure whether it was Whitearm or Oddsock who was actually leading their little group. There were times, she had noted, when the donkey would gently edge Whitearm in a certain direction by subtly angling his body across the boy's path. But it was almost imperceptible, so much so that her suspicions were as clouded in doubt as her convictions.

She prayed for understanding, an ability to see what was truth and what was fantasy. Her conviction that she was being guided by her god had grown stronger each day since the massacre outside the camp. There could be no other explanation why she had chosen to go with Whitearm rather than follow Father Alphonse. She still could not figure out what God wanted her to do, what role she had to play in this journey and where it would end. Whitearm seemed quite self-sufficient, even with having to look after all the hangers-on. He provided food almost daily, and when they walked, he did not ask her for advice on the direction they should take, he knew where he was going. So where did she fit in?

Despite not knowing what part she was to play in the journey, she felt relaxed for the first time since the rebels came to the village. Even the ever-present fear of being caught and what they might do was muted, a soft dull ache that was there amongst her thoughts, but one had to look hard to find it. Her worries now concentrated on whether they would reach their goal or not. Would they, like the Israelites in the ancient scriptures have to wander for forty years in the wilderness, spend forty years surviving on the little bit of manna that God would provide? And if they did get to the ocean, what then? Would they stay there? Be safe there?

'God will provide,' she heard the ghostly voice of Father Slater that she carried in her head say. And she wanted to believe it, but she struggled to.

The night began to make its usual sounds, soft winds tickled the ears, carrying the odd snuffling noise of nocturnal animals that were heard but never seen. The evening fire, aimed at preventing an unwanted and hungry visitor from coming, sent out a stuttered crackle of Morse Code messages, 'Don't come near or you will burn,' it said in its calm way. The slight whine of insects rang in the ears and all seemed at peace.

She shut down her thoughts, knowing that all the concerns would keep for another day.

Oddsock stared in the direction that the sun would soon rise. The dark black of the night sky had turned slowly into an inky blue that smudged the horizon, revealing bleary outlines of bushes, trees and hills. He blinked, patiently waiting for the clarity of detail the sunlight would bring.

The boy and the other humans still slept, while the other donkeys had moved quietly off in search of food where they could eat without disturbing the humans. Oddsock flared his nostrils and took in the scents that floated in the air. Each day the strange salty smell that he had first detected about a week back, was growing stronger, growing from a slither of a scent which had been so faint he was not even sure it existed, to a detectable element in the mixture of odours in the air. There was still a lot of the familiar about the surroundings, but things were changing as they walked.

It was not only the landscape and scents that were taking on different hues, but he could sense a change in Whitearm. The boy was calmer, more relaxed and confident as he walked. Perhaps the boy was also aware of the lack of evidence of those men with the bang sticks within the myriad of smells that this area brought.

Oddsock shook his head gently to remove a few irksome flies, then looked again at the man who sat weightlessly on his back. None of the other humans noticed the man and the man never spoke. He sat up straight, his whole being revealed a certain comfort in being on a donkey's back. There was a somewhat opaqueness to his presence, but he had a kind face and had always treated Oddsock well since he had appeared just after the destruction of the village.

The man looked down and smiled at Oddsock, a warmth exuding from him. Then he nodded an encouraging gesture and a signal that the day should start for the humans. Oddsock acknowledged the instruction and gave a low snort, loud enough to wake Whitearm, but gentle enough not to startle him.

It was heading towards late afternoon when Whitearm saw it. The last vestiges of the midday heat were beginning to shuffle away and a light breeze was just starting to make an effort to take the sting out of the heat. They were weary, the morning walk had been more energy sapping than usual and the midday break had felt restless. The air was hot and damp and wrapped itself around their faces, making breathing a chore.

Whitearm stopped and the trailing group almost bumped into him before they realised he had called a halt.

The girl, who sat on Oddsock's back, looked up, slowly surfacing from her sleepy stupor. One of the other donkeys gave a low bray and shuffled sideways in the pack.

'What is it?' Sister Constance moved quickly up next to Whitearm, her eyes following his gaze, trying to ascertain what it was he was staring at. The boy kept staring and she scoured the area ahead of them for a sign of what it was that had caught Whitearm's attention. Then she saw.

'Coconuts.' The boy and nun said the word together, one in almost disbelief at what he was seeing, the other with a kind of joyous relief.

'Coconuts.' The boy said it again in a whisper, as if concerned that calling out their name too loudly would cause the wonderful fruit to run away and hide, or dissolve like a mirage.

'Yes, coconuts,' Sister Constance said, her voice catching in her throat. They were nearly there, surely the ocean could not be too far off. They stood mesmerised by the sight of the palm trees, each with their private thoughts. Even Oddsock and the other donkeys realised that something important was happening and huddled closer to be part of whatever it was. A light breeze ran playfully through the group, bringing slight relief from the heat.

Then Whitearm began to run, his skinny legs flying out behind him, throwing up puffs of dust in his wake. He reached the tree and stared up at the hairy brown balls that clung to the fountain of leaves. They were high up, way out of his reach, but that did not matter, not yet. He was seeing real live coconuts with his own eyes.

They were no longer imprisoned in words spoken by the elders, they had broken free and he could see them.

The others caught up with him, Sister Constance walking quickly, aware that she could not abandon the girl and that Oddsock could not trot with her on his back for fear of her falling. Whitearm did not move from under the tree, he stood staring up at the coconuts, his eyes glowing with excitement, his mouth slightly opened in awe.

As Sister Constance drew near, he turned to her and pointed. 'Coconuts,' he said. The nun nodded and smiled her upside-down smile, her bright eyes confirming that the turned down corners of her mouth expressed glee.

'Yes,' she said and they stood a few more moments looking up at the tree.

'How do we get them down?' Whitearm asked suddenly, his smile momentarily dimmed by the thought.

'I don't know,' Sister Constance said, her smile also fading. 'I suppose we could try and shake the tree. We must just be careful that they don't fall on our heads.'

Whitearm looked serious and studied the trunk of the tree, then looked back up at the fruit in amongst the leaves. The trunk was quite thick and did not look like it would shake much. Maybe a little, but surely not enough to dislodge those beautiful coconuts. He looked round, his eyes searching for Oddsock, but instead settled on some large stones that lay on the ground nearby.

He had done that before, thrown stones up into a tree. That time it was to try and dislodge a mamba that he and Twobites had seen. At that time his friend did not have the nickname of Twobites and neither really knew the power of a mamba's venom. But that was another life, a different Whitearm, one who seldom strayed far from his parent's side, one who was protected by the comfort of the village, the elders, his family, the donkeys, cows and chickens that constituted his life back then. All that was gone, taken by the slaves of the war god in a noise of thunder. Even the Whitearm of that village was gone. That scared little boy who knew nothing of the world beyond his village except for what existed in the words of stories, that boy was no longer. He was now a young man who knew of God our Father, who knew how to hunt and fend for himself, who now knew the coconut, not as something that was wrapped up in the mystery of words, but as something he could see and soon would touch and taste.

He hurled the stone with surprising force, his thin arms disguising the strength they had. The accuracy of his throw surprising not only Sister Constance, but also himself. He had been prepared to need a good number of attempts, but the stone struck and dislodged a large coconut which fell to the ground with a satisfying thud. Only Oddsock seemed to have expected this and he gave a low snort, a kind of chuckle of one in the know and he turned to look at the girl who sat quietly on his back.

Whitearm stood still, transfixed by the reality of the moment, then broke free from his reverie and ran forward and scooped up the coconut, cradling it in his arms, his eyes not leaving the object. It felt heavy, pregnant with possibilities and he recalled the description of the elders, 'a hard wooden ball, full of refreshing juice that made your tongue feel alive and a fleshy inside, whiter than your teeth, as soft as pounded yam and as sweet as mother's milk.'

Could all this be possible? Could this hard wooden ball really contain such wonders? He shook it and heard the juice rattle inside like water in a gourd, too crisp and smooth to be pips or stones. He smiled at Sister Constance now, a mixture of his great delight at having eventually laid his hands on a coconut tinged with the slightest, 'I told you so, I told you we would find them. Look.'

The corner of the nun's mouth pulled down as her eyes lit up with the joy she was feeling. 'Yes, Whitearm,' her face said, 'yes, you have found them.' And in her look, perhaps to counteract the slight smugness in the boy's smile, there was something that said, 'God our Father is a good father, he has brought you here and delivered the coconut to you.'

Whitearm picked up on the look and his smile faltered a little, then suddenly grew.

'Here,' he said offering Sister Constance the coconut. 'We need to get God our Father to bless this, like we do with all our food.'

The gesture and request caught Sister Constance by surprise and after the initial shock, she took the fruit, tears welling up in her eyes. The boy had accepted God. She had never been sure if he had or not, his eyes had always betrayed a scepticism about her belief and his questions had been more curious than probing. But his gesture now with the coconut seemed to show a genuine acceptance that God was there, that He had protected them and that He now, as He had always done, provided for them.

She took the offered fruit, feeling the roughness of the outer shell and the sloshing of the milk that lay within, then looked at the small group that crowded around her. Most of the donkeys faced her, their docile eyes blinking patiently as they waited for the next strange thing that the humans would do, their gaze flitting between her and Oddsock, as if the one with the miss-coloured leg was interpreting what was happening.

She closed her eyes, her grip on the coconut tightening slightly as she did so, then began to pray, words of thanksgiving for having been brought safely to this point and for the gift of the coconut. While she spoke the words for Whitearm to hear, she said another silent prayer of thanks for the spiritual journey the boy had undertaken and praised her god for the point that he had reached. And as her prayers progressed, she felt a closeness to God that she had never experienced before, as if he were there with them, listening with interest to her prayers. In her mind, the role of God was played by a man not too dissimilar in looks to Father Slater, his kind eyes watching the scene with a smile of approval.

She finished her prayers and looked up, her gaze immediately taken by Oddsock. The girl on his back sat very still, watching the nun at prayer. There was a strange, almost unnatural calm about her, as if she were being held by a parent.

It was with difficulty that Whitearm managed to break a hole in the coconut. With some instruction from Sister Constance, 'You don't want it to split in two or you will lose the juice,' he persevered with a small rock and eventually broke through the hard exterior and the boy paused to enjoy the moment, then offered the fruit back to Sister Constance for her to drink first.

'No, Whitearm,' she said and smiled in her upside-down way, 'this is your moment, you must go first.'

He nodded slowly and then lifted the coconut to his lips and took a small sip of the juice. Immediately he felt his mouth begin to tingle as the cool, fresh liquid brought his tongue to life. It tasted everything like the men in the village had said it would. The urge to swallow the rest of the juice was strong, but he knew that to drink it all would sour it with his greed. He smiled and passed the coconut to Sister Constance who accepted it this time, but did not drink from it, instead she offered it to the girl who still sat on Oddsock's back, her eyes wide as she watched the proceedings around the strange fruit. A look of doubt crossed her face, then as Oddsock adjusted his weight, she lifted the coconut to her lips and took a small sip.

Her eyes lit up as the swallowed the juice and a big smile took control of her lips. But she too instinctively knew that she must share in order for the juice to remain sweet and she pointed to Oddsock's head.

Whitearm took the coconut and poured a little into his hand and then offered it to the donkey who licked gratefully at the liquid. Then, after Sister Constance had had a sip, he gave each of the other donkeys a small sip in turn, starting with the oldest. When the juice ran out, he went through the procedure of knocking another coconut down and cracking it open.

Once all had tasted the juice he split the shells, marvelling at the slippery smooth inside, as white as his teeth, just as the elders had said and sweet and soft as pounded yam. Despite his hunger for more, Whitearm limited everyone to a small piece each, remembering how his stomach had protested at his over indulgences after he had gone hungry and he did not want the pleasure of the coconut to be spoilt by its richness causing them to feel ill.

There was just one thing left to do. He picked up a stone and knocked another coconut down with his first shot. He smiled at his luck and also at the quizzical look he got from Sister Constance. She would not understand this. It was not something her god would have spoken to her about. He cracked open the shell, his skill at doing so already improved, then he slowly tipped the fresh juice onto the dusty ground as images of his father and mother, his sister, Twobites, the elders and all in the village came into his mind.

'A libation. For my family,' he said softly in answer to Sister Constance's looks, 'and the man who was bitten by the mamba,' he added as a last image came to mind.

The nun nodded and smiled her upside-down smile as he finished pouring the juice and scattered the insides around the wet patch in the dust. Once done, he paused for a moment then said, 'Now we can go to the ocean.'

The journey was easier now. They had found the coconuts so it was surely only a matter of time before they would reach their goal. That was what the mamba man had said. When they came across a banana tree, Sister Constance introduced Whitearm and the girl to the new fruit. Without the expectation that the coconut had had, Whitearm was amazed that something that tasted this good had not been spoken of by the elders. Why had they missed this one? But he didn't dwell too long on that thought, the ocean was filling his mind and he grew eager, almost reckless in moving towards this goal.

They had kept off the main roads, just to be safe, and moved alongside it, but this was becoming more difficult as the sparse foliage they had been used to, gave way to the thicker, lusher vegetation. There were people moving along the road in both directions. Not many, but they caught glimpses of them every now and then, but experience told Whitearm that he should not engage with them even if they looked harmless, like those from his village. They did not carry bang sticks like the war god's slaves did, but he would not trust them and kept his small band of followers away from the road as much as he could.

The smell of the air around them began to change, turning salty. Sister Constance said that this was the smell of the ocean. He was not sure. The elders had never mentioned the odours that seemed to grow in the air, hanging on to the heat like a parasite, not totally unpleasant, but also not totally appealing.

It was the change in Oddsock that convinced him more than Sister Constance's assurances. The donkey walked with a determination in the direction of the sea smell, almost leading the way, finding paths through the thickening tress. At times he would take them onto the road, but his nose and ears remained alert to any possible danger.

The girl too sensed the change. She rode quietly on Oddsock's back, her eyes glowing slightly with building excitement. If her attention was not on Oddsock, then she would watch Whitearm with a strange look on her face, a look of admiration mixed with a kind of inner knowledge of something others were not privy to. Occasionally she would lean back slightly as she rode, her head turned as if listening to someone.

Sister Constance noticed some of these movements but failed to read anything into them. All her energies were concentrated on moving forward and helping Whitearm reach his goal. She could not articulate why this was important, it was just something she felt compelled to do. In her mind she held talks with the departed Father Slater, searching for reasons from her mentor, but the answers she received were vague and elusive.

'Stop!' Her voice surprised her as much as it did the others. Whitearm immediately looked round to see what the danger was. The girl lost her smile and her small hands tightened their grip on Oddsock's neck while the donkey's ears shot up and his nostril flared.

'What is it?' Whitearm whispered, his eyes searching the surrounding trees.

'Listen,' the nun's mouth was turned down and her eyes were closed but her face shone with an unspeakable joy.

'What is that noise?' Whitearm still whispered, his ears catching the dull thud-and-gurgle susurration that floated to them on the breeze.

Sister Constance bathed in the sound a moment longer, her eyes remaining closed as she listened, then she opened them, revealing a light glow of excitement and she whispered, almost too scared to utter the words, 'the ocean.'

A heart beat loudly in Whitearm's ears, once, twice, thrice, drowning out the sound he longed to hear again. He seemed to fade inside himself, his whole being wrapped up within his whole being. Then slowly the moment began to thaw and the outside sound filtered through and began to flow round his senses again.

'That is the ocean?' Although he knew he was near – the coconuts had told him that – he somehow could not bring his mind to believe that he was actually hearing it, the sound, so alien to his ears, was this great sky on the ground, God's bath tub, this thing the elders had spoken of so often with such awe. He tried to feel the elation that he was sure he should be feeling, but it was blocked by numb disbelief. He had so longed for this moment but the excitement it should produce was being denied him and he felt the frustration bubble up. Then, just as it threatened to consume him, Oddsock gave a loud triumphant bray that echoed around the trees, and he straightened his legs, as if a load had been removed from his back and began to walk quickly forward, seeming to be led by some invisible hand and gaining speed as he went. The girl on his back giggled and he snorted gleefully.

The moment was broken and joy flowed into Whitearm's mind, loosening all thoughts that suppressed his emotions. He began to walk towards the sound, slowly at first, then began to gather momentum and he started to run, ignoring the sharp leaves that snatched angrily at his thin legs. The race was on between him and Oddsock, but he ran with an abandonment, the donkey was more circumspect, mindful of the small being hunched on his back, clinging to his mane and giggling uncontrollably.

'Whitearm,' Sister Constance's voice chased after him, but the tone gave away the excitement and turned a command to be careful into a shout of encouragement as she stumbled through the foliage after them, the startled herd of donkeys joining her, more out of a sense of needing to stay together than from any understanding.

Whitearm ran on, his legs beginning to hurt and the wet heat threatened to suffocate him, but he pushed forward till the trees and undergrowth suddenly disappeared. The ground under his feet turned soft and the whole world seemed to open up in front of him, the bright light of the sky dazzling as it reflected off the white sand that stretched off left and right and his breath left him with dizzying speed, spinning his head as it went. He lurched forward toward the expanse of blue sky on the ground, his body screaming at him to breath, but he did not know how to. The joy of his mind stifled him and clashed with the panic of his oxygen starved body.

Then he felt, from somewhere far away, someone at his arm, supporting him gently and a calm voice spoke his name, his real name, not the one he had been given because of his miss-coloured arm, the name his father had given him and which was so seldom used, that he almost did not recognise it.

'You are safe now.'

He turned to face the man who held him up as the air rushed into his lungs, his eyes focused on a face that was familiar to him, but he could not at that minute remember from where. His mind somehow knew that he could trust this man. He felt the strength return to his legs as Oddsock appeared through the trees and jogged over to him. The girl sat up and smiled, her eyes drinking in the scenery, then she settled her gaze on the man and, as the donkey came to a standstill next to him, she held out her hands to be picked up.

The man lifted her from the donkey's back and she rested her head on his shoulder, but she continued to stare wide-eyed at the sea, following each wave onto the beach.

Whitearm looked at the man again. He no longer looked familiar. His features in that first panicked glance seemed to have changed, but an echo of that first image remained and he slowly remembered the picture of the man on the hands-up tree that had been in Sister Constance's special room.

The other donkeys got to the beach before her and she was perspiring heavily and quite breathless as the trees gave way to the open sand. Whitearm was talking to a man who – she caught her breath – just for a brief second looked like Father Slater. But that must have been a trick of the light surely, for as she looked again she realised that it was a black man that Whitearm spoke to, not a white priest.

The sand dazzled her eyes and seemed to collude with her idea that the light had played a trick on her. She moved forward slowly, the boy's body language telling her that the conversation was an important one and she should not disturb it.

But the man looked up and noticed her, a smile breaking out on his face that mirrored her method of smiling – down-turned corners of the mouth and bright eyes.

'You must be Sister Constance,' he said, his voice smooth and reassuring. 'This young man has been telling me about you,' he answered the quizzical look on her face.

Whitearm could not have had much time to talk about her, half a minute at most, yet the man spoke as if he knew everything about her.

'You have had quite an adventure by all accounts.' Whitearm looked away, his attention on the sea as the man continued, 'But you are safe now, the war is over, the rebels have been defeated.'

She stared, not sure what to say. All kinds of emotions bubbled inside her, making her want to laugh, dance and weep at the same time. But she was still not sure of this stranger on the beach. She

still could not shake the glimpsed image of Father Slater she had
seen in him despite his features being so different now.

'The war is over?' She needed to say something to try and bring
a reality to the scene.

The man gave a brief bow of his head, acknowledging her doubts
as reasonable.

'Yes, it is finished.' The words had a familiar ring, but Constance
could not place them. The man adjusted the weight of the girl in
his arms and the child glanced up at his face, her eyes glowing with
trust and Sister Constance knew then that she was safe.

'I have some food if you would like to share. Just a little fish I was
cooking when this young man came bursting through the trees.'

He indicated a small fire a little way up the beach.

'Thank you, you are very kind.'

After they had eaten, the man turned to Whitearm who had not
taken his eyes off the ocean the whole time.

'Go on. You can go and touch it. Don't walk too far in, the water
is powerful and can take you if you are not careful. Don't let it
come above your knee.'

Whitearm stood quickly, started towards the ocean, then paused
as a small bird flew past him and settled on the man's shoulder.
Oddsock stirred and began nodding his head. Whitearm grinned
and hugged the donkey's neck before running across the sand to
bathe in the ocean, God's great big bath tub, the sky on the land
that the elders had spoken of. He no longer had to be afraid.

He paused just before the water, awe tinged with fear of this
amazing thing that surpassed everything his imagination had managed to conjure up.

Sister Constance caught up with him, the girl in her arms. She set
the youngster down next to her and took Whitearm's hand in hers.
With a child on either side of her, they took the last few steps into
the water, feeling its coolness, then as it covered the children's
knees, she bent down and gently splashed her young wards, their
laughs echoing loudly across the beach. Soon all three were soaked
and sat exhausted in the shallows, letting the gentle waves wash
backwards and forwards over them.

Constance looked at Whitearm. The mature adult who had
cloaked his features over the last few months had disappeared and
it was laughing child's eyes that looked back at her.

She then turned back to the beach where Oddsock stood alone. The man had mounted one of the other donkeys and was riding off amongst the palm trees, walking over the leaves that lay strewn across his path. Constance stared after him, watching him disappear, then slowly made the sign of the hands-up tree across her chest.